Endorse

From Summer of 1982 till Summer of 1986, I was enthralled by the life Decisions made by and for Saadri and the Buard/Weston family. Stephanie uses techniques gleaned as an MFA student to craft an authentic world of complex characters. Destinies is sure to be a page-turner.

—**Arthnise Lockhart**,
Outsource Manager, *Zurich North America*

Stephanie uses description to craft a world that is at once recognizable and inviting. This world carries the reader along to the conclusion of a novel one does not want to end.

—**Dana L. Jenkins**, Esq.

As in her previous book, Stephanie chronicles the labor of growth that is part of the lives of many young adults. She celebrates life and develops a storyline in which many readers can relate. This is a good read.

—**Rae Jenkins**, Transformational Mentor

Stephanie has long held a commitment to positively impact the community and young adults. This book celebrates the tenacity required for successful urban living. I look forward to distributing this book through my program as I did with Book One, *Decisions*.

—**Deon Davis-Harris**, Chairperson, *Not Just Hoops Inc.*

Another impactful voice is added to the cause of supporting young adults where they are and taking them where they desire. Stephanie has a love and understanding for young adults that is clearly demonstrated in this novel. Readers are taken down memory lane. These characters are so real!

—**Faith Davis**, Transformational Life Coach

I waited for Book Two because Book One was so good. I understand there are six more books planned and I am happy about that! The story, the setting, the characters, I could identify with all of it, and I became invested. I was cheering for the heroine and the hero and upset with the villain. Stephanie knows how to draw readers in, and she is building a fan club.
—**Kim Chu**, Owner and Personal Chef, *Kim Chu Cooks, LLC.*, Health and Wellness Life Coach, *KLC Enterprises*

In Book One, *Decisions*, I met the Buard family and became engrossed in their story. I did not want the story to end. Book Two brings back some of the same feisty characters and I am eager for the drama that will unfold in the plot. Stephanie crafts dialogue that helps readers understand what drives her characters. This will be a hard book to put down.
—**Michele F.**

When I opened the book, I was transported into a world that I enjoyed and did not want to leave. The characters in Stephanie's story are complex and real. I found myself responding through laughter, anger, and happiness as the characters displayed the commonalities between all human beings.
—**Cheryl Dammons**, Civil Servant

Stephanie has always genuinely loved and understood young adults. This theme is resoundingly demonstrated quite well throughout her novel. She is a third-generation educator and former high school educator who continues to maintain relationships with many of her former students. In this book Stephanie brings readers into the world of the young adult and their command of the world garners reader respect.
—**Malveata Collins**, High School Educator and Women's Basketball Hall of Famer

From page one, the voice of the misunderstood and overlooked is brought to a position of prominence. Stephanie's authentically respectful portrayal of youthful hope and love raises the status of growing in the urban environment. These characters reside in Everywhere, USA.

—**Christian Jenkins**, Health Care Professional

Life, desire, and frailty are penned to distinctly paint a visual of family dynamics and social currency in New York City. This story draws readers in from the start as the characters exude an essence of their own.

—**Arthur Gregory Pugh**, Actor and Voiceover Artist

Stephanie created a powerful book that intrigues and relates to destiny. I was impressed when I read this novel. This book was compelling. Although it is fiction this story feels like it is real, and it is relevant to everyday life.

—**Kecia Reed**, Entrepreneur and Pastor

Destinies

Buard Family Series

BOOK TWO

Also by Stephanie Dunlap-Holloman
Decisions
"Becoming" *in Travailing Women,*
The Untold Story of a First Lady

Destinies

Buard Family Series

Book Two

Stephanie Dunlap Holloman

Author Academy Elite

This is a work of fiction. Names, characters, businesses, places, events, and incidents are either the products of the author's imagination or used in a fictitious manner. Any resemblance to actual persons, living or dead, or actual events is purely coincidental.

© 2022 by Stephanie Dunlap Holloman. All rights reserved.

Published by Author Academy Elite
PO Box 43, Powell, OH 43065
www.AuthorAcademyElite.com

All rights reserved. This book contains material protected under International and Federal Copyright Laws and Treaties. Any unauthorized reprint or use of this material is prohibited. No part of this book may be reproduced or transmitted in any form or by any means, electronic or mechanical, including photocopying, recording, or by any information storage and retrieval system, without express written permission from the author.

Identifiers:
LCCN: 2022901572
ISBN: 979-8-88583-012-6 (paperback)
ISBN: 979-8-88583-013-3 (hardback)
ISBN: 979-8-88583-014-0 (ebook)

Available in paperback, hardback, e-book, and audiobook

Dedication

To my ever expanding family: husband Frank – I love the very cells that made you; daughter – Tajia (Mush) – it's our time, yeah for the creative types!; my son Jadon (Bean Bean) – God heard my prayer when He gave me you, Son; my daughter Anique (Bam) – you lit up my life the moment of your birth; my son-in-love, Jaquone (Jay)– couldn't ask for someone better to love my Mush, love you; my granddaughter Analisa (Youbaby) – Bobe loves you more than a million elephants; my granddaughter Katherine (Bunga) – Bobe loves you to the moon and beyond; and my grandson Kaiwon (King/Papa)- Bobe loves you like crazy

To Thal, my mother Jacquelynne Cheeseborough, and aunt Marilyn Leach - the best mothers a gal could have, you kept me moving and I love you very much. Dunlap Women Forever!

To the Original R. (Ronald) Kelley, my father – who loves ya baby?

To my sister Ravan (Bunky) – be ever wonderful… To my brother Qaiyim (Qai-Bear) – so proud of the man you are – love you… my sister-in-love, Tiffany (MyCherie) - you are my cherished baby doll. my cousin Kaseem (PD) – I love you like mad, Crazy Man!... and my cousin Tanya – live, laugh, and love

My baby, my cousin/little brother Christian – I love you sooooo much. Christen, Cairo and Jonnae I love you too. My cousin/big brother Andy (Howard) – my protector and confidant who I love to the moon.

To my Holloman family: Mother Ella, Uncle George, and brother Andre, I love you; my real first child/sister Danielle – my reader, test audience, and my Rider, RIP; niece Charleigh (StinkaMama) – Titi loves & is proud of you; nephew Rolonzo (Deron) – Titi loves you Modo!

I had a WONDERFUL childhood: love and appreciation to the Becton, Johnson, Maddox, Moore, Hicks, Dunlap, Jenkins, etc. families!

Contents

Foreword xiii

Acknowledgments xvii

Part One – Convergence

Chapter One – The Name is Destiny 3

Chapter Two – Us. 15

Chapter Three – My World 31

Chapter Four – As We Proceed 46

Chapter Five – Pathways. 55

Chapter Six – Commencement 66

Part Two – Fusing

Chapter Seven – Into the Groove.................. 87

Chapter Eight – What We Really Want 105

Chapter Nine – Who Am I?..................... 130

Chapter Ten – Our World...................... 149

Chapter Eleven – Help is on the Way.............. 171

Chapter Twelve – Holidays 185

Chapter Thirteen – Bon Krismis 208

Chapter Fourteen – Sisters...................... 223

Epilogue.................................... 243

Patwah Glossary 247

Works Cited 251

About the Author 253

Foreword

Whenever I am teaching a course or coaching a client, I stress the importance of the niche. The niche gives one the sense of purpose and focus needed to pursue passion. The niche, as I tell clients, is the DNA of one's dream. When a customer, consumer, potential investor sees a person's work they should immediately understand the specialty or interest that is driving the product being presented.

Destiny is defined by Merriam Webster as a predetermined course of events often held to be an irresistible power or agency. That irresistible power carries with it a sense of one encountering fate – an endpoint determined prior to one's existence. Fate impacts agency in that it lays out a path for a person that she has not chosen. Yet, destiny embodies agency in that one can choose, and that choice places one on a path. The key is to find oneself on the desired path. There are many life factors that can derail a person from her original purpose. Daily struggle, for instance, can cause a person to lose sight of possibility.

Luckily, there are individuals who come alongside others to help them visualize an alternative reality. Coaches seek to guide others to their desired states. Self-reflection and self-awareness are often acquired skills coaches can assist clients with accessing and using. These skills and many other soft skills are taken for granted and neglected as people seek to acquire technical knowledge to pursue careers. Yet it is these skills that if left deficient often lead to derailment and unfulfilled dreams in the lives of many.

Ralph Waldo Emerson said, "The only person you are destined to become is the person you decide to be." Taking such power is difficult for many who have been part of limiting realities that have beat down their beliefs about themselves and the conditions in which they live. Some have the intrinsic motivation to fight, but those trapped by negative or limiting circumstances are no less capable of making great impact. Deciding to *be* may first mean deciding to seek out help to understand how another reality is possible. Fictional stories often have the sage character who mentors the young hero for her to become a better version of herself. The sage helps the hero understand herself, her surroundings, and how to use this new-found awareness to achieve greater happiness. This is also the stuff of life; people are looking for the reality they desire but cannot seem to achieve.

It often amazes me when I find creative types who can blend reality with fiction to craft a story that resonates with truths for the reader to ponder. Destinies is more than a story; it is homage to healing and forward progression. In this novel Stephanie not only uncovers emotional, psychological, and economic issues but begins to delve into larger societal issues such as intercultural relations.

Stephanie's niche is young adults. She captures their fears, joys, and pains as one who has walked in some of their experiences. She has been a "mother" to many in her career as an educator and has been the sage in the ministerial roles she held.

Foreword

I am sure this story will resonate with many. Its characters are authentic, its setting is reminiscent of 1980s New York City, and its plot is relatable. Book One, *Decisions*, was hard to put down and Book Two, *Destinies*, will not disappoint.

I look forward to the books in this series because Stephanie has captured urban realities in a refreshing way.

-Barbara A. Palmer,
CEO of Kingdom Kare, Inc.,
Founder and Trainer of Talking Business with Barbara
Certified Business Coach
Author of No Regrets

Ralph Waldo Emerson > Quotes > Quotable Quote
Accessed March 24, 2021 https://www.goodreads.com

Acknowledgments

I would like to thank the professors I had in the MFA program of Lindenwood University who helped me think more deeply and hone my craft.

Anthony G. "Tony" Dsouza, your encouragement and instruction meant EVERYTHING.

Beth Meade, you have been a tremendous help and advocate.

William Anthony "Professor C" Conolly, your standards and expectations allowed me to challenge myself and experiment.

Anothai "Ty" Kaewkaen, you made poetry accessible; I enjoy and appreciate its crafting even more.

Christopher Candice, you've helped me enjoy all that goes into writing from the right word to the finished work.

Teran Félicie Buard
June 6, 1966

Majesty

In the presence of Majesty
I see what can be
All the purposed
parts
Divinity
designated.
Me.

So
I will not fear
for
all the capability of
He –
The One –
speeds the winds
for Me
to be.

PART ONE

Convergence

"There are no coincidences in the universe, only convergences of Will, Intent, and Experience."
~ Neale Donald Walsch

FaceBook post by Neale Donald Walsch from Dec 08, 2012

CHAPTER ONE
The Name is Destiny

Then and Now

1783 – NEW YORK

The waves of Wallabout Bay lapped the Breuckelen shoreline asynchronously with men retching and shovels clawing the earth. Even the birds respectfully restrained their tones.

"George, I don't know how you keep going. The smell has my stomach rolling." He looked around at the two-man teams digging other graves. "I say, I have the best partner for this task. Strong and quick, you are."

His name was Joris, as had been his father's and his father's father, but the British had a way of ignoring the *un-British*. He focused on the calming rhythm to complete such a vile task. "It is our small kindness to give these souls peace. A shameful business all of it." His tongue was an undeniable mixture of Dutch and English heritage.

Joris's partner grimaced and wiped at his sweat. "Let us get on with it; war is never pretty." They reached for a bloated corpse spit up from bay gases. The area was littered with sea-logged bodies seeking dignity denied them during their tenure aboard the *HMS Jersey*.

FALL 1982 – FORT GREENE, BROOKLYN

Monuments and masterpieces are consigned to the mundane as forgotten relics struggling for recognition. Concrete slabs of sidewalk obliterate paths of resistance and freedom to offer minimal space to parallel-parked vehicles. London Planetree and his comrades rise to shade the cars, trees that once provided cover and protection from so many elements. Collective voice to what came before, but no one knows their names. It is their shade that suffices.

Cast iron front-fencing extends from Italianate and Greek Revivalist brownstones to produce courtyards with iron-grilled step-down entrances tucked beneath coordinating staircases. The upper stairs lead to stoops of ornate oak doors framed in recessed archways or flanked by fluted columns. Acanthus adorns the bracketed eaves and flowerbox ledges of tall windows whose treatments demonstrate a range of modesty. It is a block.

A centuries-old retaining wall courses along a thoroughfare then ends at a double stone staircase that leads into the park. At the park's center the Prison Ship Martyrs Monument, a white marble column, rises one hundred-fifty feet, the seed of a nation. This is the hang-out. In the shadow of the structure yet casting one of its own stands the twelve-story colossus. A mini skyscraper that blends Collegiate Gothic and Deco architecture. The brick and stone of the structure testify to the national and local zeitgeist of its era. The rectangular layout hosts pointed arches, buttressed windows with tracery of curved geometric patterns, lead trimmed windowpanes, carved finials, parapets, and a caged rooftop on the tenth floor. An FM radio tower provides unencumbered reception and a crowning feature for the prestigious high school. Inside its walls, a nucleus of intelligence meld as an incubator of possibilities birthing inquiry, instigating change, and sparking a collision of ideas. The neighborhood is steeped in the tempo of revolution, past and present, where destinies converge.

Code Switching

FALL, 1982

The lunchroom spanned the length of its sixth-floor location and consisted of two sides connected by a wide section known as 'the center.' Rectangular tables with detached chairs arranged into three eating sections on each of the east and west portions of the cafeteria provided ample seating for the school's four lunch periods. Sixth period lunch was the busiest of the day.

A cast of characters assembled to provide laughter, drama, and human-interest material for the security staff and lunch monitors.

"You're set!" A player slammed the last cards on the table and gave a triumphant high five to his partner. The group of teens surrounding the game screamed.

Fawn Dennis glared at Derek Holmes. "That's what I get for playing with a Queens boy! Ya'll come high but should stay home!!" More laughter followed.

Derek looked at Teran Buard and cautioned, "You better get your homegirl; you know she gets to slicing when she loses!"

Teran gathered her things and reached for her friend. "Okay, Bruiser, don't cut nobody today. Come on; let's get to our next class without detouring through Security." Fawn rolled her eyes at Derek, leaving the table and the howling.

Derek called to the ladies, "You not off the hook, T! You owe me a rematch!"

Teran shot back, "Your momma just got her check on the fifteenth so why you trying to get it all snatched and it ain't even the end of the month!" She continued directing Fawn toward the stairwell and left the table in chaos.

Fawn grabbed the railing at the first step, bent with laughter. "Girl, you are treacherous!"

Teran sucked her teeth. "How many times does one person have to get their butt whooped before they just stop? He ain't even a challenge. The only reason you lost was because Derek don't know what he's doing." The ladies continued laughing as they headed down the stairwell to complete the last periods of their day.

----------◊◊◊----------

Seventh period history class was not the one to play with and everyone understood that from the beginning. In the fall of junior year, no one wanted to fail any classes - colleges were looking at grades carefully. Teran calmed from the lunchroom antics and walked into class focused. As she walked to her assigned seat, she peripherally noticed Bashan Watts staring at her. She made a mental note to do some fact-finding beyond the grapevine which established Bashan as well-dressed, one who kept to his own circle, yet on friendly terms with many. Teran looked at a blue Kangol resting on his desk to match a white Izod shirt and dark blue Jordache jeans. Finishing the ensemble, a pair of blue and white shell-top Adidas decked his feet.

Inventory completed, they made eye contact. His unwavering stare and the smirk he gave as if to say, "I see you checking me out" unnerved Teran. She proceeded to her seat and tried to settle down for class. Throughout the period she glanced in his direction, but he seemed not to notice her. Teran chided her out-of-character behavior and refocused. At the end of the period, she made to gather her things, turned, and once again became locked in Bashan's gaze. He broke the contact with another smirk, stood, gathered his books and hat, and strode coolly out of the room. Teran sat with her mouth agape – shocked by her loss of self-control. Then she was mad.

----------◊◊◊----------

On the Radar

Days come, days go, and some days hold a treat. This day proved exceptional as the group of young men strolled down the hall toward the staircase that would lead them to South Elliot Place, Fulton Street, and the GG train station.

Derek alerted his friends. "Brothers, feast your eyes, here cometh a nymph."

Aiden Guillaume, one of the school's heartthrobs, turned toward Derek. "No more Odyssey for you, D!"

Their laughter did nothing to contain the comment of, "I should try for her", from an unlikely candidate who received looks of surprise, and who Derek promptly shot down. "Teran is out of your league, Buddy. It's better to stick to your guppy pool."

Their amusement quickly ended as they watched Teran's approach. Bashan's own grunt burrowed beneath the appreciative sighs, lusty groans, and elated gasps of his friends. He blinked to steady his step. Her legs were smooth, firm, café au lait, and reminded him of sugar. The legs traveled to rounded hips firmly outlined in a miniskirt. She neared and her face burned its image in his stomach. He wondered over her nationality, its mixture, because she had features that spoke of another culture. Her black nor brown hair lay on her shoulders curled at the ends; it was a sanded mixture with strands of red flowing throughout. The stylish glasses she wore enhanced almond shaped hazel eyes. There was no blemish on her teenaged face, but a promise of beauty still developing. Her nose narrowed at the nostrils, and thinner lips dotted with a mole in the lower right corner of her mouth caused him to again question her origins. They caught each other's eyes, but she diverted her attention. Although they shared a class he had never been as close to Teran; beauty admired from afar can be deceiving. The truth of her desirability jolted him at the same time he realized the magnitude of her confidence and disdain for all in the group except Derek. Bashan swallowed and clasped his hands behind his back to gain equilibrium. He and his friends were sidelined, so he watched the exchange.

Teran was heading to the northeast entrance to meet Fawn. On the way she passed Bashan and Derek who walked with a group of friends. She gave a quick nod to the leering group, all too eager to respond, except Bashan who stared. Incensed, she attempted to continue walking, but Derek would not allow it. "Oh! Miss T too high post to stop and talk to a brotha?!" The young men burst into laughter at Derek's teasing.

Teran swiveled on a hip, "I said hi, D. Why you gotta start some static?"

Derek continued teasing, "You can't just walk by in that miniskirt like that, acting all flaky."

"You just want to start that's all. What's up?!" Teran engaged in the banter. Derek was her boy, he was funny, and Bashan didn't matter.

Derek smiled deviously and Teran braced herself, "Your man got you in check. You are running by brothas to meet that deadline he gave you. You gotta be at the northeast by a certain time, right?" The group of guys continued to snicker, Bashan stood with his hands behind his back- head slightly raised, as if he were inspecting their exchange.

Teran wanted to ask him if he smelled something but didn't want to acknowledge his presence. Instead, she challenged

Derek. "I ain't in check for no one and you know I don't have a man."

"Yeah, it's time you let a Queens brotha show you how it's done!" At the completion of Derek's statement Bashan gave a snort. Teran rolled her eyes to which Derek addressed, "See? That right there is what I am talking about, all that attitude. Yeah, a Queens brotha would give you some good gravy and get rid of that for you. Got too much Crooklyn in you, Queens gravy would smooth that right out."

As she turned to walk away, she answered, "You Queens boys are the ones too high post; you probably couldn't handle a Brooklyn girl."

Teran could hear the others whisper, "She dissed us hard." She hadn't recognized any voice belonging to Bashan, but she thought, 'He's probably standing there looking stupid.'

Then Derek yelled, "A little gravy would fix that right up!"

Teran yelled back, "You're still set, D!" and proceeded down the hall as the guys laughed.

Fawn was waiting for Teran at their usual location. "Where have you been? You usually beat me out here!"

"What? Are you my man now?!"

Fawn raised both brows. "Alright let's have it. What happened?"

"I saw Derek in the hall just now walking with his boys and that punk Bashan was with them."

"Bashan? You mean Shan-from-Queens Bashan?" Fawn touched her arm.

Teran narrowed her eyes, "Who else would I mean? There ain't no other stuck-up punk in this school like him, is there? I hope not!"

"I never heard anyone talk about him like that, what happened? The brotha is real chill, he don't cause static, and he is smart as heck. What did he do to you?"

Teran raised her hand to count his offenses. "First, he's in my seventh period class and when I walked in, he was staring at me like he was interested but he didn't open his mouth, so neither did I. He even stared me down after class and left without a word. Then just now he was with D and his boys, I spoke but he ain't part his lips. Then you know me, and D started getting into it, so D says something about me needing some gravy from a Queens Boy and that punk snorted like it was ridiculous or something. So, I said a Queens Boy couldn't handle a Brooklyn Girl and walked away. That stuck-up punk, he ain't that fine! He may dress nice but he ain't that fine!"

Fawn burst into laughter, "That's it? Because he ain't give you no rap? You should have said hi. He's quiet when he wanna be, he's cool, though. You just gotta get to know him."

"Well, I don't wanna know that stuck–up punk! And I ain't feenin for no rap either!" The ladies continued down DeKalb Ave toward Nevins Street train station.

----------◊◊◊----------

The Dance

The following day and many days after, Teran deliberately entered her seventh period class through its rear door so she would pass behind Bashan's desk. He turned to watch each time, which angered her, but she refused to look at him. On one occasion, before a test began, he passed a note simply stating, *"What's up?"* Teran crumpled the paper and would not look at him. Her mind reeled with thoughts of what she'd like to say: 'Ain't nobody kissing your behind, you stuck-up punk! You weren't parting your lips before so don't try to hold no convo now!' Teran took her test and thought no more of him.

As class ended, she turned to find his seat empty. Relieved, she proceeded out of the rear door. Once in the hallway she heard, *"At least let mi do someting before yuh gimme aal dis attitude, Miss."*

Bashan stood from his recline against the wall and towered over her with an amused grin. She was surprised by his Caribbean inflection; it was the first time she heard his voice. His proximity gave her a true measure of his height and she wondered how comfortable he could be in the aged classroom seats. Processing his presence and confidence, Teran did something no one would have thought possible – remained silent. Bashan looked at her and snorted the amused snort he gave during the hallway incident with Derek and others. "Don't be so mean Teran; yuh sweeter than dat."

Teran liked his lilt, but her tongue awoke, "How would you know that?!"

Bashan dismissed her tone with a nod of his head. "Anyway … how yuh think yuh did pon de test?"

She looked up into his smiling face; he was that fine. With a brief sigh, Teran decided there was no fun in fighting a one-sided battle. "I think I did good."

He gently corrected, "Yuh tink yuh did well, anyway, I know yuh did. Yuh probably get ah one hundred; yuh very smart and dats gud," then he smiled.

Teran answered with a demure, "Excuse me, I should have said *well*. Thank you for the compliment too." Then she joked. "I didn't know you were supposed to be my English tutor."

"Yuh welcum and I would rada be yuh man." He moved closer.

"My man? You don't really know me, and you want to be my man?"

"Yuh nuh haad to figure out. I know what I need to know at present. Wi find out de rest as wi guh alang." He stood with hands behind his back and watched the emotions play on her face.

Guys who liked her, to that point, had never demonstrated such self-assured poise. His confidence and straightforwardness let her know she was dealing with a different type of male. She took a long look at this young man of composure before her and thought of all the reasons she should let him down gently. Then she realized he watched her and remembered he said she was not hard to figure out. Had he taken the time to figure her out? Was that the reason for the dance the past month? In another uncharacteristic move, Teran blushed, "What am I supposed to say Bashan?"

He laughed and touched a lock of her hair. "Tell mi yuh will be my gyal; that's what yuh can say." The smirk he wore seemed to scream, 'You know you want to say yes.'

A chill shook her resolve and Teran was surprised Bashan could cause such a reaction within her. Taking a few covert breaths to calm her nerves she answered, "Then I will say yes, Bashan, I'll be your girl."

He wrapped extra-long arms around her small waist, brought them close, and kissed her lips softly. His gentleness seemed out of place on his imposing frame. One arm around her shoulder, Bashan led Teran toward the staircase to her next class. When he deposited her at the correct room Teran stared at him. He smirked, "I know yuh whole schedule, Miss, been scoping yuh fah ah while now. Meet mi at de lass soudeast window afta eight period, arite?" Teran nodded, still in shock. "Miss, I will be late fah gym." Bashan kissed her again and headed off.

----------◊◊◊---------

Scuttlebutt

Sixth period lunch came around quickly the next day and Teran was called to a private corner by one of her friends, Daphne Grant. "So, T, tell me what's up with you and Shan? I saw y'all hugged up on the third floor. I had to blink to make sure it was you." Teran's smile gave Daphne the impetus to continue. "So, it's true then, what I saw was legit? You and Bashan are together?" Teran nodded and Daphne voiced her surprise.

"Ooh, Teran, I would have thought he was too subdued for you; you know how wild you can get! But then again, he could be the right medicine for you, calm you down. We're in the Space Systems program together, Shan is a gentleman, and he doesn't get anything but A's in the class. And he can dress too, girl!! Did you know he used to go with Martina Robson?"

Teran knew Martina as a 'hi and goodbye' acquaintance, but she knew Martina was no push over. For a Queens Girl, who were notorious princesses with no street credibility, Martina was an exception. "Daph, didn't she get into a big fight a while ago?"

"Yeah, that was a few months ago. That was something else; I was there that day, and she did work. You know the Brooklyn girls try to rob the Queens girls on our way home, but Tina was not going for it. She whipped their behinds, and they did not rob *that* Queens girl. No one messes with her like they don't mess with you. Hmm, come to think of it, Shan must like them rough!" Teran playfully pushed her; when other crew members came over to where they talked, they ended the conversation.

Fawn also arrived at the table, greeted everyone, and began eating. She made small talk but kept throwing signals Teran playfully chose to ignore. Upon finishing her lunch, she directly addressed her. "T, I want you to come with me before our next class starts." They entered the stairwell and Fawn set in. "Alright, Girl, tell me what's up! About two months ago you were talking about Shan like a dog, calling him stuck up. Then today, from the sixth-floor landing, I see y'all hugged up and going down the staircase. Shoot! I ran down three flights behind y'all to make sure I was seeing right! Now, tell a sista what's up?!"

"You are no more shocked than I am Fawn. He stopped me after class, and we started talking. Next thing I know, he wants to be my man and I was so tongue-tied and stunned that I didn't know which way was up. He seems different, and that has my attention. We just started, so this is as new to me as it is for you and Daphne, who saw us as well."

"He must have kicked some good rap to catch you that fast! You need a brotha with some poise. I couldn't have found a better match for you." Fawn faltered.

"You! I should have known; how else would he know my schedule? Do I look desperate to you? Is this some kind of game? Does he win a bet?"

"Girl, stop!" Fawn held a hand between them. "He was already interested, so, no, I didn't bribe or convince him to talk to you. He genuinely likes you and he is a good brotha, and you'd better not blow this because you are so used to criminals, thugs, and woman beaters." Teran's head dropped. Fawn placed a tentative hand on her arm. "T, I am sorry. It's just that us having to fight Russell off you was too much. You know I love you and would do anything for you, so it's not about you as much as it's about what he represents. No one should go through that sort of mistreatment. Then you cut off the idea of guys after that incident but there are good brothas out here and Shan is one of them. It's time you get back out here. He really likes you, T. All I did was help him with information. He was already coming after you."

Watery eyes accompanied a lump in Teran's throat. "I know. We've been together almost all our lives and if anyone has my back it's you. Shan was so confident and mature I almost didn't know how to handle the exchange."

Fawn rubbed her arm. "So, you'll give this a chance?"

Teran nodded, "He drew me in and now I want to see how far this can go."

CHAPTER TWO

Us

News of the pairing spread through the school reaching across cliques and pecking orders. It created an opportunity for brief exchanges. Teran spoke with people she normally didn't interact with. The consensus was the pairing was a good one. Yet, Teran held pause.

As she approached history class, Teran felt her nerves flutter. She walked in and caught a pair of eyes awaiting her arrival. Their gazes met and Bashan smiled. During an off-task moment, she thought of comments made about Martina and Bashan. Letting out a breath she was startled by a note passed to her. *'You okay Miss? Yuh look as if yuh vexed. Did someone upset you?'* Teran turned toward Bashan who cocked an eyebrow in wait of a response. She smiled and shook her head; he nodded but Teran sensed the conversation was not over.

According to what had become custom, Bashan stood at the rear entrance waiting for her to exit. She sauntered over with a smile, and he returned a sly grin, "Nuh try to pretend everyting okay cause I saw yuh face." He leaned down and kissed her.

"Nothing for you to worry about, I am fine."

"Yuh gat dat rite, yuh ah fine!" Bashan openly perused her. He grabbed her hand and led them away.

----------◊◊◊----------

The Others

Twice per week, Teran's last two periods ended with a double period of physics. The teacher, a former gymnast, was widely known for using contortion and acrobatics to demonstrate the concepts of the subject. Many were eager to be enrolled in her class; Teran achieved high grades and found she enjoyed physics. Not having any close friends in the class was helpful too. The class marveled at the teacher's demonstration of centrifugal and centripetal force, engaged in activities practicing the concepts, and expressed disappointment when the dismissal bell rang. Headed toward the southeast exit, Teran could see Bashan leaning against the frame of the huge window that was their meeting place. A Kangol hat lay diagonally atop his head, the choice adopted by many of her male classmates. Teran admired his sense of style; even though Bashan wore the latest fashion, he wore them as if the clothing were tailored. As she approached, Bashan remained in recline, wearing a smirk.

His posture irked her. "Oh, so I must come to you because you're the Big Man, right?"

Bashan frowned and stood. "What's wid de attitude? I happen to enjoy watching yuh walk an de fact that yuh ah walking toward mi an are my gyal ah mo than gratifying. Or it was until yuh gimme dat Crooklyn attitude."

"This attitude was here when you met me and it's not hiding from you now or ever." Finally, a two-sided fight she could sink her teeth into.

Us

"Teran, that attitude is a front an wi both know it. I am yuh mon an nuh need dat nor do I waan it. Wi nuh have time fah fronting so lass it or lass mi."

Stunned by his direct manner, Teran stopped and stared. Part of her wanted to blast back, but Bashan's expression communicated a desire for reasoning rather than stirring up conflict. She wasn't prepared. "How did you figure me out in so little time?"

He stepped forward and embraced her. "Like I said yuh nuh hard to figure out. Cum on, let us get to know one anoda better. Put everyone an everytying else behind yuh cah dem de oda clowns nuh matta, I am here now."

Teran looked up, "Why are you so sure there are other guys?"

"As pretty as yuh are I know there have been odas. Yuh cyaan tell me differently." He placed a finger under her chin.

She shook her head, "Clowns would be right, or shall I say clown. I apologize for the outburst. A girl has to stand up for herself."

Bashan kissed her, "Flex. Teran, relax and give us time to know one anoda. I am a big pussycat yuh will see, but I do bite." He laughed as he nipped at her neck. "Nuh mo tuff gyal wid mi cah I kno betta, yuh undastan?" Teran nodded and they left the building.

----------◊◊◊----------

Settling In

Walking down DeKalb Avenue Bashan opened with, "So Miss, what's up with you?"

"Nothing much; I am keeping a low profile, out of trouble, you know, minding my business. I like how you blend your patois and American English." Teran smiled up at him as they walked along the busy Brooklyn street. He puckered toward her, and they shared a brief kiss.

"Good to know yuh keep a low profile; I nuh want my gyal in trouble. As I am comfortable, and I know you are comfortable, I will speak more Patwa. You should hear me around my family. Suh tell mi, wah yuh laik to do for fun? Hobbies, interests, I want to know yuh."

Teran wrinkled her nose, "There's that rhythm again. Were you born in Jamaica?"

"Yuh sup'm against Jamaicans?" Bashan teased.

"Yeah, I'd be in trouble if I did. We're getting to know one another, right? So, were you born there? Do you still have family there?"

"You wouldn't be in trouble, but you would miss out on a good man." Before she could rejoin, he continued. "I was born in Jamaica and came to the States when I was ten. I have a lot of family back in JA. Weh yuh ah from?"

"Born in Jamaica, Queens and raised in Brooklyn. Not as exotic as JA, as you call it, but it is what it is. My grandfather's family is from here. My grandmother's family is from the BVI and Barbuda. That's my mother's family. My father's family is mixed race and from the South. I guess you can say I am a blend of things.

Bashan nodded, "That would explain yuh skin color an yuh have brownish hair mixed wid de red."

Teran stopped, "Do you always watch people so closely? No one else ever mentions my red hair but you."

"I watch yuh cah I truly wan to know yuh. So yuh ah really a Queens gyal?"

Laughing, Teran nodded negatively, "Only through birth. I am a Brooklyn girl to the core."

"Well, I ago have to mek a Queens gyal outta yuh. I live dere so that ah weh yuh will be." He looked in a store window before checking for her reaction.

Us

Teran knew Bashan was asserting his position. She wondered if he really was her match. She would go along, for now. "What part do you live in?"

"Queens Village, do you know where it is?" The Alpha male had won and was sated.

"No, I don't, I'm not in Queens much. No reason to, my life and friends is in Brooklyn."

"You'll get used to it, it's nice." Bashan nodded his head.

Being coy she asked, "How are you so sure?"

Bashan wrapped his arm around her, "I plan to mek it nice fah yuh, real nice. Weh are wi walking?"

Teran laughed, "Just follow along, I'm planning to show you some Brooklyn sights." They walked to the Brooklyn Heights neighborhood, picked up pizza, and walked along the Promenade to find seats with a view of the East River.

Seated, they looked across the water at the World Trade Center and the South Street Seaport. Pizza slices demolished, Bashan wrapped an arm around her and pulled Teran close. He stroked her cheek. "This place is nice, you come here a lot?"

Teran nodded. She felt his hand on her face as she closed her eyes. They were firm yet comforting. She never expected his dexterity and gentleness. Derek's remark about giving a Queens Boy a try resounded in her head. She let out a long sigh and laid her head against Bashan's chest.

Feeling her relax, he stroked her brown and red-streaked hair. No one spoke for a while. He felt his skin prickle as she ran her hand up and down the length of his arm. This was the girl he knew resided behind the tough veneer. "Wah mek yuh nuh cum see mi dis weekend? It's time I get yuh out to Queens fah a while."

Teran looked at him mischievously, "I don't know Shan, nine trains and three buses, over the river and through the woods."

He laughed, "So, yuh a jokesta?! I tek a train an bus to get to school Monday drough Friday so I know transportation works bot ways it's time fah yuh to cum to my territory. Dere mo dan Brooklyn."

"I know there's a big world out here, man!"

Bashan challenged, "Then dere nuh worries. I wan to spend time with yuh widout having to sneak a kiss pon de stairwell or de promenade here. I wan yuh to meet my friends an see how I live." She agreed and they left the Promenade.

At the Flatbush Avenue train station, they prepared to separate. Bashan had Teran on a step higher than his, "How about a kiss for the road?" Without waiting for a reply, he held her steady and approached.

Derek Holmes entered the stairwell and saw them. He recognized Bashan and cleared his throat, causing Bashan to look up. "Hey D! What's up man?!"

Derek replied, "Shan, my man, everything is everything, though I ain't doing as good as you." While Derek spoke Teran turned in his direction. He took one look at her and exclaimed, "Get outta here! Shan and Teran! I'd never put the two of you together! But that's cool. Maybe you can calm her down man. She can be a little firecracker at times."

Bashan answered with, "She arite like she is."

"I'd better be getting out to East New York. It's getting late and I don't want my mother to worry. Bye D." Teran took the opportunity to excuse herself after laughing at Derek's antics.

"Hey Miss, aren't you forgetting sup'm?" Bashan took her hand as she made to ascend the stairs.

Normally Teran would not have been happy with what she viewed as grand standing, but it was Bashan, and he was quickly endearing himself to her. When he reached for her, she embraced and gave him another kiss. "Bye baby."

Bashan smirked, "Be safe an I will call yuh lata."

She resumed her departure and threw over her shoulder, "Close your mouth D." She could hear Derek carrying on, "My man! I would not have believed this if I had not seen it just now. You the man!" She shook her head as she continued.

Us

---◊◊◊---

Over the River

The sun ushered in a mild morning as Teran began her trip to Queens. She transferred trains at the World Trade Center and thought of how Fawn teased her the night before about taking the Amtrak to see Bashan. The ride was pleasant but too long for her liking. At 179th Street, Teran called Bashan who told her to go upstairs and take the bus. She waited in front of the Burger King no more than five minutes before the Q105 pulled to its stop. She boarded, paid her fare, and was about to take a seat when she heard, "Hey Teran!"

Teran looked up and into the face of the name she couldn't stop hearing for the last month. Martina Robson waved to her from a rear seat. Teran put on a smile and walked over. "How are you doing Tina? I heard about your static out in Brooklyn; I heard you did work!"

Martina laughed, "I did what I had to do. How are you doing?"

"Well alright! I'm okay, I can't complain."

"Are you going to see Shan?" Teran nodded. Martina continued, "He really likes you. You're all he talks about."

Teran knew the two were still friends but wasn't aware of how close Bashan and Martina were. This time she smiled more to cover her discomfort with Martina's familiarity than out of wanting to be friendly. "Really?"

Martina laughed again, "Yeah, really. He is sweet, Teran, and he'll give you anything in the world. Be good to him."

Feeling a little insulted by the comment, Teran came back with, "Well, why'd you two break up? Did he do something to you?" There is an unspoken code in New York that one must be assertive or become the one who is stepped on. Teran never allowed anyone to step on her, and she was not about to start. She would control her participation in this conversation.

Martina seemed to maintain her stride, "No, he didn't do anything. We just thought it was better for us to be friends. He's a good guy and not into playing games, I'm sure you can appreciate that."

"I can't blame him because I do not like games either; they waste too much time. For a good month we seemed to dance around each other, and I felt like that was a game. I was not enthused with him, but now I understand he was checking me out." Teran felt better about being in control of the information she would share. There was no sense in being angry with Martina; Bashan was another story. "Now that I am getting to know him, I see that he is a gentleman." Feelings she was developing for Bashan would never be Martina's business.

"You two are going to be the couple – I know it. I am happy for him and for you." Martina smiled and Teran thought of how pretty she was. That Bashan could pull the ladies was evident. Martina's stop came as she finished her statement, so they said their goodbyes and Teran was left alone to her thoughts…

Russell Davis grabbed Teran by the hair to threaten in her ear, "You know what happens next don't you?!" Teran let out an interrupted scream as his hand quickly covered her mouth. Tears clouded her eyes as he continued to pull her hair, dragging her backward toward his front door. She reached out to stop their momentum knowing he would really hurt her if he got her alone. She managed to grab the banister and began to kick backward. The third kick connected enough to sting Russell, "Owww! Girl!" He let her hair go and she screamed. "Fawn!"

Fawn raced around the corner and was on Russell faster than Teran could register. She shook herself free and they jumped him in the hallway outside his front door. Teran determined it was the last time she would need rescuing.

She almost missed her stop but as she prepared to disembark, Teran looked out of a window to find Bashan waiting. Grins broke out on both their faces. Bashan wore a brown

Us

Kangol, Cazal frames, Brown Clarks, a brown leather jacket over a beige Izod shirt, and brown pants. Teran was proud of how good he looked and saw a woman on the bus looking at him too, "Is that your boyfriend?"

"Yes ma'am."

"He looks well put together. I am glad you have a young man who knows how to carry himself. You seem to make wise choices and I hope you continue to do so."

Teran beamed at the woman's appreciation for Bashan's appearance. In the exchange with the stranger, Teran could identify with pride Bashan felt as they faced the surprised Derek on the subway steps.

He greeted with "Hello Miss." as she disembarked.

"Hi yourself!" She walked into his outstretched arms. They kissed briefly and began walking.

"Suh how did yuh find de ride out here?" Bashan pulled a strand of the hair she wore straight with curled ends.

"It's too long – two trains and a bus – I don't know how you do it!" Teran shook her head with disdain.

Bashan watched her and laughed lightheartedly, "You'll get used to it once yuh live here a while."

Teran stopped and looked at Bashan, "What makes you think I'm gonna live way out here?"

Bashan's answered with confidence, "Time will tell eff yuh will or eff yuh won't. I know I am staying here, I nuh coming to live in Brooklyn!"

"What's so wrong with Brooklyn?! You go to school there and I live there. Brooklyn is a beautiful city!" Teran broke away to stare at him.

Bashan shook his head and grabbed her hand, "Brooklyn ah cool but I love Queens, so I am staying out here. And my ooman will tan wid mi weh I live."

With a wrinkled brow Teran observed, "You have to be in control, huh, Bashan? And I noticed you slipped more of your patois in there."

"You undastan me so I relax, an I am de mon here. A mon cyaan let de ooman walk all ova him wen de Bible seh him ah de head." He stopped Teran from countering. "Yuh probably controlled yuh oda boyfriends. Half of de dudes up at de school ah fraid to talk wid yuh. Dey tink yuh wud ave dismissed dem an hurt their pride." He shook his head and laughed.

Teran's mouth dropped, "Are you serious? The guys at the school are afraid of me?"

"Maybe I should not seh fraid but dey ah reluctant to approach yuh. Was dat all yuh heard mi seh? Bout de oda guys? I watched yuh an I knew yuh needed someone ooo could dominate but love yuh at de siem time."

"Wow! I am that bad that I make others reluctant? And because of this you have appointed yourself my loving dominator? Am I supposed to be okay with this?"

"Don't misundastan mi. I am miself fram beginning to end. I know what I want an I go afta it. I know I must be firm wid yuh because yuh a strong ooman. A strong ooman can make a strong mon great and he needs dat support. I need dat support." He jingled the hand he held.

Fawn said in Bashan Teran likely met her match, and while she could respect his strength, she would not be overshadowed by him. "I have goals and plans too, so I suggest we find some compromise. Things will not go well if it's all about me supporting your dream at the expense of my own."

Bashan smirked, "Wi can make bot sides fair an equal I just won't be de ongle one leggo everything."

"You do seem to be letting go of everything like too much information. That is why Martina had the nerve to talk to me about how well to treat you."

Bashan raised a brow, "Yuh talk wid Tina when?"

"I saw her on the bus ride over here. That is when she took it upon herself to inform me you two best friends always talk about everything including me. She then added how she wanted me to treat you well because you were a good guy and you really liked me." Now Teran had hands on her hips.

Bashan laughed and grabbed her into an embrace, "Teran ah jealous! Gyal yuh have nuh worries an nuh need to hear from anyone else how I feel about yuh. Yuh neva have to fret about mi hiding my true feelings from yuh."

Teran narrowed her eyes and broke the embrace as she looked up at him, "Yeah, but she did."

He pulled her back in, "Miss, neva mind dat wi ah togeda now because I want to be wit yuh." He kissed her lips quickly, grabbed a hand and led them up the street.

----------◊◊◊----------

Shop Around

Bashan led her toward a brown brick two-story detached home. The bright white awning above its door held drops from an early rain. They ascended four steps and entered an anteroom where he took her jacket and hung it on a coat tree.

Teran suddenly felt she was among Redwoods. Mary Watts stood five feet eleven inches, with her feet in slippers, in an archway leading to the living room. She was solidly built with even proportions, had flawlessly dark skin and sported shoulder length curls. Bashan was a six-feet-three version of his mother.

"Shani ooo yuh did bring home?"

Moving a hand to her lower back, he brought them closer "Mumi, this ah Teran, mi girlfriend."

"It's a pleasure to meet you, Mrs. Watts." Teran's extended arm awaited a hesitant engulf. She kept her smile in place as she glimpsed a twitch at the left corner of Mary's mouth.

"How yuh duh? Shani tells mi yuh have family in the islands?"

The contact was brief and now she stood under Mary's perusal. "Yes ma'am, on my grandmother's side they are

Caribbean. I don't know them." Another jerk lowered the woman's lip. Teran forged ahead. "I live in Brooklyn, but I was born here in Queens."

The thought that, in 1982, one still had to prove her worth irritated Teran. And what further annoyed her was how she explained herself to this woman.

She had to be ten when she first noticed the beauty of Brooklyn's tree-lined streets. She walked with her mother towards her grandparents' century-old brownstone in Clinton Hill. How she smiled every time she approached the row of houses where the Jacksons resided in the middle of the block. In this home she learned their family had been part of Brooklyn's history; it was a history of which she was proud. She was no transplant, but a true New York native.

"Shani told me yuh go to the prep school as well?" Bashan eased the ladies into the living room and helped Teran sit on the beige linen Churchill couch.

She focused on Bashan pretending not to see Mary's brow knot watching them. "Yes, I do, and we have the same history class. That's where we met."

The woman settled in a brown brocade chair opposite the couch. Her strong hands gripped each armrest as she pushed back into a reclining position; her legs crossed at the ankles.

Bashan stood, smiling, and moved to the end of the centered marble-topped coffee table. "Mumi, Teran ah smart an gets good grades aal de time." Then he left the living room.

Mary nodded. "That's nice to hear. Shani also gets good grades."

"Some of our friends said he gets nothing but A's in his Space Systems classes." Her grandmother taught her how to agree with the disagreeable.

Bashan came back with two glasses of iced tea. He set one on the coffee table then settled a glass next to Mary. She beamed at her son. "He has loved planes since he was a likkle bwoy. He always had a plane in his hand."

Bashan offered, "Teran is in engineering too, she takes electricity courses."

"So, yuh are going to kip that up in college, Teran?" Narrowed eyes awaited an answer.

"I am not sure if I will major in engineering. The first two years I will take general courses until I can make up my mind. I may find something else that interests me."

Mary sat forward in her chair. "Dis generation tinks they have aal de time in de world. Dere ah sup'm to be said about making up one's mind and sticking to de plan. Shani has a plan, and I nuh waan him distracted." She focused on her son, "Don't kip yuh friend out too lang, Shani." Mary nodded toward Teran and left the living room.

When she would bring Bashan to the red brick project building where she resided it would not measure up. It was apparent he was used to something different. It had to be different for her. She was going to have a different life, and no one would be able to look down at her.

Teran grabbed Bashan's hand and was about to speak when she heard another voice, *"Shani, ooo duh yuh ave in dere?"* Mary's twin walked into the room with a dimpled smile, *"Ah dat Teran, Shani?"*

Bashan stood and she reached his shoulder. They grinned, "Yah. Teran, dis ah mi sista Armentha. Mentha, dis ah mi girlfriend, Teran."

Teran stood and made to shake the woman's hand but was swallowed in an embrace. "Wah gwan? Shani told mi aal about yuh. How did yuh like de ride out here? Shani said yuh called it ova de riva an drough de woods - wi laughed at dat one."

She instantly liked this sister. "The ride was long, but it was peaceful."

"Wah gwan?"

Teran turned to yet another of Mary's clones. Yet this one was shorter at five feet seven inches and slenderer in build than Armentha. Bashan introduced her, "Ivee, Teran ah mi girlfriend. Teran meet mi oda sista, Iverine."

Teran moved forward but sensed this one would not embrace her and was correct. Iverine stepped backward but extended her hand, "Wah gwan?"

"Hi, nice to meet you." Teran felt a chill.

Iverine nodded and dropped her hand. She never smiled. "Shani, wat happened to Martina?"

Armentha turned toward her sister. "Ivee, dat question nuh appropriate at dis time."

Bashan countered, "Teran knows Tina, wi guh to de siem school."

Iverine snorted, "Yuh ah trying to guh drough aal de gyal dem dere at de school, Shani?"

"Nuh Ivee - it is mi an Teran now." Bashan blew out a breath. Teran placed her palm behind him and rubbed his back.

Mary reentered, "Teran ah mi pickney pon dem bess behavior? Dey ave home training but act laik de devil at times." Teran smiled and Iverine sat in a matching brocade chair.

Mary looked at her daughter, "Ivee, wi mus get going."

"Okay Mumi, nuh a moment to rest."

Mary quipped, "Rest wen yuh ah ded!" They left the living room.

Armentha addressed Teran, "Excuse mi sista, de Queen of Sheba, Teran. Shi can be a bit much at times."

Teran nodded, "Thank you Armentha, I guess she really likes Martina. I can see why – she is pretty and smart. What's not to like?"

"Call mi Mentha. Yuh ah priti an smart too, suh dats wah mek Shani choose yuh. I have laundry to duh, yuh two have fun." She walked out of the living room.

Teran sat on the couch absorbing all that transpired when Bashan lifted her into an embrace. He was moving before she registered the song playing in the background. The balladeer

Us

crooned about how the woman loved him as Bashan whispered, "Yuh meet mi madda an sistahs. What yuh tink, Teran?"

"I think you're really comfortable because you are speaking to me as if you're speaking to them." She snickered and laid her head against his chest as he led their slow dance.

Bashan's laugh resonated within his chest. "Yuh ah in mi yard. Wah mek yuh nuh answer mi question?"

Teran looked up at him. "Slow down; I am learning this Patwah. I like your house and I like your family, but I don't think they all like me."

He rubbed her back, "They will get used to you."

"Thank you for speaking English."

"I am speaking English."

"You're English, but I need you to speak my English."

Bashan stopped dancing and stepped backward. "Yuh here fi get fi know me."

"Yes, and I am glad I am here, but let's not pretend your mother and Ivee like me because you and I both know they don't. Even Mentha knows that. What makes you press me for an answer?"

"There's that mout again. Yuh rude!" Bashan walked over to the stereo system behind the couch and turned the music off."

Teran volleyed at his back, "I'm rude and you are trying to put what happened on me. Is Martina Jamaican too? Because you know that's what this is about, right?"

Bashan extended his legs over the back and flopped into the couch. "Tina is from Guyana and has nothing to do with this."

"Shan, your mother does not like that I am not Caribbean."

"But you are."

"Oh, does that make me acceptable? I am from New York, born and raised in New York, there have been Jacksons in New York since Dutch colonial days. I know who I am, and I do not have to be Caribbean to be acceptable."

"Teran, yuh mi gyal an dats acceptable fi mi. Why the argument?"

"I want you to be fair and be honest. This is not about me liking them. Call this one right; they do not like me, and I do not appreciate the reasons why." Teran sat in the brocade seat vacated by Ivee.

Bashan sat up and clasped his hands before him. "What yuh tink de reasons ah?"

Teran crossed her legs. "Ivee likes Martina, and I am not Martina. Your mother wants you with a Caribbean girl; one who knows her Caribbean roots."

"Babi, they will get used to you." He walked over and kneeled in front of her.

"Shan, that's a hard pill to swallow that they would have to get used to me. I have done nothing to merit this freezing out. But I do not want to fight with you about it either."

He approached her with a smile. "Don't fight with me. We go through this together. We go through everything together. Okay?"

Teran returned the kiss but held him off afterward. "Shan, I have been through some things in the past and I have promised myself I won't go through being mistreated again. If we are going to be together, I need to know you will protect me. I would not let anyone hurt or disrespect you."

"I didn't expect this, Babi. It happened suh fast. Forgive me. Yuh have mi protection."

Teran smiled and ran a hand down the side of his face. "That's all I ask."

He drew her out of the seat and into his arms. "Mi waan fi mek ih up. Yuh need mi fi translate?"

Teran grinned, "No, I think I can get this by context."

CHAPTER THREE
My World

The Brethren

At Burger King, Bashan fed Teran a French fry and made her blush. He laughed, "Wah mek yuh suh modest afta de time wi just spend togeda?"

Teran lowered her head, "Shan! Stop it!" She grabbed the soda they shared.

He continued laughing and whispered in her ear, "Miss strong ooman one moment an melt inna mi arms de next minute." Teran choked on the sip.

"What are you doing to that girl, man?!"

Bashan looked up to find his best friend walking toward them. "Way! How yuh livin?!" Teran sipped again and looked on as a dark brown, mustached young man of six feet came toward them smiling. Bashan introduced, "Wayman Morrison, dis ah Teran Buard, mi babi. Teran, dis ah mi bess bredren, Wayman."

Wayman cocked his head, "Hey, Miss Teran, I gotta get a hug." She stood and obliged with Bashan looking proudly upon the interaction. "You got my man's heart, so I hope you know that." Teran blushed and Wayman added, "I see why too with your cute little self!"

Bashan removed Teran from his friend's embrace and sat her on his lap. Wayman slid into the opposite side of the booth. He watched the couple for a moment then took a fry. "You two ready to hit it?" Teran gave Bashan a puzzled look and Wayman replied, "We are hanging out, Lady. Show you how we do it out here. Brooklyn isn't the only one that knows how to live you know!" They left the restaurant.

Teran was further surprised by Wayman jumping behind the wheel of a dark blue four-door Buick Skylark. "You drive?"

"Yeah, Shan drives too. We got our licenses a week apart."

Bashan smiled at her, "Yuh ah out here to get to know mi betta an see how I live, rememba?"

They settled in the car and Wayman turned up the radio. As if WBLS spied the quiet time the couple enjoyed earlier that afternoon, the deejay began to play a slow jam to which they danced. Bashan turned toward Teran, who was in the backseat, and blew her a kiss. She blushed and averted her eyes. Wayman shook his head, "I don't even have to ask."

Bashan offered, "She can be shy. Let's go over to Jamaica to get the hats we talked about."

The Jamaica Avenue shopping mall held vendors selling clothing, pagers, new electronic gadgets, and a host of other wares. Teran was overwhelmed but enjoyed being there. "This is almost like King's Plaza in Brooklyn, but King's Plaza has actual stores."

Wayman joked, "Bet you didn't think we had this kind of shopping out here, did you? We have to get you out to Green Acres. You'll really like that because it might be more like your King's Plaza."

"That sounds like a plan! I am looking forward to that. I notice the Queens folks dress a little differently at school. Bashan walks around like he's on the runway."

Wayman laughed, "I like that sense of humor. Yeah, we like to represent out here. You dress well yourself."

"Brooklyn always comes high."

Bashan added, "Way, she is high post. Dissed a group wit mi an odas deh at de school. Dat mini she wore killed wi dead!"

Wayman laughed until he held his stomach. "Man, B, I remember you told me about that! Girl, you are tough. You are good for my man here because you bring him a challenge."

"So, Martina didn't challenge him?"

Wayman's brow raised. "Whoa, that's right, Tina goes to the same school." He waved his hand. "Don't worry about Tina, Lady. Shan and Tina wanted different things and that happens. It's history and no need for you to worry about that. B is with you, and he is happy with that; so am I."

Bashan grabbed Teran's hand. "I told yuh nuh worry. Tina is a friend. Yuh ah mi Babi." He wrapped his arm around her neck and kissed her cheek. "Help me get a hat."

"See, T, he is all about you. Don't worry about no other girls. We have a lot ahead of us today and you two have a future. Let's get these hats and go to the next stop. We have a party to go to later, Lady. You might find something you like."

"Yo, Way, quit! Yuh hit mi inna de pockets." Teran pinched him and they laughed on the way to the booth containing men's clothing and hats.

----------◊◊◊----------

Queens

Wayman brought the couple back to his home. After he parked at the curb, Teran opened her door.

"Miss, weh yuh go?" Bashan grabbed the door and gave her a frown.

Wayman got out, pushed his lock down which engaged all of the locks, and closed his door. "Hey, T, you know my man has to be the gentleman. That's how we Queens boys do. I know you not used to that with those Crooklyn guys."

Teran snapped her head as Bashan helped her out of the car. "Alright, y'all got one more dis for Brooklyn! For the record, there isn't a thing wrong with the Brooklyn guys; they are not soft."

"Yuh call mi soft, Miss?" He leaned on the door frame.

"Shan, you know there is nothing soft about you. Stop dissing my city."

Bashan snorted, "Way, shi love Brooklyn, but shi will be wit me out here. Facts."

"Take charge, B, that's my boy!"

Teran fired, "I will be where I want to be, and not where he tells me to be!"

"That's right, you tell them, Girl!" Cherise Morrison descended the four steps leading from the detached home's front door clapping her hands. "They are always trying to act like they run the world."

Wayman answered, "You would jump in and make it a fight. Teran, this is my sister Cherise. We call her Cheri; Teran is Shan's girlfriend."

Cherise walked to the car and stood next to Teran. "I'm glad I get the chance to meet you. Shan has been talking about you a lot and about how he is getting you out here to meet us. I like you already because you are no pushover."

Wayman addressed Cheri, "Where you on your way to?"

"I'm supposed to meet up with D-D and Nina on Jamaica Ave. Nina needs shoes for tonight."

Wayman dismissed the last comment with a wave. "Nina is the last person to need any more shoes. Kennith told me she must have almost eighty pair already." He turned toward the house and headed down one side to its basement entrance.

Bashan answered Teran's unspoken query. "Kennith ah anoda bredren and Nina ah his ooman." He reached for her hand and led them toward the side of the house.

Cheri followed them down the side of her home. "Teran, you want to go with me to meet them. We can have some girl time and do some shopping."

Bashan answered, "We just came from the mall."

"I already know she can answer for herself. Aren't you coming to the party tonight out on Utopia Parkway?"

Teran pulled Bashan's hand, "Shan wouldn't help me find anything for the party."

"Yuh didn't see anything you liked, rememba?"

Cheri offered, "Let's go on the avenue. There are more stores there and I am sure you'll find something. Cough up the bucks, Big Man, you know she needs to look fly. Besides, with your job you know you can afford it."

Teran gasped, "You didn't tell me you have a job. So, you drive, and you have a job. Is there anything else I need to know?"

Bashan dropped her hand and wrapped an arm around her shoulders. "Yuh cum here to learn about me. Of course, dere mo to find out."

Cheri tapped Bashan's arm. "I need to go meet D-D and Nina. We need to leave."

Bashan stared at Teran a moment. She could see he was thinking about something that made him hesitant. When he dropped his arm and entered the basement Teran's confusion was evident. *Did he just leave me standing here?*

Bashan returned and placed some bills in Teran's hand as he kissed her lips. "Mek sure yuh ah priti fi mi tonight, Babi." He turned her toward Cheri and gave her a pat on the backside.

Teran turned to thank him, but he was gone. So, she turned to Cheri who watched with amusement. "I guess that is that. Let's go." Teran placed bills in three different locations.

"Shan has his ways, doesn't he? He and my brother have been friends for about five years now and as long as we have known him, he has had his own ways. I actually like that he does his own thing. Too many dudes out here try to put up a front, but Shan does what he wants to do. And something tells me you follow your mind too. I think this will be interesting for you because you both seem to have met your match."

The ladies resumed their walk toward the street. "We just met, Cherie, and you are already making predictions. How are you so sure?"

"I know Shan and I have seen him operate. He is different with you. You are different than anyone I have seen him with before."

A stabbing pain hit Teran's gut. "Don't tell me, Martina, right?"

"Martina?! Oh, you know names, huh?" Cheri began to laugh but stopped when she looked at Teran's expression. She placed a hand on Terna's arm, and they stopped walking. "Teran, you have absolutely nothing to worry about. Shan and Tina were not tight like you and Shan. They didn't fit and they both knew it, so don't worry about her or anyone else."

"Well, my God, how many *else's* are there?"

Cheri let out a guffaw this time. "Girl, you are crazy! Look, Shan can pull them, and he has pulled them, but they didn't stay. It's easy to see he feels a lot for you."

Teran thought about the day's events. "Maybe that explains his mother."

They continued walking to the bus stop. "You met Shan's mother? Miss Mary is a little hard, but you get used to her. She does warm up a little more."

Teran nodded, "I met his sisters, too. Mentha is cool, but that Ivee acts like her mother."

"Uh huh, Queen of Sheba! But everyone likes Mentha. Even Shan likes Mentha, but his sisters will do anything for him. Ivee will break someone's neck over Shan. It's like she can dog him out but no one else could even think about doing him wrong. Ivee is a trip!"

"And they talk about Brooklyn girls?!"

"Right! Brooklyn, Queens, Bronx, Manhattan, we are all New Yorkers. You know that's the notorious Jamaican temperament. Anyway, what do you think you want to wear tonight?"

"I guess you'll have to give me an idea of what I should wear because I don't know jack about this party. If Shan had told me, I would have brought clothes with me. Would you mind if I took a shower when we get back?"

"That's fine. I have my own bathroom because my brother stays downstairs. We will have privacy for you to get ready. We are going to the Basilica tonight. It used to be a church, but they moved to a different location and rent this building out for events. You know the code is to get fly."

----------◊◊◊----------

Through the Woods

Bashan watched with pride as Teran walked through the crowd outside Basilica. Her transformation shocked him. She came down to Wayman's basement in a red blazer that had a three-chain closure. Above the left breast of the jacket sat a lion's head with a ring through its mouth from which three attached chains extended to the right pocket of the blazer to be gathered in a rectangular clasp. Beneath the jacket she wore a black tank top and black miniskirt atop fishnet stockings and red short pumps. She pinned her hair into a French roll with several loose strands and completed the look with a headscarf that complemented her ensemble.

Kennith poked him in the ribs, "Your girl is fly, Shan. She is pretty too. You had better keep an eye on her because these dudes will try to rap to her in a heartbeat."

"Nuh happening Ken cah shi in mi sight aal de time." Bashan moved into the crowd before calling over his shoulder. "Ken, yuh take yuh own advice yuh nuh see yuh gyal?!" He motioned toward Nina off to the side talking to a guy.

As Kennith moved toward the two Wayman suggested, "Ken, you won't go nut out here tonight man." Kennith nodded his head and kept moving.

Teran felt Bashan's presence before she recognized his citrusy scent. She turned and looked into his face. "Are you following me, Sir?"

"Look at the love birds out to party tonight! Can I get one dance with him, Teran?" Martina walked over and hugged them both. Teran felt the stab again. She stood before them in a pink jersey mini dress with three black belts of varying glittered patterns hung from waist to hip atop fishnet stockings and black slouch boots. Her hair was pulled to the top of her head and allowed to muss forward in tight curls. A gold nameplate hung on her chest. She looked at Teran and smiled, "I like that outfit Teran! Where did you get that jacket? It is bad! Shan you will have to watch her tonight."

"Thank you, Martina. I like your outfit too. I found this jacket today on Jamaica Ave." It was difficult to keep smiling, but she did, especially since Bashan stood by proudly watching the exchange. Martina moved on and Teran had to fight from letting out an audible sigh of relief.

Cheri came up beside her, wrapped her arm around Teran's arm, and addressed Bashan. "You are not holding her hostage. She is hanging out with the girls. You can come and find us later." She marched Teran into the party.

D-D had secured a table and Cheri led them in that direction. When they arrived, D-D announced, "I hope there is no static tonight because Nina's ex is here and had her in a box outside."

The ladies sat down; Cheri responded. "Can we go out without all of this craziness. I swear, she and Ken always have some crap going on. They are a pain in the butt. All I know is I will have words for Nina if my brother gets into a fight. This is Teran's first night out with us and I want her to have a good time."

As D-D shook her head, the pineapple waves in her hair glistened. "We usually know how to act Teran. It's those two that always bring the static. Wayman had better not get into anything else. I already told him I am not having it."

Teran asked, "There have been problems before? If Wayman was involved, then Shan must have been involved too, right?"

D-D nodded, "The parking lot at the movie theater a while back. We were out and Kennith got into it with some guy over Nina and those tight Jordaches she was wearing. I told her about squeezing her big behind in these jeans. Well, if you're flaunting it, you can't get upset when someone is attracted. The guy said something about wanting a piece of that butt and he and Kennith got into and then Way and Shan were in it, of course, because the guy has friends. It was a mess, and I was pissed."

Teran shook her head, "And they talk about Brooklyn?! Shan and Way had better not say another thing about my city because I can go see a movie in *peace*."

Nina arrived at the table and flopped into a seat. "Every time I turn around it is something. Wayman and Bashan had to get Kennith because he was ready to fight Tyreece."

D-D sucked her teeth, Teran caught her breath, and Cheri blasted. "Who are you mad with exactly? Why would you be in Tyreece's face anyway? He is your ex who obviously wants you back and you find it okay to be in his face at a party where everyone and his mother is attending, and you think Ken should be cool with that?"

Nina rolled her eyes, "Don't start with me, Cheri! I did not ask or try to be in his face. But I didn't want to make a scene, so I heard him out and told him no dice. I am happily with Kennith." She looked into her bag.

D-D stopped Cheri from replying because she saw Nina was upset. "We need you and Ken to get this straight because Way and Shan keep getting dragged into this stuff and that's not fair to any of us." Nina cried and D-D consoled her.

Scandalous

The group had a system of dancing and watching the table. Teran and Cheri sat at the table laughing and sipping on sodas. The most popular reggae tune boomed over the sound system and a roar exploded inside the Basilica. The sounds were becoming popular, but Teran didn't listen to much of it and certainly did not dance to it, so she watched. The crowd gyrated and Teran was surprised by the movements. She heard Cheri stammer, "Oh, crap," and looked out on the floor to see Bashan dancing. The stab let her know before she left the table to investigate, ignoring Cheri's calls to come back.

Bashan wound his body as he dipped low, and Martina matched his movement by arching backward. They came up from their whines and met face to face. The movements were graceful and sensual, Teran watched as they stepped closer. Bashan grabbed Martina's thigh and she held his waist as they renewed a whine that almost took Teran's breath. She walked over and screamed, "Are you finished screwing her on the dance floor?!"

Bashan stopped and let a wide-eyed Martina go. Teran felt tears so she struck him in the chest and turned to leave the dancefloor. No match for his longer steps, Bashan had Teran around the waist in no time. He half-walked half-carried her to the table where he sat down and placed her on his lap. She slapped his face. "Nuh hitting, Teran. Wi nuh do that!" Cheri left the table.

"Let me go, Shan."

"Calm down, Miss. I was dancing."

"That was not dancing. That was screwing standing up!"

"That is how we dance in the Caribbean."

"Well, you had better learn how to dance like an American."

"It's my culture, Teran."

"You grinding on your ex-girlfriend is not culture. It's disrespect."

"Teran, it's only a dance."

"Okay, then let me go and let me find someone to grind on since it's only a dance. I am sure the brother I danced with earlier wouldn't mind showing me a thing or two."

"Nuh vex me, Teran."

"Nuh vex me, Bashan! You must be out of your mind all on her like that and I am sitting right over here. That tells me you are out doing whatever you want to do when I am not around. Now, that may fly with the Queens girls and the Caribbean girls, but you are dating an American girl from Brooklyn, and you will not be disrespecting me like that!"

"Yuh finished?"

"NO, brotha, I'm just getting started. I do not and would not disrespect you. I get culture, but y'all were going at it out there. If you two still have coals in the fire let me know so I can bow out gracefully. I am not interested in static, especially when I am so far from home."

Bashan held Teran firm on his lap. "Weh yuh ah, ah weh yuh will be. I am with yuh, Miss, an nuh want nobody else. No coals in the fire. It was dancing. If it went too far, I apologize, but it was a dance and nuh mo." Teran looked away. "Miss, watch mi, yuh aal mi want." He turned her face toward him. "Yuh aal mi want, Teran."

Wayman, D-D, and Cheri walked over to the table and sat down. He looked at the battling couple, "Everything cool you two?"

Bashan looked at Teran, "Everyting cool, Miss? Yuh forgive mi?" Teran shook her head and he kissed her. "We cool, Way."

Martina walked over and addressed Teran. "Hey, T, I am so sorry if you did not like me dancing with Shan. I thought you were okay with us dancing since I asked you earlier."

Teran felt Bashan tighten his grip, so she'd remain in his lap. She nodded her head. "It's okay, Tina. I'm just not used to the dancing yet."

Bashan added, "Yet."

Martina smiled, "So, are we cool? We don't have any static, do we?"

"No, Tina, we are cool, no static."

"You are sure, T? Me and Shan are only friends. He doesn't see anyone but you."

"I'm sure, we are cool."

Martina said good night and the group gathered their things to leave.

Kennith and Nina drove Cheri home. Wayman, D-D, and Bashan decided to drive to a diner not far from Basilica before driving Teran to Brooklyn. They rehashed the evening while eating.

"Way, this gyal giv mi the business at the party. Told me, '*Nuh broda, I jes getting started!*'"

Wayman laughed, "Cheri found me and said I had better get to the table because Teran was spitting fire when she saw you whining with Tina. What were you thinking, boy?"

"Yuh know the song came as shi asked mi fi dance."

D-D laughed, "Yeah, and my girl danced your behind right off that floor. We saw her run up on you and then you run after *her*."

"I apologize for causing a scene. I just couldn't stand there and let it go down like that." Teran lowered her head.

D-D reached for her hand, "Don't apologize. Shan is your man and you served them skanks notice tonight. Trust me, they will think twice about approaching your man. And he'll think twice before grinding on some heffa!"

Bashan grunted, "Shi have nuh worries. I kip telling her."

D-D waved her hand, "She had to let her position be known. You men handle things your way and we do too."

Teran shook her head, "For real, right?!"

Bashan looked at Teran and pulled at a strand of her hair. "Shi ah a firecracker."

Wayman agreed, "And she is time enough for you."

----------◊◊◊----------

"Nuh touch that door, Miss!" Bashan jumped from his seat to help Teran from the car.

Outside her building Teran almost bolted. The minute they entered her neighborhood she tried to melt into her seat. She moved her hand away from the door and looked at D-D who was laughing. "I had fun with you tonight, T, we have to do this again soon, right Wayman?"

"Of course! My man Shan will have her out with us, and we will come scoop her up. There's no doubt about that. You are part of the crew now, Miss T!" He parked, cut the motor, and jumped out to open D-D's door.

Teran stammered, "All of you don't have to get out. I can get into the building from here. It's late and you need to get back home."

"Flex, Babi." Bashan ran a large hand down her back and kissed her temple. "I will take you to your door. Hug Way and D-D so we can go."

Teran turned into the smiling D-D's outstretched arms. "I had a good time tonight and I look forward to our next hang out. Again, I am sorry for the outburst."

"Girl, please, do you think I would have been copasetic with Way grinding on his ex? You did well tonight because I probably would have done more." D-D squeezed Teran and let her go.

Wayman stepped up, "Stop apologizing, T, you staked your claim just like Shan staked his. Trust me had that been you we would have been getting Shan off the dude. Don't let him fool you. You stood up for yourself and he respects that; I bet you won't have any more problems out of him."

Teran laughed and announced, "Brooklyn Girls Don't Play That!"

Bashan held up his arms in surrender before reaching for her hand. "Let's go, Babi. It's late. We still need to take D-D home." They walked toward the building's entrance. "What floor are you on?"

Teran stopped walking, "You're right, it's late. Go get in that car and go home. I am fine. My apartment is on the second floor. Nothing is going to happen to me. I am fine."

Bashan frowned, "Yuh tink I would put yuh out and drive off? What kind of man would that mek me? Wah mek yuh feel shame?"

"I am fine, so you don't have to baby me."

"Yuh ah fine an yuh ah mi Babi, suh mi pamper yuh. Sup'm wrong wid that?" Bashan still had her hand and pulled her forward to walk. "Wen do mi meet Mumi an Daddy?"

She could not hold the groan that escaped her throat. "Soon, I guess."

"Wah mek yuh nuh wan mi fi meet dem? Teran what is wrong?"

She laughed, "You going in and out of that Patwah is something else and I must be used to it because I am following along."

"Nuh change topics. What's wrong? Yuh feel shame yun ah inna de project here?"

"I don't like living out here, but I am here, so I make the best of it." Teran sighed and lowered her head.

Bashan jiggled her hand and brought it to his lips where he kissed her knuckles. "When I saw you in school I was attracted to your strong personality. I did not worry about where you lived, and I am not worried about it now. I see my Babi."

"I realize you had no idea where I lived, but I didn't realize we lived so differently. Then, your mother's disposition kind of opened a scab for me and this is my scab."

My World

"My mother will come around once she gets used to you. She doesn't know you right now, that's all. You don't like it out here then we move when we graduate, okay? Mi say yuh weh mi ah, ooman, undastan?"

She wrapped her arm around his waist. "Yes, I want to be where you are, Shan."

CHAPTER FOUR

As We Proceed

Antics

Teran sat eating a cafeteria-prepared beef patty that tasted nothing like its Golden Krust brethren.

Her older sister, Saadri, sat next to her. "Are you hungry, Sè?"

Teran was about to answer, but Derek took the opportunity to tease her. "You are tearing that patty up, girl, it must remind you of your man." Everyone started laughing; about twelve ate together that day.

Before she could reply, Saadri asked, "Who's her man?"

Derek responded with, "You don't know? Everybody knows she's with the big Jamaican!" At the girl's puzzled look Derek blurted out, "Bashan! Shan-Doo!"

Roy Sharp, another lunchmate, exclaimed, "Get out of here! I would have never put them two together!" By that time Teran was red as a beet.

Derek continued, "I wouldn't have either until I saw them hugged up at the train station. I almost passed out on the stairs when I ran up on them, and he was all proud running the show, *'Give your man a goodbye kiss.'* And Teran just grinning and jumping to do his bidding. Y'all should have seen it. I wish I had a camera." The laughter exploded, various people spoke of Bashan getting her used to beef patties, her using a ladder to kiss him, and how their children would be tall with big mouths.

Once the laughter ebbed, Teran asked Derek, "Do you have a problem with me being happy?"

Derek teased, "No, not at all. We are just having some fun. I am glad somebody could calm your wild butt down. He is crazy over you too. Think he's Mr. GQ saying. *'T says she enjoys climbing this mountain*!" Everyone cackled; Teran smiled.

Saadri leaned in, "And now I know why you have been a ghost lately. When were you planning to tell me?"

Teran finished her meal. "You are preoccupied with the Godfather and have no time for me."

Fawn sat across from the sisters and saw Saadri's eyes narrow. "Saadri, you know Teran is always Miss Independent. Her nose is open, and she barely has time for me, so I have to track her down at lunch."

"So, I am not the only one in the dark here? Well, after school *today* we will catch up, right Sè?"

"Wi, Sè, we will talk after I say goodbye to Shan this afternoon. Wait for me just a few minutes and we can ride home together." Saadri hugged her and left the group.

As they gathered their things Fawn began in a low voice. "T, I hope you're not upset about the teasing. People are genuinely happy the two of you are together. You're a lot mellower, and Shan is real chill. Makes me think some gravy might have been dished out. Gravy tends to make things mellow out like that."

Teran burst into laughter, "Fawn you're a trip! I'm glad you didn't say anything like that with my sister at the table." They said their goodbyes and left for their next class.

Fawn laughed lightly, "Umm hum, I may be a trip, but I'm right, aren't I?" Teran continued laughing and wouldn't answer. Fawn continued, "Okay, I already have my answer. Just don't be stupid and slip up."

Teran answered, "I have college ahead of me. How's Reggie?"

Fawn rolled her eyes, "He's fine. He asked about you and Shan and wanted to know when we were all getting together. You know he has his birthday party coming up so make sure you two are there."

"That will be cool. Shan loves a party and Reggie certainly knows how to throw one. What can we get him? You like Shan's hats; maybe we can get Reggie one. What's his favorite color?"

"I like the way you completely evaded my inquiry. Reggie's favorite color is blue. Do we have a quiz today?" She and Teran had the same teacher at different blocks.

Teran offered, "You made an assessment to which I counter assessed by saying you're a trip because you are. So, then, we need to look for a blue Kangol for Reggie. I will have to go in my piggy bank for this one. Also, I hope you studied because we did indeed have a quiz." Fawn groaned as they continued down the stairwell.

Teran made to enter history and found Bashan waiting for her beside the front door "You're not usually here. Hi, how are you?"

He grinned, "Waan to surprise yuh. Meet me at de soudeast exit afta school, arite?"

Teran smiled, "Of course –" Before she could say more Bashan kissed her and excused himself.

Teran stared after him when Martina walked up and said, "Aww how sweet, following her man into class."

Teran swiveled, "Hey Martina, what's up?! He moves so fast sometimes that I have to stop a minute to process." They both laughed as Martina continued down the hall.

As We Proceed

----------◊◊◊----------

The last period of the day was one of Teran's electricity classes. An all-star cast of cutups assembled in the class including Fawn and Derek. The teacher didn't mind and even found comic relief in their playfulness, as long as the students completed the work. Often a dry eye couldn't be found after a barrage of caustic quips, comments, jokes, and ranks passed between the crew. The day promised to be 'brutal'. As Teran entered the room Derek sang out, "Day-o!" All went silent and Teran tried to go to her workstation peacefully, he would have none of it. "Come Missa Shani-man tally me bo-na-na" At the sight of Teran's blushing face the crew broke into a peal of laughter.

She exclaimed, "Okay Derek, I'm going to tell Shan how you messin with me!"

Derek feigned indignation, "Me and the brotha are cool. Why you tryin to mess that up?!" He followed with a facial expression that caused Teran to laugh along with the rest of the group.

She main'tained, "Okay, D, you are getting yours."

The group calmed long enough to receive a circuitry mini lesson before working on follow up projects. Fawn and Teran worked together as the class jibed and ribbed the period away. Particularly entertaining were the antics of Carl and Sheri who went head on with quick wits that left others gasping for breath. Sheri roasted Carl about being a warped Panamanian and Carl called her a wild Yankee who needed a horse bit and prong for taming. When Sheri saw Teran laughing she threw her a torpedo. "It ain't gonna be funny when that crazy Jamaican starts going off. One blood fyah and you outta there!" The crew roared. As if on cue the last period's bell rang and again there wasn't a dry eye in the room.

While exiting the room Teran spoke with Fawn, "Sheri is sick in the head; my stomach is hurting. I just didn't like the comment about Shan going off on me?"

Fawn, still laughing, responded, "You know Sheri was just messing with you. Jamaicans have that reputation for quick tempers, so she used it, that's all." When Fawn saw the concern on Teran's face she understood, "T, don't get worked up by the comment. Shan is cool and easygoing. He doesn't act crazy with you." Teran lowered her head and Fawn stopped them on a landing, "T, Shan is not Russell."

Teran looked at Fawn, "I know that, and I have not treated him differently or wrongly because of Russell being a fool."

Fawn led them down the staircase, "I'm glad to hear that. Shan is completely different but then I don't have to tell you that. Sheri wouldn't have said that if she knew it would really have upset you. Relax, it was just a joke."

"I know she meant no harm." Teran sighed, "I just feel like there's more I don't know. Like when I was in his room, I saw pictures of his older cousins and they were Rastas."

"Oh, so you have been at the gravy table! So, is Shan a Rasta? There's nothing wrong with that. You say they are older, so it probably explains why he's so mellow and mature. The dude is cool and if he were any different, we all would have known by now. You never hear anything crazy about him. He's a mellow dude."

"Why are you so interested in my gravy? I don't know but I ain't saying a word!" Teran walked ahead of Fawn. "I have to go to meet Shan then meet my sister. You know I can't keep Sè waiting too long. Please tell her I will be there shortly, and I will call you tonight."

Fawn stopped her progress. "No problem. Listen to me carefully, and don't try to play with him. If you're about him then be all about him. That's only fair. Just like you don't want it don't give him a reason to be jealous or to go off. You know you don't have brothers who could fight that big dude. You'll be walking around here busted up if he jumps on your behind! He is crazy about you too! Chile - he'll bruk ya neck!"

Through laughter Teran answered, "Uh-oh, the Guyanese is coming out! You know full well I have my sisters and we can do quite a bit of damage if need be. Remember, we have my sister's enforcer who will take care of him, too." Fawn nodded as Teran defended, "Besides, he broke up with Martina and he didn't act up on her so why would he do that with me?"

Fawn stepped closer, "T, others see what you apparently don't. Now I'm not saying he didn't care for Martina because they remained friends, but I know he is really into you. Many of us see it, even Martina sees it! The two of you are really close and I know he never got that close to her. We all know he's more mature than most of the guys running around here. We can see with you it's not another notch in his belt. He's into you in a way you are not used to, and I need you to understand this. He seriously cares for you, Teran." They walked the rest of the way in silence; Fawn gave Teran more to process.

Parting on the first floor, Teran began to make her way toward the southeast to meet Bashan. Fawn called to her, "Hey T, I just want you to know you have something special, so you'll treat it that way."

Teran returned, "I know, and good lookin out!" The ladies went their separate ways.

----------◊◊◊----------

Harsh Winds Blow

Jordache jeans, navy Clarks, blue Izod, navy Kangol, and black leather bomber on a six-feet three-inch frame waited for Teran's arrival. He saw her approaching and began to smile; he stood beside a window waiting for her to come to him. Teran thought about them, the events of the afternoon, and where their pairing would lead. She walked up and tiptoed to kiss him. Bashan wrapped large hands around her waist and brought them closer. In one smooth motion, he perched Teran on a nearby window ledge. Bashan watched her smiling face and sighed as he opened with, "We need to talk."

Teran straightened at Bashan's accent-limited statement, "What's the matter, Shan?"

Bashan moved beside her, sat on the ledge, and took her hand. "I'm having some problems at home and gotta work them out. Do me a favor and don't call the house for now. Let me call and meet up with you until I let you know things are better."

Teran's heart began to throb, "Are you breaking up with me? Just tell me! You don't have to go through a story!"

"Yuh ah listening to mi?! Teran, yuh neva heard dat fram mi!" Bashan gave a grunt, "Mi am trying to explain bout fi mi crosses an yuh ah trying to run wey?! Were yuh listening to mi at aal?!"

Teran swallowed and calmed her voice. "Okay. I am just shocked, and I don't understand. What's going on?"

He took her hands again, "I'll explain everything when I can. Just do what I asked for now, okay?"

"Yes." Teran submerged the apprehension she felt because whatever was going on had put a strain on Bashan she'd never seen.

He took her down from the window. "Dats fi mi strong ooman. Mi just need fi yuh support rite now." As they parted, Teran felt something was extremely wrong. She did not know what to tell her sister about this development.

Teran was no closer to understanding the magnitude of Bashan's plight when he withdrew from school. What little she did learn came from the sporadic conversations they had between Bashan working and going to night school. This strained relations between them and caused Bashan and Teran to see very little of one another. She dared not speak to anyone about this because she had so little information. Her sister kept her as encouraged as she could but was busy with her own challenging love life. When asked by friends of Bashan's well-being, Teran would say he was doing fine. Derek and Fawn made statements about the change in her own behavior, but Teran would shrug it off to stress from senior year concerns and developments that evolved in her family.

Saadri, her second oldest sister, was the most level-headed and faith filled of Damas Buard's three daughters. So, when she started dating the neighborhood hustler all heck broke loose. It was a double whammy because Saadri also announced she would not attend their father's alma mater but would stay in New York to be close to her ailing mother. Then, their oldest sister, Veronique went on one of her *to-heck-with-everyone-leave-me-alone* kicks and it sent their father into a tizzy. She was in college but not at their father's alma mater. His focus on their drama worked to Teran's advantage as she was not scrutinized as closely concerning Bashan and that suited her fine except for his disappearing act. Even her mother was preoccupied with the umpteenth return of her husband. Butch always garnered the lion's share of Nadine's attention, and that was the problem because it left, she, her younger sister Ayana, and her younger brother Talib more or less on their own. Teran always stepped in to keep their train on the track. The problem was that this time she had no energy to do the dance with her parents, her older sisters, or her younger siblings because she was barely holding it together.

Several days without hearing from him turned into weeks before the calls ceased altogether. Against his wishes Teran called Bashan's home several times. Since their first tenuous meeting Mary had grown cooler toward Teran until she finally became rude. On Teran's last call Mary commented, *"De Yankee gyal dem duh run afta de men, yuh should slow dung an let dem run afta yuh. Den yuh ah vex wen dey trifle wid yuh an don't marry yuh! Mi ago tell Shani yuh called."* and hung up. Teran stopped trying to make contact. She dried her tears and resigned to Bashan never returning her calls. Spring flowed into a long summer of empty activity.

When senior year arrived, she felt better able to cope and decided to enjoy the time left in school as she prepared for college. Her turn came as her father, Damas, announced he would only pay for school if she attended Xavier University in New Orleans. She needed help from her mother to justify staying in NYC and still have her father pay school. Yet, she knew her mother was too preoccupied to give this support. Her mother's husband was still trying to smooth things over with Nadine so he would not engage in a battle with Damas. Her grandparents were on fixed incomes but promised to do what they could, and they encouraged her to attend the City University system so they would be able to help her more expediently. Teran found herself having to make the same serious choice as her sisters before her.

CHAPTER FIVE

Pathways

Fall 1983

The senior year parties, trips, and laughs promised to make the year the most memorable for Teran. Derek and Fawn strung together clues that helped them confront Teran who admitted to the breakup. They were supportive and Teran assured them she was fine. She was having fun, she drank, and nothing would spoil her good time. Yet, she was unprepared for what she experienced in her mother's kitchen while cooking the night's meal.

School was eventful and hilarious so when the phone rang, Teran was ready to evaluate the day's occurrences with Fawn. "What was in the air today?! It was sheer madness in the place. Sheri is a straight up lunatic!"

"Teran, it's me, Bashan." She stood speechless. "Are you still there?"

"Bashan? How are you?" Heart racing, Teran wondered how she kept her voice from wavering.

"Better now that I hear your voice. Missing yuh aldough, yuh miss mi, Babi?"

Teran frowned as she prepared for battle. "Bashan, I haven't heard from you in months, and I mean months! So many that I've lost count. I've called and you didn't return my calls, and your mother completely dissed me on the phone. You just left me high and dry! Now you are calling and acting like nothing happened. I don't believe this." Then Teran's voice and hands trembled.

Bashan's voice was steady but that he slipped into Patwah confirmed his anxiety. "I know yuh ah vex an mi deserve dat but mi ave been drough ruff times. Dis whole time I ave been tinking bout yuh an having yuh by fi mi side. I had fi get drough dis ting suh wi could be arite, mi nuh waan notin fi cum between wi anymore. Yuh ah wat kip mi guh fi guh get drough aal of dis."

Teran shook her head, "You asked me to support you and I tried to, but you cut me off. There was no communication whatsoever. You say you miss me, but you hurt me when you dropped out of my life."

"Mi neva dropped yuh. Yuh ah still fi mi gyal."

"Are you serious Bashan?! How do you think I could still be your girl when you haven't said a word to me in months! Things have changed and I have changed. I am not the Teran you dawged out!"

"I neva dawged yuh out Teran. I just went drough hell an was trying to protect yuh."

"I needed you to talk to me Shan! You made all the decisions and didn't let me in on them. Did you really think I was supposed to sit on the sidelines waiting for you to notice me?"

"Teran, please?" She swallowed as she heard the waver in his calm. She was about to respond but he continued. "Tell mi sup'm, yuh ave let anyone touch yuh since mi ave been wey, nuh lie to mi?"

She frowned, "What are you talking about?"

"Anyone yuh let touch yuh?"

She gasped, "Are you serious?! Is that what you're worrying about? Whether I've been with someone else? That's none of your business! If you're not minding the store, then you can't worry about who gets the goods!"

Bashan became irritated, "Nuh vex mi pon dis phone ooman! Watch fi yuh mout gyal an show mi de respek mi demand as a mon. Yuh will neva speak to mi wid disrespect mi won't allow it!"

Teran's temper flared. "You have a lot of nerve calling here with this kind of crap. You should be begging my forgiveness, instead you're worried about who I might be with and how I should talk to you. Newsflash – I'm not with you! That's all you need to concern yourself with."

"Nuff, mi said mi had nuff! I am trying to get wi bak pon de rite track, an fi yuh ruining it wid fi yuh mout. Nuh show fi yuh ignorance cah ih time wi taak tings out."

"My mouth! I am supposed to shut up and let you waltz in like nothing ever happened. *You di mon an mi just di ooman, arite?* Unbelievable!"

He ground out, "I am trying to stay calm and keep from leaving you alone. This is not how civilized people talk things out. You are pretending to be tough, and I told you about this very thing when we first started out. If you cannot control your mouth you are going to lose a good man who wants to give you the world."

Teran heard every word, and each cut her, peeled the scabs away, and made fresh the rawness of his abandonment. Sitting on the side of the tub crying, running into the bathroom at school crying, turning up the music crying, crying. The burn twisted her ache to anger. "Ladies and gentlemen, he can speak English!" She heard him inhale and it elated her to have the opportunity to create a raw spot of her own. "You are trying to control your temper, you are trying to stay with me, you are trying to be civilized. Then take your civilized self and step! I won't die if I'm not with you. You disrespected me by treating me like yesterday's trash or some play toy you can put on a shelf." Teran stopped preparing the meal and began pacing.

He groaned. "Babi, that's low; if yuh only knew wat I ave been drough but mo wat I ave been able fi duh yuh wud realize wid yuh nasty attitude dat yuh ah fighting a gud mon. Maybe yuh ah too used to de Crooklyn guys."

"No, you can't turn this around on me. What type of attitude were you expecting? Was I supposed to pant like a dog for you to pat my head because you finally decided to act like you knew I was living? Instead of insulting me you should be trying to really talk to me. But no, you want to know who I'm with. Bashan maybe you should get off your high horse and realize you screwed over a good woman. I was willing to stick by you but that didn't keep you from leaving me with no explanation."

"Okay, Teran," Bashan sighed. "I'm sorry for hurting you when I thought I was protecting you."

"Bashan, that's not an apology. Let me make this clear, you broke my heart when you completely stopped communicating with me. As close as we were, to get to the point of hearing nothing from you was hard to deal with. I have finally come to terms with that and now here you are acting like I should be glad you called."

"Okay, I am sorry for hurting yuh and not communicating wid yuh. I had to make some hard choices and I never meant for yuh to be hurt. But, Babi, I am calling now trying to get us bak pon de rite track. Dis was tough but if wi can mek it drough dis den wi ave a solid relationship an can get drough oda tough times. I need mi strong ooman by fi mi side."

"Thank you for your apology, Bashan."

"I can hear yuh reluctance, Teran."

"You haven't let me finish. We can't pick up where we left off. We need to start over."

"Wat yuh ah talking bout, Teran?! Ah dis som relationship advice yuh gat fram fi yuh bredren? Dey waan yuh fi mek mi pay an beg, rite? Yuh did get sum Dear Abby advice?"

Teran looked at the phone in her hand. "Dear Abby would probably tell me to tell you to take a long walk off a short pier, but I haven't done that so don't push me."

"But it is what yuh want to say to me, right? Teran, nuh romp wid mi like I am an idiot or a sapps cause mi know every inch of yuh, rememba?"

"No, you definitely are not the stupid one here. You may have known every inch of me as you put it, but you didn't know enough not to treat me like crap. I apparently didn't know but an inch or several inches of you!"

"Yuh tink dis ah just bout jooks? Maybe it was for yuh, but I am trying to show yuh sup'm different. Yuh ah mi Empress. But okay, Teran, yuh win – mi ago ketch yuh lata." The dial tone signaled the battle was over and Teran again felt as if she lost.

Teran checked on the meat she put in the oven and brushed tears with her forearm as she remembered the second call.

When the phone rang again, she thought they would have a chance at reconciliation. It was Fawn. "Hello?"

"Girl, you know I make my afternoon phone call. Why was the phone busy?"

"Fawn, I thought you were Bashan. He just hung up."

"Get out of here, girl, what did he say?! Are you two back together? What was his reason for dropping out of sight like he had?"

Teran answered matter-of-factly, "He said he went through hard times, wanted to know if I had been with anyone, said he missed me, wanted to be with me, and no we ain't together!"

Fawn sputtered, "What? Are you at least talking again with the goal of getting back together? What happened? He misses you and I know you miss him. What's the problem?"

Teran rubbed her forehead, "The problem Fawn is that he called and assumed I was going to run back into his arms. He didn't even think to apologize to me because he didn't think he had a reason to apologize. In his mind, he made tough decisions for us but, Fawn, he never let me know anything. He just left me guessing and abandoned. On top of all of that he wanted to know if I was with anyone else. What kind of macho crap is that? You left me and then don't want anyone else to look at me?! I am not running back to him because he notices me now. I am worth more than that."

"T, did he explain what went on? Do you know any of the decisions he had to make? Aren't you the least bit curious about what happened?"

Teran lashed out, "This doesn't sound much like support, Fawn. Whose friend, are you? You're spending a lot of time defending Bashan."

"Teran don't even try it! I am your friend and his friend too. I saw two people born for each other. I watched that brotha around you and I knew he was on the up and up. So, if he had to step off from you like he did then he had one heck of a reason and you need to find out what that reason was. But I can tell by your tone here that you didn't do that."

"Uh-uh, not again, no one is turning this around on me. That dude hurt me and asking me who I was with should not have been the first thing out of his mouth. I should not have had to explain to him why he owed me an apology and then get a forced act of contrition from him. I don't know what his reasons were, but I do know that I am the one who bore the pain of his abandonment. I had to cope with that."

Fawn was also battle ready. "Yeah, you and the liquor got you through, right?"

"Fawn I don't need this."

"Do not hang up this phone, Teran, or you will lose a friend today." Fawn waited. "I have never lied to you. No one is fooled by the drinking and many people who care about you have asked me several times to say something to you about it. Heck, Saadri almost strangled you behind your binges. You must chill out on the drinking, Teran. You're too smart for that and you know that's one of the reasons why your mother and Butch haven't been together."

She sighed, "As hard as this is to hear I know it's from a good place. I'll chill."

"I gotta be up front and honest with you, T. As for Shan, I don't know what happened, but I am hoping that you two can find your way back to one another. You know as well as I do that the two of you had something special. Both of you have healing and learning to do and when that is complete then I hope you two get back together."

Teran shook her head, "He sounded pretty final on the phone so I wouldn't hold my breath if I were you."

"You both need more time. Don't close the book on the two of you. Ya'll were too good together to be finished." They hung up.

Teran wished he never called. Then she wouldn't have to face her pain, again.

----------◊◊◊----------

Moving On

Application time came and went and Teran found herself having to make some tough decisions of her own. Her mother was unable to afford for her to go away and her father would only pay for her to go to Xavier University - his alma mater in Louisiana. Refusing to succumb to his ultimatum, Teran took her grandparents' advice and decided to stay in New York for college. She submitted applications to local colleges and waited. Bashan hadn't called and she didn't try to contact him. As she promised Fawn, Teran enjoyed the good times but left alcohol out of the equation.

Another day in the lunchroom clowning with the crew validated her decision to enjoy herself and forget about Bashan. The crew ranked on one another, played cards, and howled with laughter. Roy Sharp was among the group – he had to have been the funniest person in the crew. He was 'roasting' Jason Ellsworthy about being made to shovel horse manure on a class trip after breaking curfew with a female student. Jason and Teran were nemeses who tolerated one another for the sake of the crew. Teran was laughing so hard she cried, "I didn't know about that! Roy, you are crazy!"

Jason sneered with, "You were passed out drunk in your room - you lush!"

Teran knew he was trying to get serious; she also knew her overindulgence was the reason Fawn intervened. Not feeling up to another battle with Jason she replied, "Yeah, I was. You got that, J."

However, Jason wanted to hurt her, "Yeah, I know I do, you lush. That's why B ain't with you anymore!" All activity stopped as the crew looked at Teran.

Fawn attacked, "You ain't got to tell her business! She wasn't laughing any harder than anyone else and you ain't said a word to nobody but her! You trying to start some crap, but you will have two to tangle with today!"

Roy added, "And they gonna light you up, Mr. Ed!"

The crew began laughing again but recovered quickly. Derek asked, "You good T? The last thing I knew Shan was trying to get up with you."

Jason threw in, "Man that has been finished! B has been dealin with my sister for a while now. I told him he was gonna want a lady sooner or later."

Teran had enough, "Yeah, but what you should be tryin to teach your sister is not to settle for leftovers! Then again, as ugly as she is, that's the best she can do!" Uncontrollable laughter erupted as the two-edged sword struck again. Jason was hot but knew no one would allow a full-blown confrontation. Instead, he rose, visibly gave Teran the finger and left the lunchroom.

Fawn patted Teran on the back, "Sometimes that mouth of yours pays off! You got him good," while wiping tears from her eyes. Teran laughed too, but her heart felt as if it had been suctioned through her skull. She left for class fighting back tears.

----------◊◊◊----------

May brought responses and excitement filled the air as many declared the schools they would attend in the fall. Fawn and Teran relaxed on Fawn's Crown Heights stoop. It was a welcomed change from Brownsville. A slow, soothing spring breeze hinted of the upcoming summer, and Fawn's long brown hair blew lightly. Teran was deep in thought.

"You know Fawn, it's funny how life throws you curve balls. Everybody is going away, and I'm stuck here. I wanted to live in a dorm and walk on a campus like my sister. I should be getting ready for California and Stanford right about now, but Damas and Nadine have managed to kill that dream. P'er won't pay and Mon Mon can't pay."

In her wisdom, Fawn consoled Teran. "When life doesn't give us what we thought we should get we must learn to work with what it hands us. In the end things may work out for the best. Your staying here is not the end of the world. You get to be near when your godchild is born."

"What?! You're pregnant?!" Fawn nodded and Teran rushed on, "And here it was you were telling me not to get caught out there." Teran inhaled and looked out into the street.

Fawn touched Teran's shoulder, "It's okay that you still think about him, T."

Teran straightened her back, thereby, removing Fawn's hand from her shoulder, "So when is my godchild coming? How did Reggie take the news? Your parents?"

Fawn shook her head at Teran's reaction but decided to pursue the happier line of conversation. "He's excited and wants to get married. My parents are happy about that. They are talking about going back to Guyana and leaving the house to us. They'll be here for their first grandchild though."

"Oh, my goodness, Fawn is going to be a wife and a mother. You are in the Big Leagues now, girl."

Fawn grabbed Teran's hand; the opportunity was too evident to pass up. "We are both going into the Big Leagues, T. This is what I've been trying to tell you all along. High school will soon be over and so will all the games and laughter. We both must make choices about the kind of life we want. I want to be a mother and a wife. What do you want?"

Teran tried again to pull away, but Fawn held on. "You think I'm running but I'm not. I want a man who will love me, and we will be there for one another. I want to be in a rewarding career and yes I want the house and kids."

"Bashan is that kind of guy."

"Fawn he moved on and so must I. He didn't think he had anything to apologize for and that was selfish. You don't just throw people away and that's what he did to me."

Fawn let her hand go. "T, can someone do the wrong thing for the right reason? I mean, can you mean well but mess up."

Teran rolled her eyes, "Yes Fawn; of course."

"Then why can't that be what Bashan did and why can't you give him another chance?"

"Fawn, I haven't heard from him since the phone call and Jason let the whole world know Shan is with his sister now. You have been trying to defend him, but he never tried telling me about this 'right' reason to do me wrong. So, what do you want me to do about that?"

"Nothing, but if the situation ever presents itself, get the closure you need so you can move forward." Teran nodded as they listened to a popular rhythm and blues song.

CHAPTER SIX

Commencement

June 1984

Graduation day felt surreal for Teran – a day she dreamed of, yet it didn't feel as special as she expected. Her family was there to celebrate with her, including her father and sisters. She, Fawn, and Derek walked out together. The ceremony proceeded without much excitement and afterward everyone parted to dine with their families. Troy Jackson, a fellow graduate, and crew member was having a party later that night and it was the designated meeting spot.

----------◊◊◊----------

Déjà vu

Fawn and Teran met up to travel together. Teran found herself on the 'E' train and the memories began to emerge. They inundated her conscious causing her heart to throb with an ache too long untended.

"T, come on girl, this is our stop!" Fawn pulled Teran off the train. "What's going on with you, girl, snap out of it!"

Teran regained awareness on the 169th St. platform. "I'll be okay, let's go."

They walked toward the exit with Fawn shaking her head at Teran's obvious distress. "How long will you do this to yourself, Teran?"

Irritated, Teran faced Fawn. "Do what?! Monje' (*my God*)! Can we just go out and party without a lecture of what Teran is not doing right?!"

"Then do right!"

"What do you want from me, Fawn?!"

"I want you to live, Teran! Take a chance and live; forgive him and live." She passed Teran and ascended the staircase. Teran followed behind. On the street, they boarded a waiting bus to Troy's house.

----------◊◊◊----------

Walking up the block they heard the music. Teran broke their silent war with an excited, "Ooh you hear those beats, Fawn? This party is going to be jumping!"

Fawn didn't want to fight her friend, "We are going to get loose tonight, T!"

Teran cocked her head, "You won't be getting but so loose carrying my godchild."

Fawn waved, "Girl, this baby is tough as nails. Besides, I am only 9 weeks, so I have plenty of time to slow down. Tonight, I celebrate – we're all high school graduates!"

Troy met them at the basement door in a pair of black leather shorts and a black nylon tank top. Teran had never seen him look so good. Fawn verbally echoed her thoughts, "These Queens boys sure know how to dress!" She looked Troy up and down as she spoke. Teran's mouth fell open.

She leaned over to Fawn, "Ahem, you are pregnant with Reggie's baby. Remember him?"

Fawn narrowed her eyes, "I know my own condition but I ain't dead or married yet so I can admire. Don't disturb my groove!" She left Teran staring at her back as she went to dance with Troy.

----------◊◊◊----------

It was 12:30 when they left the basement for the cooler rear yard. They were laughing about the funkiness of the packed room as they climbed the stairs. Fawn slapped Teran's hand when she tried to help. "I ain't crippled." They continued laughing.

Troy called, "Ya'll having a good time?" As they both turned toward Troy to answer, they saw Bashan among the group of assembled young men.

Teran froze. As Fawn answered, "Everything is good, Troy! Hey fellas, what's up Bashan!" Teran walked in the opposite direction. Fawn waved, smiled, and turned to see Teran gone; she caught up with her. "So, you saw him. That's a bad jogging suit he has on! Where does he shop?"

"At Cocky Bastardville – I don't know, girl! Who cares? Are you ready to leave yet?" Teran wrung her hands and closed her eyes to breath, focus, and gather her nerves.

Fawn grabbed her arm, "Now we just talked about this! Don't nut on me out here!"

Teran opened hazel-turned-green eyes and ground out, "We are getting ready to be the main attraction out here if you tell me off, defend him, or grab on me one more time! You are the one nuttin out, not me."

Fawn saw the emotions her best friend struggled to check. She decided to call a truce and joked, "Sometimes you feel like a nut!"

Commencement

Teran finished the line, "Sometimes you don't!" They started laughing. Teran continued, "I'm good, but shocked and mad cause I still feel the butterflies. I can't shake this dude."

Fawn smiled, "Then don't try to shake him. I bet you he feels the flutters too and we shall soon see because here he comes." She waved in Bashan's direction and walked the opposite way to give the couple space.

Teran took a breath, turned, and took another breath. She prayed her tremors were unnoticeable as Bashan walked toward her clad in a maroon and white striped nylon Adidas shorts set, matching sneakers, and baseball cap. She grinned.

Bashan saw Teran's smile and was happy for the welcome. He admired her one-piece pink linen shorts romper. Slender, shapely, caramel brown legs tapered into beige leather espadrilles. He shook his head and grunted. "Well Miss, yuh ah a high school graduate now. Ou does it feel?"

"On the one hand, I feel free but then it feels unreal that it's all over. College and a job are next, so I think I'll get over the shock soon enough." Teran laughed nervously, "How are you, Bashan?"

"Much betta now dat yuh nuh arguing wid mi but gi mi such a priti smile." He placed his hands behind his back and openly examined her from head to toe. Bashan snorted, "Gyal yuh ah wearing aal dis pink an looking suh sweet." He stepped closer, ignoring his strategy to move slowly. With a groan he released, *"Eeee, Teran, dem de sweet suga legs dat wrap round mi suh, yuh rememba? Wah gwan?"* He buried his nose in her hair and inhaled.

Teran closed her eyes and swallowed. She could smell his cologne and it caused a burn to grow in her stomach. "Shan, I'm glad you're well. Can we talk?"

Bashan took her hand and led her to the rear of the yard, "Glad yuh aks." He found two lawn chairs and placed them close to one another in a treed area that would give them privacy.

Teran sat and crossed her legs. Bashan watched her with blatant desire and her nerves quivered again. When he sat, she started, "Two wrongs never make right and so I want to apologize to you for our last conversation. I shut you out and was very nasty. You never had the chance to explain what happened. We both needed that for closure. I was still hurting, and I wanted you to know and feel it too. That wasn't the best way to handle things. The last few months I have had time to think about everything and I know this is an opportunity to make things right. So, I am sorry for my response to you."

Bashan leaned forward and took both her hands. He studied her features a moment. "I am willing to do whateva I need to duh fi mek dis up. It was never my intention to hurt yuh. Trust me, I felt this in the worst way wen wi had de lass conversation. It was wrong to think I could come bak widout dere being any repercussions. To expect yuh to deal wid de craziness widout a word from mi was nuh fair to yuh. But wi ah outta high school now an reddi fi tek pon de world. The only thing I am concerned wid now ah dat wi dweet togeda. I love yuh, Teran; and nutten has or will change dat."

Teran squeezed his hands, "Shan, I love you too and I forgive you and I want this separation to be over and I want to be with you."

Bashan pulled her onto his lap and kissed her with the tenderness and urgency of a man at his end. When he finished, he took a breath, "Cum now, gimmi de bad news. Weh yuh guh for college this fall?"

Teran was still reeling from the kiss. "What? Hunter, in Manhattan, why? Where are you going?"

"Irie!" He grabbed her into another long kiss. "Wi ah bot here inna New York, I started Nassau Community in February."

"When did you graduate?"

"December; Babi if yuh only knew how hard I had to work an double up to finish early." He looked at her smiling.

Commencement

Teran rejoined, "You're right, I don't know. I don't know what in the world happened. You have a big gap to fill in." She lay on his chest as he reclined them in the chair.

The feel of her in his arms was so distracting. He really didn't want to rehash the hell he'd been through but they both needed the closure. One hand on her hip and the other caressing her back, Bashan was in heaven. "Okay, fair enough. We hung out with Al who I only deal with because of Wayman. We were out on the island at a party, and he got into some static. Of course, the dude's boys jumped in, so Wayman had one guy, I had a guy, and Kennith had another. Al cut the guy he was fighting, and the guy had to go to the hospital. Police came to the party, and everyone acted like we were the menaces. We didn't start the beef, but it was something Al was involved with from before the party. Nassau County pressed charges against us and we had to get lawyers. Mumi was not having it and told me I had to pay for my own troubles. I widdrew from school to get a job and went to school at night. With the classes I already had, my counselor told me I would not be in there as long as I thought. They let me enroll in spring, I took summer classes, and I was able to finish in the fall. The whole time I worked a full time and a part time job so I could save for an apartment. I had plans to pay the fees for the lawyer, get my apartment, and come for you. During that time, I focused on getting it all over with. Sometimes I would plan to call yuh an would be suh tired I would fall asleep, when I woke it was time to guh to de nex ting. After ah while I felt it betta fi get miself togeda and come fi yuh correct. When I called yuh I was ready, but yuh were not and as much as it was killing mi, I had to give yuh de time yuh needed fi get ova what I did."

The smell of his cologne made Teran bold enough to kiss his neck. "Umm hmm, give me my space and go messin with Sharon Ellsworthy."

Bashan looked down at her but tightened his hold. "Ou yuh did know bout her?"

"Jason announced it in the lunchroom one day, he used it to try and dis me. You never knew we don't get along. Anyway, he put it out in front of the whole crew. Me and Fawn almost kicked his behind up there. It probably was a good thing no one let us at him because I would have pushed him out of the window."

He kissed her forehead, "Dat was foul. Truss mi, I will get him straight. As for Sharon, she and I ah only friends; yuh ah mi ooman always. Shi knew yuh to be mi Empress from de start."

Teran tried to sit up, but Bashan stopped her. "Are you serious?! You told her about me, and she still stayed with you? What kind of mess is that? I would have told you to step and go get your woman you want to be with so much."

Bashan laughed, "That's what yuh did! Yuh told mi to step off!" Teran joined in the laughter.

"Shan, from here out, don't just make decisions for both of us. Let me know what's going on so we can go through things together. Do we have a deal? I want to be able to stand with you."

"I like the sound of that - fram ere out. Yuh have mi wud; wi will talk about and wuk things out togeda. Yuh ah reddi fah mi, T? Cah I neva waan smadi as much as I waan yuh, inna everi way."

With difficulty she responded, his hands were roaming down her leg and back. "When we were apart, I wasn't in the best frame of mind. I started drinking and partying and talking to other guys. I wasn't a nice person and wasn't the Teran you knew. Once I realized how crazy I was and how many people I was worrying, I got my act together. I don't want anyone but you, Shan."

Commencement

He nibbled her neck, "That was because I was gone, but Daddy ah home again an nuh gwon noweh. Nuh mo of eni of dat foolishness," and continued to caress her hip and back.

"Shan... uh., Shan, we are in public. Mmm" He captured her lips again.

----------◊◊◊----------

At 2 a.m. the party crowd thinned. Fawn stretched along the fence and Teran knew it was time to be getting home. Troy, Bashan, and a group of former schoolmates were huddled together laughing and joking. Teran walked over and made a general announcement, "Okay fellas, we're headed back to BK."

Troy called Fawn over, embraced her, and grabbed Teran by the waist. "MY girls! Ya'll made school all the way live. We gotta hang out over the summer. Fawn, you take care of my baby and Teran, you be good to my man here." He kissed them both on the cheek. The group followed with hugs and kisses and set tentative plans for summer events.

Bashan wrapped an arm around each of the girls' necks, "Well it's time fi take mi ladies home, check yuh lata!"

Derek, as usual, began clowning. "Oh yeah, T ain't ride in the 'Callo yet! You are going home in style tonight, Miss Brooklyn!" Everyone laughed and decided to see Bashan's new car.

Teran raised an eyebrow and whispered to Bashan, "I didn't know you had a car." Bashan looked down at her and smiled. The crew walked out of Troy's yard to admire the black 1980 Monte Carlo parked a few steps away from the gate. Black tinted windows, black racing tires with maroon stripes, front bucket seats that swiveled and a sunroof faced the group of teenagers. The compliments and gazing from the crowd had Bashan grinning ear to ear. Teran watched the scene and wondered how he could afford such a car; it was a limited-edition model.

She whispered to Fawn, "I hope Shan hasn't gotten into selling drugs. We already have one resident hoodlum in the family."

"Stop, T, that car is bad. You are riding in style, you got it made." Fawn laughed and waved her away. "And you need to stop talking about Najid; you know Saadri loves herself some him!"

Teran smiled, "I hope everything is cool because I don't want him or me in the middle of anymore craziness. Sè is going through so much with Ace; I can't go down that path."

"You won't repeat any mistakes. Shan ain't into nothing like drugs; he's too smart for that. From what I hear he is working and banking his money to spend on you!"

"Ladies!" Bashan opened the passenger side of the two-door. "Yuh chariot awaits." He swiveled the seat and helped Fawn climb into the back. Teran smiled as he helped her sit. Bashan watched her closely, then closed her door and strutted around the car. Teran rolled down the window with the automatic button so she and Fawn could say their final goodbyes while he started the engine.

No sooner than they pulled away from the curb, Fawn reclined. Teran draped her sweater over Fawn's shoulders. Bashan noticed her shiver, "Yuh ah cold Babi? I can give yuh my jacket." She nodded and they removed his jacket as he drove. Settled back into the seat Teran snuggled into the jacket's warmth and looked out of her window. He placed a hand on her thigh. "Yuh nuh seh nutten bout de cyar, Teran."

Teran chose her words carefully. "I like it, I really do, but I'm wondering how you got it. This is a lot for a nineteen-year-old."

Bashan shook his head in agreement, "Fair enough, it was a gift from mi fada. He rewarded mi once I sekkled de business wid de lawyers. Aldough he nuh laik wat went dung he liked the way I handled de responsibility. He bought imself a new BMW and give mi this cyar. I wasn't going to turn it dung!"

Fawn yawned from the back seat, "I told you he wasn't selling drugs."

Teran turned toward her, "You're supposed to be asleep."

Bashan added, "Yuh thought I was selling drugs? Yuh should know mi betta dan dat, Teran. I'd rada work fah mines."

"I didn't know what to think. This car is so fly. I just didn't know what to think." Then she turned to Fawn, "And you, back there, I don't need comments from the Peanut Gallery. You just worry about resting my godchild."

Bashan placed his hand on Teran's stomach. "It would be beautiful fah wi fi have a babi. When ah wi going to mek one? I hope it's soon." Teran stared wide-eyed but made no comment.

Fawn cautioned, "It's no race so don't rush. You two just got back together so wait until you are ready. Besides, T is starting school in the fall. I know she's not ready yet."

Bashan laughed good-naturedly, "Yuh ah an old soul Fawn, I am glad mi babi has yuh as her bess bredren."

Fawn thanked him, "Thanks, Shan, and for the record, I am a friend to you both."

Teran looked out of the windshield and thought about how their lives were changing forever. She covered Bashan's hand, which remained on her stomach, leaned into the seat, and closed her eyes.

"Yuh ah getting tired?" Bashan squeezed her belly.

She smiled, "This has been a long and eventful day. I am getting pooped."

"Should I take yuh home or can wi find someplace fi nyam an celebrate?"

"Let's find something to eat and celebrate. Then we go to Crown Heights because I am staying with Fawn." Teran kissed his hand and smiled at him.

Fawn watched the couple and was grateful they were back together again. "My parents won't mind you crashing on the couch Bashan. Mumi will make a good breakfast in the morning."

Teran shook her head, "All she does is eat and this pregnancy is just getting started."

Fawn slapped Teran in the back of the head and the threesome laughed.

----------◊◊◊----------

Heating Up

Although they worked within walking distance Fawn and Teran didn't see much of each other. Reggie and Fawn prepared for a wedding and impending parenthood while Teran and Bashan spent any free moment they could together. Reality set in for Teran as she found herself responsible for helping her mother with random bills and rent. She held no stock in promises of repayment for loans and struggled to save as she intended. Teran knew she would need to leave home soon. Adding to her anxiety was the fact of not having been able to save what she wanted for Bashan's birthday. She had to settle for treating him to a movie and dinner.

She came to enjoy the ride from downtown Manhattan to Queens as it gave her time to relax. She settled into the routine of walking over to the World Trade Center to get on the first stop of the E train where she'd be guaranteed a seat. Bashan faithfully picked her up from the train station. This evening was no different. As soon as Teran came up from the subway she spotted the Monte Carlo a few steps away. She bent, knocked on the window, and waved. As she got in Bashan spoke, "Hey babi wah gwan? Wah ah wi doing tonight?"

Teran smiled and kissed him. "Happy birthday, my love! I thought we'd go to the movies and get something to eat afterwards."

Bashan agreed, "Mi need fi mek ah few stops before wi duh dat." He drove them to the mall where they looked around. Bashan ended up getting a new beige Kangol. Teran looked around as well; she spotted an attractive ensemble: a flair, cream, rayon skirt; a cream and gold rayon blouse; and gold leather sandals. The entire outfit came to about eighty dollars, which was more than Teran could afford at the time. As she admired the outfit Bashan commented, "Dats de kind of ting mi would laik to see yuh inna."

Teran smiled at him. "Yeah? Making demands, are we? Why don't you get it?"

"Fah wah? Yuh neva duh nutten laik dat fah mi!"

Teran's mouth flew open. "I was only kidding. Why'd you go off on me like that?"

Bashan maintained his tone, "Smadi has to snap yuh outta de dream world yuh live inna. A couple does fah one anoda. Ih show dey care." He reached for Teran, but she pulled away.

"So, Sharon and Martina and whoever else must have been buying you things. Now I should fall in line, huh?" Teran challenged with hands on her hips. She kept her voice low and lethal.

Bashan stood in front of her with hands behind his back. He looked down at her and nodded, "As a matta of fact dey did."

The bravado was too much for Teran. She hissed. "Well good for them that you walked out on them with the clothes on your back that they bought. And good for me that I haven't been stupid enough to do it." Bashan again reached for her; she stepped out of range and hissed. "You tell Sharon and all the others for me that they can keep on buying for you." She started walking, "I'll take the train home. I don't need this and did not deserve it either." He walked behind her. She pivoted and stepped into his chest, "I give you what I can Shan – me!"

Bashan snorted, "Teran yuh nuh a skettle but yuh ah my ooman, sleeping wid mi nuh mean I mus buy yuh tings." It came out harsher than he'd meant, and he could tell from her tear-streaked green eyes he'd gone too far. He quickened and grabbed her hand as she fled. They exited the mall with her tugging away and fighting tears. "T don't fight wid mi, please. Cum, wi ago to de cyar an nuh mek a scene."

Once in the car she unloaded. "I came out here tonight to treat you to the movies and dinner because it was all I could afford. Every time I look up, my mother's hand is out. I can't even save what I want to save to get out of there. But that didn't have anything to do with you and how I wanted to spend your birthday with you. I don't even know how to shop for you. I never bought clothes for a man before. Here I was trying to make sure you knew I cared, and you go off on me in the middle of a store." She reached for the door, but Bashan wouldn't let her leave.

"Yuh ah rite babi, I planned fi taak wid yuh, but de store triggered sum foul feelings. Guys always talk about ou de gyal dem use us and will especially use their bodies for manipulation."

Teran fired, "I'm not trying to use you. You threw other women in my face!"

"Yuh broadcast dem up. I kip telling yuh ih just mi and yuh but yuh kip bringing up dere names." Bashan rubbed his hand over his face. "Teran wi agreed dat wi would taak, suh cum let us taak." She nodded and he drove off.

When he turned onto 91st Avenue her stomach muscles tightened. In her mood, Mary Watts was the last person she wanted to see. Teran remained silent.

Bashan led them through the anteroom into the living room as Mary walked toward the kitchen. *"Shani, yuh ah home soon. Yuh did ave company?"*

Teran stepped from behind Bashan, "Good evening, Mrs. Watts."

"Teran ih been a lang time. Wah gwan?"

"I am well, thank you for asking."

Mary stepped closer, "Yuh ah sure? Yeye wata, Shani wah happen?"

"Mumi mi an Teran just need fi taak bout sum tings dats aal." Bashan defended.

Mary turned to Teran, "Shani mek yuh cry, Teran?" Teran sighed but gave no answer.

"Wi need fi taak bout sum tings dats ih Mumi." Bashan led Teran to sit on the couch. Mary walked into the kitchen and Bashan followed.

He came out with a glass and handed it to Teran. She thanked him. "Wen fi mi mada cum bak please tell har yuh arite suh I won't ave anoda heachache tenight." Teran looked at him but remained silent.

Over Bashan's shoulder Mary called, "Teran yuh feel betta, Shani vex yuh?"

"Thank you, Mrs. Watts, I do feel better. We are talking." Teran smiled in Mary's direction but could tell she still wasn't Mary's choice for Bashan. The discomfort returned and she lowered her eyes.

Bashan looked from his mother to Teran and read the signals. He was disturbed, "Wi gwine fi de movies just now."

Mary responded, "Nuh kip har out too late Shani. A young gyal should be inna shi gates at a propa time."

"Okay Mumi."

----------◊◊◊----------

Back in the car Bashan felt the strain of the evening. "I want yuh to meet my fada. Im lives inna Baldwin. Wi cyan guh to de movies any time."

"If you'd rather do that it's fine with me. This is your night; I really want to make sure you enjoy it." She lowered her head and sighed.

"Teran."

"Shan, I don't know what else to say. I feel like I don't measure up tonight with you or your mother."

"Yuh ah mo dan enough fah mi. My mada nuh matta."

"Shan, she's your mother."

"Shi nuh matta wen ih cum to yuh. Cum wi guh and see my fada."

----------◊◊◊----------

They parked in front of a stone and brick two-story home on a well-maintained block. Teran was impressed, "Do many blacks live out here?"

Bashan took her hand as he led her up the walkway. "Nuh enuf but my fada has been living here a while."

Crandall Watts opened the door after the second ring, "Well eff it nah mi son de birdday bwoy! Wah gwan? Mi ena wondering eff mi wud get de bly fi see yuh or eff dis priti gyal wud get aal of fi yuh attention cah shi wud ave aal of fi mi. Cum inna an nuh kip mi waiting; ooo ah dis gorgeous creature and did shi 'ave a sista?"

"Daddy, dis ah Teran, mi empress, and Mary ah de ongle one ooo need fi yuh attention, nuh har younga sista." The men laughed and hugged. It was easy to see the special bond between them.

Teran extended her hand, "Good to meet you Mr. Watts."

Crandall brought Teran close, hugged her, and squeezed. "Ih gud to finally meet Shani's empress ooo mi ave heard suh much bout. Yuh ave fi mi bwoy running round half crazy ova yuh and mi see wah mek im behave suh, cah mi wud be worsa. Cum gi Poppa a gud sweet kiss, priti gyal." When he kissed her lips, she was surprised.

Bashan reached for Teran, "Dis ah fi mi ooman, mon, kiss fi yuh own dung inna Queens Village." Crandall laughed as Bashan pulled her into his embrace; Teran was glad for the rescue.

Commencement

He guided them to seats in his living room before speaking, "Suh yuh ah celebrating a birdday. Twenty now, dat ah a gud age, everyting still ahead of yuh. Aldough mi cyan quite believe yuh ave grown up suh fass wen mi taught yuh suh nuf tings as a pickney. Yuh mek mi feel lackan ole mon an ole mon dem need grandchildren, but afta a while. Teran yuh ah tirsty? Shani, get har sup'm fi jink."

Teran felt the loss of Bashan's warmth as soon as he left the couch. "Thank you. You have a nice home."

"Tenk yuh dahlin. Yuh ah deh at school? Wah yuh ah taking?"

Bashan returned with a glass for them to share and handed her the drink as she responded to his father. "I am starting Hunter College in the fall and will be studying elementary teaching. I have always thought about being a teacher." She took a sip and handed the glass back to him.

"A teacha? Dat a gud profession! Dere ah plenty of need fah teachers out here pon tim ahland. Wen yuh finish mi ago taak to som of fi mi friends an see eff wi cyan find yuh sup'm out here. De pay an de living ah betta out here, nuh need fah yuh fi affi bodda wid de city pickney. Shani de two of yuh should move out here, ih a betta standard of living. Tink about yuh pickney."

"Mi just getting har use to Queens win eve chat bout di Island. Wi ah waiting pon starting a family. Teran ah nuh redi yet but eff ih happens mi ago be willing an excited fi tek care of de babi."

Crandall became excited, "Eeee, Teran, di Island a gud place, even betta dan Queens. Mi kip telling Mary but shim eaz haad – dat stubborn ooman." He sucked his teeth and continued, "Tings betta Shani?"

"Nuh really but mi focus inna different place – Teran, wuk, school, and di future. Mi own place soon, dat mus happen." Bashan leaned back on the couch with his arm across Teran's shoulder and his ankle over a knee. Teran listened carefully to catch the content as they spoke faster.

He sucked his teeth again, "Mary neva change an neva learn dat wah mek mi nuh THERE. Shani guh soon mi will help yuh out. Teran yuh live wid yuh parents?"

Teran was relaxed in Bashan's armpit. It took a moment to register Crandall's question. "Oh! Yes sir, well, I live in Brooklyn with my mother. She and my stepfather are separated right now." She could feel Bashan watching her and sensed he was in a better mood. She hoped it would last.

Crandall nodded, "Yuh like Queens?"

"Shan is in Queens." Everyone laughed at that.

"Shani cum an let mi ave a wud. Wi mus excuse wi self an cum bak shortly, please mek yuhself at home." The men pardoned themselves and Teran leaned into a pillow on the couch.

"Babi? Teran? Babi, wake up."

Teran opened her eyes as Bashan shook her. She was disoriented. "Did I really fall asleep? How long were you two gone?" Teran stretched and shook her head.

Crandall looked on with concern and mirth, "Yuh waan fi tan ova fi yuh ooman look tired."

"Wi had a tuff evening but wi ah fine now. Yuh gud babi?" He lifted Teran from the couch and embraced her as he stared into her face. She smiled up at him and he kissed her lips.

"Did I really fall asleep? That's embarrassing." Teran shook her head.

Bashan grinned, "Yuh ah fine. Wi ago touch de road, cum."

Crandall nodded as the couple said their goodbyes and made Bashan promise not to keep Teran away from visiting soon. Again, the older Watts kissed, and hugged Teran before Bashan and she headed for the car.

----------◊◊◊----------

As Bashan rounded the vehicle after settling her in, Teran looked at the gas tank. He positioned behind the wheel while she reached into her purse and withdrew a twenty-dollar bill. "We should need gas by now Shan. Stop at a station and fill up."

He looked at her offering and looked at her, "You don't have to don't this, especially since I acted suh crazy earlia."

Teran insisted with a smile, "I accept your apology and I want you to use it. We've been all over the place this evening."

Bashan returned the smile and kissed her on the mouth, "I can do it with twelve." He drove a short distance to a gas station.

When he left to care for the car she sat and thought of the evening's events. She realized that if she remained observant, she'd learn far more than Bashan would say. He demonstrated his feelings but really wasn't the talker she expected him to be. Teran felt good about the epiphany.

PART TWO

Fusing

"Why am I as I am? To understand that of any person, his whole life, from Birth must be reviewed. All of our experiences fuse into our personality. Everything that ever happened to us is an ingredient."
~ Malcolm X

Malcolm X (2015). "The Autobiography of Malcolm X", p.159, Ballantine Books

CHAPTER SEVEN

Into the Groove

They stopped at a diner on the island before returning to Queens. A hostess led them to a booth and Teran slid over to accommodate Bashan. Once settled he draped his arm around her shoulders. "Wah yuh ah inna de mood for beside a salad? Yuh nyam lacka bud an mi affi get yuh fi nyam mo food. Yuh need fi nyam gud Jamaican food."

Teran laughed, "Why does it bother you that I like salad? It's too hot for heavy food in the summer. Salad fills me up without loading me down."

"I nuh care wah yuh sey ih bud food." Bashan frowned, "I waan a cheeseburga and sum fries. A double chocolate milkshake sounds lacka plan."

"It will be salad and iced tea for me. I think I'll do a chef salad. That has egg and turkey and ham. If I eat like you, I will be big as a house and then you won't want me."

Bashan gave the waitress their order before he turned to Teran. "Dat will neva happen! I will always luv everi inch of yuh. Besides, yuh badi will change once wi ave wi pickney and mi ago still luv aal of yuh "

"Well, I will make sure to keep the inches to a minimum, so you'll have just enough to love."

Bashan cleared his throat, "Ih time for mi fi leave my mada's ouse. Tings ah nuh gwine well dere at aal. Inna truth tings nuh ave been well fah a lang while. Since my fada has been gaan tings have nuh been easy. Now I'm outta school, suh deres nuh mo fi kip mi dere. I am free to start my own life wid my Empress."

Teran frowned, "But you dealt with your problems like a man, so why are things still strained?"

"This is mo bout my fada nuh being dere, but since I am dere I get de lion's share of de boderation. I try fi tan gaan most of de time and cum home wen I feel she has gone to sleep. I am saving for my own apartment; I know yuh ah having trubble too suh wah mek wi nuh move inna togeda?"

Teran frowned as she processed the question. "You mean live together, Shan? I don't know about that. I want to be married and I want my husband to be the only man I live with."

He considered her words, "Yuh ah reddi to be my wife? Dats final yuh know because dere will be nuh divorce?! I am mo dan reddi to duh dat but I waan mek sure yuh ah reddi too."

"So, are you saying you'll give me time to try some other guy and see if I really want you or not?" Teran held her head down to keep from laughing aloud.

"Raatid! Yuh ah aal mine and ongle fi mi gyal!" Bashan playfully choked her.

She let out the laugh, "Then why act like you want me to be ready. If we live together what would be different from being married. Are you planning to go somewhere?"

He brought their faces eye to eye, "I am exactly weh I waan be. Yuh nuh know just how much yuh ah inna my skin and how I nuh function rite widout yuh. No, I am staying rite weh I am cah yuh ah de one ooo kip mi going. Yuh shud know dat what I do, I do for us." She kissed him. He reared back and looked at Teran. "Wa'ppun to *'wi ah inna public Shan, tap!'*" He mimicked her voice.

"I don't sound like that!" She swatted his arm. "Okay two can play at the game. *'Teran mi waan sum sugar yuh ah mi ooman!!'*" Bashan laughed.

"Very gud impression. I luv yuh Teran. Yuh affi know dat." He played with her curls.

"I know Shan. I love you too. But we gon have a problem if you mess up my hair!" She moved her head out of his reach.

He sucked his teeth. "Yuh females an fi yuh hair!" He laughed. "Eff I mess it up mi ago just pay fah ih fi be don again."

Teran shook her head, "You wouldn't have to. I do my own hair."

"Beautiful, sexy, and talented I see, and saving mi whole heap of money!" he pulled another curl. She swatted his hand and laughed.

Teran became serious; she needed to try her hypotheses. "So today was more about you and your mother than me. But you want our relationship to also go further. You need some things from me." She may have been off track, but she felt better about making the step toward trying to understand why things had gone awry earlier in the evening.

Bashan allowed the waitress to distribute their food on the table before he graced it and began answering Teran's probe. "Dat was a gud assessment, Babi, and yuh ah correct. Add that I waan tings dat nuh cum fass enough suh my patience ah being stretched. Teran, I waan a pickney. Ih wud mek mi suh happy fi watch yuh wid a belly fah my babi an bring it inna de world. I have a whole heap fi give and I know I would be a gud parent. I waan us to create our own fambily."

Teran listened carefully, "Shan, I have no doubt you'll be a very good father. You want to do better than your parents and I understand, but you must see my side of things too. I do want to have your babies, but not right now. I grew up being responsible for my sister and brother and I need time to focus on me. I have enough room to care for you right now, but a baby is too much. I want to go to school and put myself in a better position to take care of a family. I wouldn't dream of putting all the weight on you. I've seen that and I know that does not work. It's one of the reasons why Butch and my mother have had such a roller coaster relationship. To be honest, I have my concerns with Fawn and Reggie having this baby so soon after Fawn finishing school. She has not done any living yet, however, I support her because she's my fourth sister. When I see all of this, I take note and try to do better by not putting unnecessary pressure on myself. I want to be an equal partner in our relationship, and I have this time in my life to prepare for that. A baby would add pressure and responsibility I cannot handle right now. Please be patient, Shan. It will happen, but not now."

"I never heard yuh express yuhself like this. How can I rush yuh wen yuh put it like dat? What about marriage? Duh yuh tink yuh ah reddi for dat?" He bit into his cheeseburger.

"That's a big step too, but it's more within our reach than trying to have a baby we're not ready for. We can set up our futures together. The two of us can share a can of beans and huddle in a blanket if we needed to but we can't do that to a baby." Teran ate her salad.

Bashan laughed, "Jokesta, yuh kno I will neva ave *us* inna blankets and beans. I wud wuk four jobs before dat wud happen, but yuh mek yuh point."

"I just thought of pigs in a blanket." They chortled heartily.

----------◊◊◊----------

Back in the car Bashan noted, "Yuh quite de jokesta tonight. Yuh gud? I waan guh fi guh by Wayman's ouse."

His eyes sparkled with the excitement one's birthday brings. She had not the heart to admit to her tiredness. "This night has been about you. While we didn't get to the movies, we have had plenty of drama. I would love nothing more than to end it with some fun and see you laughing with your friends."

He brought her close and kissed her. "The best part of this night ave been with you." Bashan drove out of the parking lot smiling. Within twenty-five minutes they parked outside Wayman's Hollis home and walked into his basement.

He led Teran by the hand to the side of the house where they walked down a narrow lane to the side door. Bashan gave a special knock and walked in. He led Teran down a flight of stairs before exclaiming, "Hail up! Wah gwan?" Everyone turned in the direction of the stairs and greeted Bashan as he smilingly announced "My ooman wid mi fi celebrate mi earthstrong."

Over the hum of the full basement, Cheri, Wayman's sister called, "Happy birthday Shan! T! What up girl?!"

Teran walked around Bashan to embrace her. "Cheri-baby! How ya livin?!"

Wayman addressed Bashan, "My man! Happy birthday, I know you're doing good!" They nodded conspiratorially as they shook and gave one another brotherly pats. He then grabbed Teran, "I know you don't just see Cheri standing here."

"Hey, Way!" Teran giggled as he bear-hugged her.

Al, Wayman's friend and the bane of Bashan's existence, commented, "She must be a very special lady with all this attention she's getting. You are the queen tonight Miss Lady! How does it feel?"

Teran only managed a smile as Bashan interjected, "She ah my empress everi day, Al."

Al faced Bashan and threw up a mock surrender before offering. "Just making conversation; happy birthday, by the way." The young man turned his attention toward

Teran – introducing himself, "I'm Al-Ski lady, what's your name again?" He extended his hand toward her.

Bashan moved Teran to his side. "My empress ah Teran. Wah gwan, Al?" Teran watched the exchange and became uncomfortable.

She moved to the bar area with Cheri who promptly poured them drinks as Teran took a corner seat. "Okay girl, tell me what's up with that Al and Shan? There seems to be some tension between them."

"You're right, they are only cool because of my brother. Otherwise, they really don't chill. Al has always had this competition thing going with Shan. It's like he can't stand to hear Shan having anything good going for him. Stay far away, T."

"I'll be sure to keep my distance because he looks like he would come at me to get to Shan. Not that he would get anywhere because I love my baby and I am not interested in anyone who doesn't mean him any good."

"Yeah, he would be foul enough to do that. You peeped him well."

Teran kept a safe distance from Al and in close enough proximity to Bashan to send the message no foolishness would be tolerated. Wayman's reel-to-reel played a popular "slow jam".

"Eeee, dat ah wi Miss!" Bashan scooped Teran off the stool she'd occupied near Cheri and others. Wrapping his arms around her, he pulled Teran against him and began a slow winding of his hips. His movements molded her to his frame, and they were moving in unison quickly. Bashan allowed his hands to gently caress her back, hair, and hips. Other couples joined the dance, conveniently pushing Bashan and Teran into a corner of the basement.

As they danced, she whispered, "You are being bad. Did they teach you how to dance like this in Jamaica?"

He held her tighter before responding in a deep, sexy voice. "Mi learn a lot inna JA an I intend to show yuh aal of ih."

Into the Groove

A mid-July heat baked downtown Manhattan even though it sat at the convergence of the East and Hudson Rivers. Teran walked down Chambers Street toward the meeting point she and Fawn established. She received looks and comments she ignored for the most part. As she approached Church Street she heard, "Good golly, Miss Molly! Does your man know you're out dressed like that?!"

Teran turned to watch Fawn walk toward her. "Ooh, your nose is spreading!"

Fawn volleyed with sarcasm, "Thanks for the compliment. That won't be the only thing spread once Bashan sees that skirt! You are wearing the Tale Lord right off that thing!" The two laughed as they walked toward one of their favorite pizza shops. "So, how are you two doing?"

"We're doing alright. You would be proud of me. I had a few revelations that helped me get us through some potentially sticky circumstances. We're talking about getting married." Teran ordered a slice and a small fruit punch.

Fawn ordered two slices and a ginger ale. "You two are not playing! Have you set a date?"

They found a table and sat. Teran shook her head, "We are early in our talks, but I think the date will come up soon."

Fawn listened and watched Teran as she ate. "So, he's more ready than you are? Is that why you sound so blasé about this?"

"I'm reserved and taking it one step at a time. Shan really wants a baby and asked me to become pregnant a couple of weeks ago. I know him, this will come up again. Now I wonder how long I will be able to keep him distracted from the subject, especially once we're married. He can be a lot to handle at times. When I think I have him managed something comes up and I'm back at trying to figure him out. What I do know is that I am going to finish school, move out, and save some money before I entertain having a baby. Moving out looks more like my priority every day. I am thinking about working full time and going to Hunter at night so I can save and get out of there quickly. Butch and my mother are doing that 'Baby, I'm ready to come back' dance again and I am not up for it. Although, he needs to help her pay some bills, so she'll stay out of my pocket. I remind her I am not the bank of Teran and that I am trying to move. You know how that ends, an argument, but I am not there to pick up Butch's slack. I refuse to do it."

Fawn shook her head, "I am sorry things are that bad for you. You know you can always stay at my house."

"I won't do that Fawn. You are getting ready for this baby and Reggie is about to be your husband. You have enough to deal with. I am managing my mother for now. I had to tell her the other day that I was not there to replace Butch. They need to get their stuff together. Talib needs his dad. Ayana could use some stability too. Right now, I'm the rock and I didn't sign up for that role. I have helped all my life, it's time for Teran."

"My girl has grown up overnight!" Fawn smiled, "I am proud of how you're progressing."

Teran sighed, "Circumstances warranted me growing up. I don't have time for carefree, careless mistakes."

Fawn checked her watch, "Speaking of time, we'd better be heading back. Can you come over this evening and go over some of the wedding stuff with me?"

"Sure, that would be fun. We haven't been together in a while and our time is growing short."

Teran got back to the office and left a message for Bashan who was unavailable. She tried to reach him on her break but had to leave another message. The extremely busy afternoon caused five o'clock to catch many unaware in her office. Before leaving to meet Fawn, Teran checked for messages from Bashan, but there were none. True to her word, Fawn awaited Teran's arrival beneath the municipal building and they caught the number four train to Utica Avenue. On the way to Fawn's house, the ladies stopped and picked up Caribbean food for dinner. Teran laughed to herself then focused on Fawn, "I came over here to get away from a Caribbean to end up eating the food."

Fawn replied, "I thought you came to spend time with me?"

"Yeah, that too." Teran joked.

----------◊◊◊----------

Fawn's floor was the staging area for swatches, pictures, and samples as they went over details for the wedding. "September 12th is our day. It will have cooled off by then and I won't be too big. The colors are pearl and grey, and it won't be a large wedding. Small and sophisticated – that's what it will be. You can pick the color of your dress from the swatches in the far corner over there."

Teran walked over to the swatches and chose the color that immediately caught her eye. Fawn responded with, "That one is my favorite. It is so different. We are going to get your shoes dyed that color as well."

Teran nodded, "With this variety of shades, what will be the color of Reggie's cummerbund?"

"He will have a pearl cummerbund and the groomsmen's cummerbunds will match your dresses." Fawn showed her the color.

"Wow, Girl! Can you believe we are talking about your wedding?"

"I know, right" Fawn blushed. "This feels so right. I am happy about this and couldn't think of anything else I'd rather do at this point."

Teran watched her, "That is beautiful to hear."

"What about you, T?"

"This is all about you marrying that crazy Reggie. Stop worrying about me. I am fine and my stuff will work out all around. Isn't it funny how we both ended up with Jamaican men?"

"That's easy to understand, you always wanted to be like me when you grew up." Fawn laughed as Teran stuck out her tongue. "But seriously, T, I am concerned. You look like you have the weight of the world on you, and I hope Bashan hasn't put some of that weight there." She led them to chairs.

"Shan's weight is there because I choose to deal with it. The other weight I am handling a step at a time. All in all, I am managing, and you don't need to worry about me. I am not going to break down or jump off the Brooklyn Bridge or anything like that. It's the reality of life and I am making it mean what I need it to mean for me. Someone very wise taught me that." They smiled and hugged.

The evening quickly faded into night as the ladies cemented plans for the wedding. They cleared Fawn's room of material and laid on the carpet listening to a songstress declare her love for the man of her dreams. "The invitation is still open. This house is big enough for us not to get in one another's way. My parents will leave after the baby is born. We wouldn't charge much either since it's paid for. Ooh let me get the phone… Hey Shan, yeah, she's here. Cool…. Okay. Bye."

Teran looked at Fawn, "He didn't want to speak to me?"

"He's on his way over. He called from your mother's house. He sounded upset." Fawn watched Teran sigh and queried, "Are you sure everything is okay with you two?"

"Fawn." Teran groaned. "We're good. You can't behave and I've just been around you a few hours. You expect me to live here? No way."

Fawn waved her off. "I want you two to be okay, is that a crime?" They continued to listen to records.

----------◊◊◊----------

Twenty minutes later, Bashan rang Fawn's doorbell. Fawn left her second-floor room to answer the door. "Shan, how ya livin?! Long time no see stranger. What? You don't love me and Reggie no more?"

Bashan hugged her, "Fawn, wah gwan?"

She led them to the kitchen. "You're looking good as usual. Have a seat. Would you like something to drink?"

Bashan sat at the kitchen table and hung his beige Kangol from the chair. "Yuh ave sum juice? Yuh ah guh start fi show yuh pregnancy soon. Ih inna yuh nose now. Yuh look gud, weh Teran?"

Fawn handed Bashan a glass of apple juice, "Yeah, I am starting to grow. T's upstairs in my room. We've been going through some final wedding stuff and listening to records. She's straightening up for me. I wanted to talk to you anyway."

He wore a concerned expression, "Everyting aright?"

"I'm concerned about the pressure T is under at home and trying to maintain a relationship with you. She won't say it, but I think it's getting hard on her. Now that I look at you, I see you are not having it easy either. What's going on and how can I help?"

Bashan smiled, "Yuh ah a gud bredren. Wi affi guh drough di tuff times togeda dats aal. Nutten fah yuh fi worry bout."

"Are you pressuring her about a baby?" Fawn stared at him.

Bashan waved his hand, "Nuh pressure fram mi, wi chat bout dat an nuff of oda tings but no pressure. Listen, yuh ave a babi coming and wedding fi plan. Neitha one of us a guh burden yuh suh yuh may as well tap aksin." Bashan smirked. "Yuh cyan help mi wid har birdday surprise. I will call yuh lata inna de week."

Fawn nodded, "Bet. I think I hear T."

Teran came downstairs and smelled Bashan's cologne. "Fawn, where are you two?"

"We're in the kitchen." She waited for Teran to appear then exited to give them privacy.

"Hello, my love. What brings you here this evening? You couldn't do without me, huh? You are getting spoiled Bashan Watts!" She tiptoed and kissed him.

He looked at her and snorted. "Spoil yuh sey to a mon ooo shows concern cuz his fiancé neva at de train station like she seh she wud be. A mon ooo waits almost two hours den drives to Brooklyn to find har nuh at home but chillin at har bess bredren ouse. A mon should be screw but give har a kiss and ah happy fi see har? Mi spoil?" He kissed her again.

Teran stepped back, "Shan, didn't you get the two messages I left with your co-workers?"

He frowned, "I neva get any messages and yuh seh yuh leave two?"

Teran held up her fingers, "Two."

"Now mi vex an smadi a guh tell mi wa'ppun pon Monday. Meanwhile, wah gwan? Fawn fi taak bout mi pressuring yuh."

Teran shook her head, "She is fishing, don't worry about that. We talk about all we need to talk about. I am learning it's best to keep our business to ourselves."

Bashan smiled and embraced her, "Dats my babi. Yuh get de hang of dis."

"So, does that mean I can get a real kiss, Mr. Watts because the others were unsatisfactory?" They embraced for a proper greeting.

Fawn entered the kitchen, "Now that's what I'm talking about! Here's Reggie!" The couple turned toward Fawn and Reggie and greeted with smiles.

"Wah, yuh fighting? Nuh quarreling wi celebrating tenight. Shani ou yuh stay? Mi ave nuh see yuh in a while." Reggie gave Bashan the customary dap.

He turned and kissed Teran's cheek before giving her a bear-hug.

Teran squealed, "Unhand me you brute!"

Bashan joked, "Mi cyaan squeeze yuh ooman cah yuh ave har belly swollen wid a babi suh lef mine alone!"

"Shani, suh ou yuh tink mi did, shi ave belly nuff?" Reggie preened as he rubbed Fawn's stomach.

"Yuh did a gud job wid har belly!" They high fived as they chortled together.

Fawn waved them off. "Reggie, you bring the car or the van?"

"De van, Momma, wah mek yuh aks?"

Fawn rubbed her stomach, "Let's go to City Island. I want some seafood. Teran you want some seafood?"

"We picked up food on the way in and now you want seafood. I guess we can leave that food in the refrigerator because the fellas probably have not eaten."

"I ate some of my food while you crashed on me."

"Good grief, girl! I took a cat nap, and you ate in that space of time?"

"Yes, and now I am hungry again so let's go."

Reggie grimaced, "Bench and Batty here wit dere routine. Dem nuh be separate, suh cum wi tek dem an let dem nyam. Dem tek nuff of funds fi support Shani, yuh know?"

Bashan grabbed Teran about the waist, "Dere holes inna mi pockets now an wi nuh even ave a babi. Lawd a massi shi taking all mi funds. Watch dis – Teran yuh waan seafood?"

"Yes! I could go for some shrimp and scallops." Teran's eye glistened.

Bashan nodded, "Cyaan kip nutten inna mi pockets, yuh see it?"

Reggie motioned to lead them out of the house, "Well, dem waan nyam sum bikkle suh cum, wi touch di road."

"Wi cum." Bashan turned to Teran as they entered the hall, "Guh get yuh tings, Babi." He didn't see Fawn motion for Reggie to stop and watch them.

Teran responded, "I have my purse, I'm ready."

He frowned, "Weh yuh bag wid yuh wuk clothes?" Fawn began laughing. Bashan looked from her to Teran. "Wah gwan?"

Teran bit her lower lip as she rolled her eyes at Fawn. "I don't have a bag, Shan. We came here straight from work."

With brows raised, Bashan questioned, "Weh yuh wuk clothes ooman?" Teran motioned at her attire and Bashan shook his head. "Yuh wuk laik dat, Teran!"

"Shan, it's a skirt." She patted his arm.

He grimaced, "A short skirt, Teran. Everi mon inna Manhattan had sup'm fi sey bout yuh batty inna dat skirt! Nuh! Save dem fi mi alone, yuh undastan?!" Teran nodded and Fawn's enjoyment rang out in a belly chuckle.

"Shut up, girl! Let's go!" Teran walked past Fawn and out the door behind Reggie who was shaking his head and laughing. Bashan watched her walk and grimaced again.

He turned to Reggie, "Mi ooman running round de place inna dat ting widout mi." He sucked his teeth. "Teran, tap rite dere. Wi ago fi de cyar togetha." Fawn closed the front door with tears in her eyes. Reggie had to lock the house and help her down the stairs because her laughter was uncontrolled. On the street Bashan took Teran's hand and Reggie held Fawn about the shoulders.

Reggie spoke, "Shani, wi ago inna mi van. Wen wi cum back wi drop yuh at yuh cyar." Bashan nodded agreement and they led the women to Reggie's waiting van.

At the van, Bashan lifted Teran and watched as she moved over to make room for him. The skirt rose on her legs and his heart fluttered. He got in behind her. "Teran." She looked at him and smiled as she settled herself. He scowled, "Dis ah too much, Babi. Nuh widout mi anymo."

She placed a manicured hand on his cheek. "It's all for you," and kissed him. "I won't wear them anymore without you." He nodded and wrapped an arm around her legs.

Fawn looked over her seat, but Reggie interrupted, "Fawn, too nuff yuh cyaan be di mada hen ova dem relationship? Rememba tidday fi mi, tomorrow fi yuh."

Teran added, "Thank you Reggie!"

Fawn laughed, "I love you Teran."

"Yeah yeah, that and fifty cents won't get me on the bus!" Teran rolled her eyes but started laughing, "Miss Always-have-to-be-right."

Fawn looked out of the front windshield, "I told you Shan was going to have a fit. You don't realize how you wear that skirt. All that butt you got in that skirt is dangerous. Men were walking and tripping and almost killing themselves when we were out at lunch!"

"Stop it girl before you upset Shan!" Teran gave him a refuting look.

Fawn turned toward them and laughed. "No, for real, one guy walked straight into a pile of garbage. You had that brother getting ready to get jumped by some rats!"

Reggie howled, "Betta de rats dan Shani!" The van erupted. Reggie turned on the music and the foursome jammed on the way to City Island.

----------◊◊◊----------

Friday night in the summer found the streets of City Island busy with people walking, shopping, drinking at the bars, and eating in the many establishments dotted along the main street. The seafood mecca, a Pelham Islands hot spot sandwiched between the Eastchester and Pelham Bays, sat in the northeastern section of the Bronx and bordered Westchester County. Reggie drove them to the restaurant at the end of the main street. They were fortunate enough to find a table near the water. Frog legs, crab legs, scallops, shrimps, clams, cole slaw, and French fries filled the table along with sodas and condiments. Fawn talked about the wedding, Teran talked about school, Bashan talked about the future, and Reggie talked about Grumman.

"Shani, wah yuh taking inna school?" Reggie asked as he reached for a frog leg.

Bashan took a gulp of soda and replied, "High school – space and aeronautics. At Nassau ih liberal arts fah now."

Reggie perked, "Yuh still ave interest inna aero?"

"Yah mon, mi workin at Kennedy now, cleaning planes, loading luggage pon di tarmac. Mek nuff funds fah mi empress an get wi own place." He squeezed Teran's leg under the table.

Reggie began to tell Bashan and the ladies about the Minority Mentoring Program at Grumman for those interested in aerospace engineering. Bashan expressed interest and Reggie promised to give him one of the information packets he'd gotten from personnel once they got back to the van. Fawn had been quiet, so everyone glanced in her direction. Mouths dropped as the trio watched her consume the seafood and fries.

Bashan commented, "Mon yuh a guh fi need Grumman an den sum to feed har. Look at her!"

Reggie laughed, "Shi ah getting bigger too. I need nine incomes fi support har appetite. Ih nuh ova yet!"

Fawn spoke up, "I gotta nourish my baby and that's what I intend to do."

Bashan looked at Teran, "Mi hope yuh nuh nyam laik dat wen ih fi wi time."

Teran agreed, "I don't want to eat like that either." Everyone laughed as the group finished their food.

----------◇◇◇----------

It was after midnight before they got back to Brooklyn. Reggie gave Bashan the information packet and dropped him and Teran at the Monte Carlo before taking Fawn home with him. As they got into the car Bashan began, "Now dats wah mi waan bad. Im taking im ooman home wid im. Mi waan to duh dat fi wi. Wah yuh tink bout dat?"

Teran rolled down her window, "Are you talking about marriage because I am not living with you. I want to be married; if we love one another then we need to make that commitment and not play around with things."

"Yuh feel like wi romp round?"

Teran could sense his mood change. "I know we're serious about being together. The next step is to make a commitment to one another through marriage. I don't want to act married and not be married. A lot more people are doing that these days but that's not what I want. My Granmè Mazie used to tell us that we were not to be trifled with. If a man loved us and wanted to be with us, then he should love us enough to marry us."

Bashan rested his head on the back of his seat and looked at Teran. "Dat de first time mi ave hear yuh mention yuh granmada."

Teran added, "She's my father's mother."

"Shi here inna New York? Wen duh mi meet har?"

Teran shook her head, "No she's not here. Anyway, I would rather be married."

"Wah mek yuh duh dat?" Bashan frowned. "Yuh nuh tell mi much bout yuh fambily. Did sup'm happen?"

"Shan" Teran placed her hand on his knee. "I really don't want to talk about this. Fawn and Reggie are getting married in about a month and a half. I agree that they should, and I want to be married also, not because of them but because for me that's the way things should be."

He could see pain in her eyes, and it frustrated him that he couldn't get through to her. "I want fi marry yuh Teran and want to be de one yuh can share everyting wid." She reclined in her seat and Bashan knew she would not open to him right then. "Wah type of wedding yuh wud like? Wen yuh tink yuh wud be ready fi get marry?"

Heart beating fast with excitement, her head whipped around. "I'd like something small and elegant with a nice honeymoon. Around spring would be ideal." Bashan listened intently as he drove them toward Utica Ave.

"Wah bout March or April of nex year? Wi should be able fi pool enuff funds to duh likkle and elegant. I kno fi wi parents wi help as well." Watching the sparkle in Teran's eyes gave him relief.

"I can go through Fawn's things and get some idea of what we might want to do and how much we need to spend. We can plan things out together." She snuggled next to him as he drove.

He placed a hand on her thigh, "Dis sounds laik ih involved but ih woman's bizniz. Tell mi wah di cost an wah yuh need mi to duh."

By a quarter after one Teran was in her mother's apartment showering and preparing for a well-deserved rest.

CHAPTER EIGHT

What We Really Want

Two weeks later, Teran awoke on a Saturday morning, cleaned the bathroom and the bedroom she shared with her sister Ayana and ran some errands for her mother. By one o'clock she was surprised she'd not heard from Bashan who'd promised to take her shopping for a ring set. She called his house, but no one answered. Ayana asked Teran to accompany her to Pitkin Avenue for some shopping and she obliged. They returned home at four and Teran was upset that Bashan still had not called. She warmed a late lunch for herself and ate while watching a movie on the television. Sated and relaxed she stretched on the couch, and it wasn't long before she dozed off.

    A knock on the front door woke her. She sat up a little disoriented and looked at the clock over the kitchen table; it was after six. "I'll get it." On the other side of the peephole a refreshed looking Bashan stood. She opened it, "So nice of you to show up."

He walked in and kissed her cheek. "I kno yuh vex. Dis ave been a lang crazy day. Yuh look like yuh did sleep. Wah yuh do today?"

"Cleaned, ran around for my mother, shopped with Yana, ate and fell out. Oh, and I wondered why a certain someone played me to the left."

He sat on the couch and motioned for her to sit next to him. "Let mi see weh duh I start, flat tire pon mi cyar; Wayman's battery dead; mi parents start quarreling; mi sista's tek opposite sides; had to guh fi mi fada's house an chill him dung; run out to de airport fi pick up mi overtime check; cashed and banked de check; pay a couple of bills; showered and rested; now, here telling yuh bout my day. Still vex wid mi?"

"Not with all that going on. Are your parents, okay?" Teran rubbed his back and Bashan grinned, sated.

He enjoyed her attention. At the mention of his parents, Bashan waved. "Both of dem eaz haad an Mentha an mi let dem know ih."

"Hmm." Teran sat back as Bashan rose to greet her mother and sister.

"Shanidoo what's up?!" Ayana walked into Bashan's outstretched arms as he grinned.

"Yana, I am gud, wah bout yuh? Teran spend all my funds shopping today?" He patted his pockets.

Ayana's brown eyes brightened, "She left you a little. She tells you everything, you should already know that." She swatted his arm.

Bashan laughed, "Hail Mrs. Gregory. How yuh duh?"

Nadine leaned against the wall separating the hall from the living room. "I'm well Bashan. You're looking good. How's your family?"

He nodded, "Everyone doing well. I dress fi take Teran fah har birdday."

Ayana protested, "It's not until Wednesday. You spoil her and it is going to bite you. Teran won't let you stop."

"Whose side are you on?!" Teran playfully challenged Ayana.

Ayana feigned annoyance, "Shan did this? Shan said that. Shan likes when I wear this. Shan bought me that. Shan took me here. Shan is taking me there."

Nadine laughed, "Yana, you are sounding jealous."

"I'm not jealous of Pipsqueak and the Giant. I'm just telling him how rotten she is and how she was pouting today because he didn't call her at the break of dawn!" Ayana motioned about their height difference with her hand and Nadine howled.

"Awoah!" Bashan placed his hands behind his back and nodded with a smirk.

"Pipsqueak and the Giant?! Okay Ya, you will get yours back! Wait until you finally get serious with someone, oh wait, you are too busy going through them like the express train to 125th Street!" Teran mimicked a nonstop train with her hands and the subsequent fallout of victims mowed down. Bashan laughed aloud.

"Oh no, shi tek de brothas dung!" The group laughed again before he asked, "Weh Talib?"

Nadine stood up from the wall, "He's with his daddy. Ya'll are too much, let me get in here and put something together," and walked into the kitchen.

"Ma, I'm going to meet Tracy and Peaches and we are going to the movies. I'll be back later." Ayana walked to the closet and grabbed a sweater and her purse.

Nadine called, "Don't come in here too late Ayana Niquel!"

"Umm she called your whole name." Teran whispered.

Ayana whispered her reply, "I know, right," before replying aloud, "Okay, Ma." The three in the living room laughed. "Bye ya'll. Teran, don't get pregnant." Teran threw a couch pillow at Ayana who laughed, walked into the hall and left for the evening.

"Well Miss, yuh ready fah an evening wid mi?"

Teran jumped up to go into her room, "I was ready this morning when we were supposed to be ring shopping." He stood and grabbed her around the waist.

Nadine walked into the living room, "Where are you two headed off to?"

"We will kip it simple tenight wid dinna and a movie. Then we'll probably hang out wid our bredren afta." Bashan beamed.

Nadine sat in an armchair. "So, when is this wedding taking place? Whatever happened to the custom of the guy asking the father for the daughter's hand? All I know is that you two are getting married. Ayana told me and Teran confirmed."

Bashan frowned and took a seat on the couch. "My apology Mrs. Gregory, I neva meet Mr. Gregory. Wen Teran and I taak wi gat excited an just start to mek plans. I mean nuh disregard."

Nadine smiled, "It's okay, Bashan, Butch hasn't been around." Teran visibly bristled. Nadine shot her a look and continued. "Teran could have taken you to meet her grandfather. I don't expect you to know all this, but Teran should have done more."

"Ma, why now?" Teran sighed and shifted her weight to one hip.

"When is a better time? Yana and Talib are out of the house and you're here by some miracle. Surely you can spare me a few minutes to say what I need to say?" Nadine withered Teran with a look that sent her to the couch beside Bashan.

Bashan watched the scene and added it to the catalog of questions he had. He settled Teran next to him. "I am willing to chat wid any male fambily memba yuh wud laik Mrs. Gregory. Please know I mean no disrespect. Disya a big step. I love yuh dawta and I cyan provide fah us. Right now, I am saving for our first apartment, wi ah saving. We'll ave ih by de time wi gat marry. Teran makes mi happy an I waan fi spend mi life wid har."

Nadine watched the couple. "I admire you both, Bashan. Teran is independent and I like that, but it also causes me concern because she can be very bull headed at times. You seem to mellow her out and it's a nice complement. She loves you too, of that I have no doubt. I just want to make sure you both understand the commitment you're making. Marriage is serious and it's more than the honeymoon. You are together day in and day out, not just on the weekends hanging out and having fun. There are bills and responsibilities waiting for you."

Teran's arms were folded, "You sound like you're trying to talk us out of it." She looked at the coffee table and Bashan knew she was pissed.

Nadine forged ahead, "There are those whose marriages didn't last because no one talked to them beforehand, or they wouldn't listen." Nadine paused for effect. "I understand you are twenty, but Teran is only now eighteen so taking this big step cannot be treated lightly. If you're going to do it, I want you to last. I want you to go into it knowing that it is hard work but very rewarding. As a mother, your mother, and soon to be mother-in-law, it is my responsibility to tell you these things. Bashan, you have my blessing with my daughter. When is the wedding? Have you set a date?"

Teran slid closer to Bashan and placed her hand in his. She looked at her mother and said, "May is the month."

Nadine frowned, "This coming May? That's only ten months away! Why – Teran?!"

"No no, I am not pregnant! We talked and settled on a spring wedding. It will be small and elegant. We don't need that long to plan small and elegant." Bashan and Teran exchanged smiles.

"The two of you also need to hold off on any babies. You both need to complete school; it will put you in a better position to take care of a family. Marriage is hard enough without the strain of finances and screaming babies adding to it. Promise me you'll finish school before the babies come."

"Mrs. Gregory, yuh ave my word dat wi will wait. I plan to apply fah a training program an wid dat, school, and Teran, I ave mi hands full. We will wait fi start our family." Teran was shocked to hear the words. She smiled at Bashan, and he returned the warmth.

"Okay you two, get on out of here. I have my house to myself, and I want to enjoy it." Nadine stood from the chair and held her arms out for Bashan. "Welcome to the family. We'll have to do dinner so you can meet the rest of the gang."

"I wud laik dat Mrs. Gregory." He winked at Teran who gathered her things and they left.

----------◊◊◊----------

In the car Bashan held Teran's hand, "Yuh ah happy?"

"Of course, I am," she grinned.

"Yuh neva like it wen yuh mada mentioned Butch. Wah gwan?" He watched her carefully.

Teran closed her eyes and shook her head. "Butch is not my father so there would be no need for you to ask him anything and she knows that!"

"Teran."

"Shan, I -"

"I aready know, yuh nuh waan fi chat bout it." Bashan started the engine and turned onto Rockaway Avenue as was their custom.

Teran looked out of the window and sighed before turning back to him. "Shan, I need to tell you a lot and I know it. I missed you all day and now that we're together I don't want to take up our time with that drama. I promise we will have a time set aside to get down and dirty but not tonight. Okay?" She sat back as he caught a succession of green lights and had them cruising toward Linden Boulevard.

He looked over at her and grinned, "Yuh rite, tenight nuh de night. Dis ah yuh night, Miss." He took her hand while she turned on the radio.

They crossed over Linden and continued, "Shan, where are we going? I thought we were headed to Queens?"

He shook her hand, "Flex, relax, cah dis a yuh night."

Teran continued to watch as Bashan took Rockaway Avenue into Rockaway Parkway and the Belt Parkway. She smiled as he turned off the highway for Riis Beach "So we are going to have a romantic evening on the beach?"

Bashan smirked, "Sup'm laik dat." He parked and grabbed a blanket out of his trunk.

Teran questioned, "Where's the picnic basket? What are we supposed to nibble on?"

"Teran, mi say dis a yuh night, suh flex. Wi nibble one anoda. Cum ya." He held out his hand and she didn't disappoint.

As they walked down the boardwalk, Teran spied a large crowd assembled with music blaring. "Ooh Shan, a beach party?!" He nodded.

They walked directly toward the group. When they were within a few feet the music stopped and Fawn, Reggie, Wayman, and Delores appeared before the crowd, "Happy birthday T!!!!!"

Teran covered her mouth. "Shan?! You did this? Was this what you were busy with today?"

"Greet yuh guests an tap playing Twenty Questions."

Teran hugged necks and kissed faces for several minutes. Many of their former classmates were in attendance. Then she came face-to-face with Jason Ellsworthy who brought his sister Sharon. "Hello, Teran, happy birthday."

She wanted to ask why he decided to come and bring his sister but realized he most likely wanted to ruin her party. Instead, she spoke. "Hi, Jason. You must be Sharon, I'm Teran." Teran held out her hand and Sharon gave it a weak shake. "You two enjoy yourselves." She didn't wait for either to respond and walked away seething.

Teran made her way to Bashan who was standing with Wayman, Delores, Derek, Reggie, and Fawn. "Shan, did you know Jason is here with his sister?"

With a frown he asked, "Ou wud I know dat? I neva invite him."

Fawn stepped next to Teran, "Okay, let's go get his butt!"

"Hey, Fawn, weh yuh tink yuh a guh an yuh belly? Bote of yuh tan here. Dere nuh be any trubble eff yuh two tan weh wi cyan see yuh, Bench an Batty." Reggie took Fawn by the hand and wrapped an arm around Teran's shoulder.

Wayman agreed, "T, this is about you tonight. That clown won't ruin a thing, even if I have to say something to him."

Delores stood next to him and nodded. "True that! You know I am down but not tonight, so enjoy yourself. What did he just call you?"

Reggie answered, "Dem Bench an Batty cah wen yuh see one yuh see de oda. Dem de seat an de backside." Everyone howled.

Bashan cleared his throat. "I cyaan tek no bodderation tenight. I a guh speak to him." Bashan moved to leave the group and Teran tried to leave with him. Reggie wouldn't allow her to follow. Bashan addressed her "I believe I am de mon an nuh need my ooman fi fight my battles. Rememba, I protect yuh and watch ova yuh; yuh nuh de king of de relationship." Teran stood in place; Bashan left the group with a concern-etched brow.

Sharon saw Bashan approach and smiled brightly. "Hi, stranger, long time no see. I met Tara. She's cute." Sharon spoke the word cute hesitantly. Bashan snorted.

"B! How ya livin?!" Jason held his hand out for a dap, but Bashan folded his hands behind his back.

"Okay, suh yuh here, J? I know yuh and Teran," he threw a corrective look at Sharon, "nuh laik each oda. Ow yuh find out bout dis?"

Jason cocked his head, "Come on man, you know word of a party always travels."

"But dis ah har birdday party, har surprise birdday party. Yuh pick tenight fi show up. Wah gwan?" Bashan stretched his arms to accentuate his growing irritation.

"Yo, B, I thought we were cool? I heard about a party, and I came out. Me and sis here are out for a party. We didn't know about it being someone's birthday. So, what's up, we not invited? You are doing us like that, B?" Jason stepped closer to Bashan as he reasoned.

Bashan nodded, "Nuh mon, yuh out dis far, suh enjoy de night. But J, dis ah Teran's night an I nuh waan nuh craziness fi spile ih. Sharon, yuh ave a gud time." He walked back to his group.

Fawn spoke first, "I hope you told him he is about to catch a beat down!"

Delores added, "I don't like the way she watched you when you walked away. I can make a trip over there and let them know the deal."

"Naw, D-D, we are here to celebrate. We don't want to nut out here and the cops come bustin heads. We are here for Teran, and we are going to have a good time. So, stop that frowning and worrying because you're too pretty for that." Wayman grazed Teran's cheek with his knuckles.

Bashan embraced her and kissed her lips. "I neva tell dem to lef but I mek ih clear dis ah yuh night. Dem say dem undastan suh I lef dem." Bashan led Teran to a spot where they spread out their blanket. He laid on it and pulled her down next to him.

The evening progressed and they mingled with the crowd. Teran saw Sharon make several plays for Bashan's attention. Each time Bashan said something and moved on. Teran did all she could to remain peaceful but then she caught Jason's snicker and knew things may get dicey.

Someone had gotten hold of a well-known DJ's mix tape and jammed a popular tune. The party took on greater energy as everyone danced. The birthday girl danced with Roy Sharp, so Sharon took the opportunity to dance with Bashan. The breakdown of the song came, and the DJ mixed it into an extended set. Crazy Sherrie was dancing with her boyfriend Carl (to everyone's surprise the two had gotten together) and yelled toward Teran in a mock accent, motioning with her head. "*Gonna be some gwon on if ya don get ya man, gul!*" Roy and Teran turned toward Bashan and Sharon. She was stepping close and grabbing at him as he moved away and tried to thwart her advances. Teran had enough.

She shot across the sand and heard Bashan say, "Sharon, cut ih out," while Sharon giggled and continued her pursuit.

Teran spun the young lady around "He said cut it out." and slapped her. "Now I'm saying it!" Sharon lunged for Teran who sidestepped and punched her squarely in the face with a left hook. The young lady dropped and screamed. Teran's lefts were known for the damage they caused when she'd have to defend herself or prove a point in the neighborhood or at school. She was about to move in for a more complete assault when Bashan grabbed her by the waist and carried her away from Sharon. Roy grabbed Sharon who arose and tried to go after them.

Jason rushed over once he realized what was happening and tried to go after Teran as she was in Bashan's arms. Troy Jackson grabbed him, "Yo, J, cool it! It was fair. Don't do that!"

Bashan deposited Teran with Reggie and went after Jason, "Rass! Yuh try to lick har?" Bashan swung and connected with Jason's jaw. Jason fell backward and Bashan was on him. The young men threw blows and rolled in the sand faster than anyone could get to them. Teran stood rooted and afraid of anger she had never seen from Bashan. Many in the crowd were equally stunned by his ferocity and power. Jason fought back but was not up to the challenge in this scrap.

Wayman broke the stunned silence, "Reg, we'd better get him before he kills that dude." They both moved to break up the struggle.

Troy stood by Teran and Fawn, "He's crazy for disrespectin Shan's girl like that when everybody was trying to keep static down to a minimum."

Sharon tried to help her brother, but Reggie stopped her, "Gyal, move wey fram dem; yuh mus waan fi gat licks. Dem screw an yuh nuh guh near dem laik dat!"

Carl and Sherrie moved a crying Sharon out of harm's way. "Get him off my brother!"

The guys had to make several attempts to get Bashan off Jason. Reggie saw that Teran began crying and decided it might work to their advantage. "Shani, too nuff! De mon gat de idea! Yuh waan yuh ooman see yuh rage laik dis? Teran ah crying. Im gat de point!"

Assisted, Bashan rose from Jason's bruised face, "He cum out here fi disrespek mi fiance an dragging im sista round. Wah de point, mon?! Teran ah mi empress, shi mi! Aal mine an dere nuh cum between dat! Guh yuh wey an tek yuh sista – wi ave nuh mo bizniz togeda."

Sharon shot a nasty look at Bashan before she ran to her brother. In her loudest voice she commented, "And to think I believed you was about something. I'm sorry I ever met your sorry behind. It wasn't all about her when you were sleeping with me! You weren't about her then!"

Bashan spewed, "Suh wah mek mi did call yuh har name eff it did aal bout yuh?"

Sharon's eyes were wet as she left with a bloody Jason.

Teran couldn't believe what she'd heard. "He called her by my name?"

"Daag, that's embarrassing." Delores shook her head.

Roy Sharp chose that time to quip, "Ya'll belong together. Ya'll could make a lot of money in the WWF for tag team wrestling. Bodies flyin, people screamin, shoot, I thought I was at the Garden!" Everyone laughed as Bashan gathered Teran to him and prepared to leave the beach.

----------◊◊◊----------

The rest of the summer was productive, eventful, and hot. Several classmates threw departure parties and barbecues to celebrate their transitions to college life. Teran attended, wished them all well, and came to terms with the different path her life took. On Labor Day, three couples got together for a picnic in Bear Mountain. Fawn was four months pregnant by then and showed neatly. Reggie, Wayman, and Bashan took turns working the grill while she, Delores, and Fawn played cards, talked, and listened to the radio after they set out food and paper goods. Once all the meat was cooked, the fellas joined the blanket.

Reggie kissed Fawn lovingly, "Just tink Momma, inna few days wi will marry. Den yuh ah mi own!"

Fawn smiled, "Yeah, but I been yours all the while."

Reggie playfully answered, "Now dat wud be true, but wah oda wey ih could be?"

Teran interjected, "She could have been with someone with some sense!"

"Cum now, Teran, yuh know yuh love mi too," Reggie feigned offense. Teran blushed as he playfully stroked her cheek.

"Wah gwaan?" Bashan pretended jealousy. "One ooman nuh nuff, mon? Lef mine alone!"

Teran turned to Fawn, "Lord these accents and sayings. I'm around it so much I don't have to figure anything out anymore."

Fawn laughed at the comment, "Chile you in the middle of it. You better get used to it!" As they laughed privately, the fellas watched them.

Teran responded to their looks. "Yeah, we are talking about you two and how the accents come out so hard when you're around one another. The original islanders when ya'll are together, americanized when ya'll are just with us."

"Yuh see, Shani, dat ah de problem wid de Yankee gyal, dey ave too much mout an need fi chill dung. Wah mek yuh nuh tape har mout shut?" Reggie reasoned as Teran looked on in shock over his suggestion.

Laughing, Bashan proceeded to respond. "But, Reg, shi does fight like a Jamaican gyal. Shi will box yuh!" He mimicked Teran's beach maneuver and Reggie held his hands up in surrender. Fawn laughed aloud.

Teran flushed, "I don't believe you," and swatted Bashan's arm. When she made to withdraw, he prevented it and pulled her to sit on his lap. "Bashan!"

He sucked his teeth, "Bashan wah? Yuh mine and I waan sum sugar, dat American enough."

Teran lowered her head, "Not here, stop, we are in public," she gave him a quick kiss and tried to leave his lap.

He grabbed her waist, "Yuh wait fah our wedding, mi tonguing yuh dung!" Teran looked at him in alarm and shook her head vigorously. Bashan grabbed her and pulled her down on the blanket. "Yuh nuh ave a choice cuz mi ago duh dis." He grabbed her head and descended on her lips as she let out a protest.

The other two couples were watching them howling. Wayman cheered, "Take over boy, that's it! She knows she loves it!"

Delores came to Teran's aid, "Fight him, Teran!"

Fawned rebutted, "D-D please! Teran is a punk when it comes to Shan."

Teran resisted as best she could before giving into Bashan's tender assault. When he received her response, he finished the kiss and let her up for air. A red-faced Teran sat up attempting to hide her embarrassment.

"I didn't realize she was so shy. Shan, you shouldn't tease her like that." Delores patted Teran's shoulder.

Fawn added, "Yeah, she's always been shy, but I don't understand why. He's her fiancé and we all know they kiss."

Reggie threw in, "Knowing Shani, dey duh more dan dat!"

Wayman gave a dap to Reggie, "True that!"

Bashan gathered Teran into his chest and she buried her face. "Lef mi babi alone. Shi nuh laik scenes." He turned his attention to Teran. "I just waan a gud kiss fram yuh, forgive mi?" He kissed her neck and the six settled down for a game of spades.

The ride home was relaxing as Reggie steered his custom van down Palisades Parkway. Fawn reclined in a swivel seat near the rear. Teran was seated closest to her followed by Wayman and Delores. Bashan sat in the passenger seat so he could guide Reggie out of the park and back to Queens.

Delores looked at Fawn and Teran and commented, "I see why they call you Bench and Batty. You two are like Siamese twins."

Fawn responded, "No, not us, you should see Teran and her sister. Their family calls them twins because they look and act so much alike."

Delores asked, "Oh, she and her younger sister look that much alike?"

Fawn answered, "No, it's her older sister." Then she had a thought. "T, are you going to have your sisters in the wedding. Is Pe'r Damas walking you down the aisle?"

Teran answered without thought, "I haven't planned that far. It's definitely something to plan for."

"When's the last time you talked to them?"

"Who, Fawn?"

"Your sisters, heck, your dad."

Delores queried, "How many sisters do you have Teran?"

Teran answered, "Three altogether; two by my father and one by my mother. I also have a younger brother by my mother."

Reggie turned the music low and chimed in, "Mi neva kno yuh had more dan Ayana, Teran. Wah yuh oda sista's names? Weh ah dey?"

She proceeded to answer the questions and could feel the tension rising from Bashan who watched the road.

"Saadri lives in Brooklyn and Veronique is in North Carolina."

Wayman entered the discussion, "I like the way you said that – Veronique, sounds French. Are you and your family French?"

Teran swallowed, "I'm Creole on my father's side. So, yes, we are all Louisiana French on that side."

Fawn was too excited to detect the growing friction between Teran and Bashan. "Like I said, she has a sister that looks like her twin. That is Saadri. The other one, Veronique, is a strawberry blonde! They are so cute. You should see pictures from when they were little girls. Teran and her twin looked like little Indian babies and her oldest sister looked like she was Spanish. What's the breakdown on you guys again?"

Teran looked out of the window and swallowed as they crossed the George Washington Bridge; she felt she was moving into bad territory with Bashan. "Veronique is the oldest and six months later Saadri was born. I came six months after her. It's Saadri and I that everyone says are twins."

Delores commented, "Wow! Your dad was busy!"

Fawn clarified, "Pe'r Damas is fine! I know why he was busy!"

"Damas, dat Butch?" It was the first time Bashan spoke and Teran knew he was fuming.

Proudly Teran spoke in Creole, "Non shae, mâ pè çé Damas." Fawn grinned while the others in the car looked at Teran in shock. It was all entertaining for Teran until she viewed the blazing hurt in Bashan's eyes when he slowly turned in her direction. Her attempt to lighten the weight of her disclosure failed. She offered, "Baby, my father is Damas Buard not Butch Gregory, he is Ayana and Talib's dad."

Bashan shook his head and turned toward Reggie, "Wi ago tek de Cross Bronx Expressway fi de Major Deegan."

Fawn proudly announced, "My girl is completely different when she hits Natchitoches Parish. We spent a summer down there with her translating for me. Wait until you meet Granmè Mazie; she is a beautiful woman and doesn't speak a lot of English although she can. I love her father's family and Pe'r Damas is a trip flirting with all the women!" Teran shook her head at Fawn's animation.

The Triborough Bridge took the group into Queens where Bashan then instructed Reggie to maneuver onto the Van Wyck Expressway and into the Hollis area. Reggie pulled in front of Wayman's house and to everyone's surprise Bashan left the van with them. Teran excused herself. "Hey baby, what's going on? Where are you going? Are we getting in your car? Are you leaving me behind?" She chuckled nervously.

"Wah de big deal? Ih nuh laik I mean dat much to yuh."

Teran tried to touch him, but he moved out of reach. "Shan. Don't do this, we had such a wonderful day."

"Nuh duh wah? Yuh sit inna de van an speak anoda language dat mi neva kno yuh speak! Inna fact, mi neva kno bout nutten yuh volunteered todeh! Ou dat yuh fi be marrying mi but mi cyaan get yuh fi tell mi basic tings bout yuh – yuh a Creole an mi nuh kno. Yuh ave sistas mi nuh kno exist an one even live inna Brooklyn. Yuh fada nuh Butch, but alive an apparently well. Yuh ave a grandmada Mazie ooo speak Creole an mi still inna de dark! Yet mi suppos to waan fi spend mo time round yuh? Smadi mi suppose fi marry."

"Ok, Shan, you have every right to be angry with me. I did not finish telling you my family history and I really don't know why. I guess I was so absorbed in what we were doing at the time that I put it on the backburner and never took it off. I didn't mean to withhold the information."

Bashan, hands behind his back, snorted, "Teran, yuh really waan fi marry mi or dis sum sort of fantasy relationship? Mi yuh ticket of escape fram de projects an yuh mada? Mi or de idea yuh cum afta?"

"What are you talking about? I love you, Shan. Of course, I want to marry you." Teran again tried to close the distance between them.

Bashan stepped away, "Yuh nuh gat ih and I affi teach yuh everyting. Yuh love de idea of marriage but yuh nuh inna love wid mi. Mi nah let yuh mek mi look laik an eediat."

Tears clouded her eyes, "Because I left out some details you act like this and say these ugly things to me?"

He snorted, "Leave out de details? Yuh life de details? Teran gat yuh head outta de clouds! Mi nuh yuh knight inna shining arma fi save yuh fram de witch. Mi a mon ooo loves de ground yuh walk pon but mi nuh a sapps an yuh won't treat mi laik a clown. Yuh will share my bed but nuh share yuh life wid mi?! Dis ah ridiculous!" He placed a hand on the door to the van. "Get inna de van. I need yuh to guh home an tink bout wah yuh waan. I chat wid yuh lata."

"Shan, please don't act like this. Let's go and talk. I don't want to leave fighting like this. Please let's talk." She grabbed him around the waist.

He inhaled, opened the door, and commanded, "Get inna di van, Teran! I need space fi tink, odawise ih ova rite now."

Fawn gasped and Reggie grabbed her arm to quiet her. Wayman held Delores and gave her a silencing look. Teran left all propriety, "I made a big mistake and I'm sorry, why are you doing this?!" Bashan looked up into the air. Teran became desperate, "Mâ shae!!!!!"

It was his undoing. He grabbed her by the arms, "Wah yuh waan fram mi Teran? Mi nuh begging yuh like a dawg. Nuh eva duh dis again! I will be yuh usband an nuh badi had betta find out nutten else before mi again, yuh undastan?!"

"Mo shagrin be; I am sorry. It won't happen anymore. Let's go and talk and I will tell you everything and more. I love you Bashan and you are more than a knight in shining armor. You're my friend and lover and I will talk to you. Again, I am sorry."

The onlooking foursome sighed as the couple kissed unabashedly. Wayman teased, "For a second ya'll had us worried, but when girl broke into that French, we were all like putty!"

Bashan laughed, "Yah, did mi undoing. Ou cyan yuh tan vex wen yuh ooman cyan bruk out inna priti language laik dat?" He closed the van door.

Reggie chimed, "I guess mi an Fawn getting pon de BQE by fi wi lonesome selves?"

Bashan agreed as he walked them to the window where Fawn sat, "Yah, mi and Miss ave a chat waitin pon wi. Beside shi gud as a Queens gyal now."

Reggie offered, "Shani, wi know making up di best part!" After they dapped one another through the window Fawn pressed her forehead against Teran's and spoke.

"I'm sorry, T, I didn't know."

"No worries, this had to come to a head. It's time to tell the sordid story. He better still marry me after this or I'm taking him out – he will be at the bottom of Jamaica Bay!" The ladies laughed and everyone said their goodbyes.

----------◊◊◊----------

Bashan, who'd parked at Wayman's house, drove them to Baldwin. This time he opened the home with a key. He led them into the den and left Teran to find his father.

"Hey priti gyal, wah gwaan?" Crandall walked into the den with outstretched arms.

Teran stood and walked into his greeting, "Hi, Pe'r Crandall!"

"Mi laik dat Teran! *Peeer* Crandall. Wah yuh call Mary?" He beamed.

Teran's frown came unbidden. "I call her Mrs. Watts."

"Suh yuh an Mary nuh gat alang? Shani, wah wi a guh duh bout di ooman?"

"Mumi nuh seem fi warm up to Teran."

"Yuh will be marry soon. Wi affi be fambily. Dis a nuh gud. Wi affi fix dis." Crandall shook his head and walked to an oversized armchair where he sat heavily. "Teran, I mek nah excuse fi Mary cuz shi de mada an mi wife. Shi can be haad fi deal wid but shi frighten by suh much change, shi feels as eff shim losing everytig rite now."

Teran leaned into Bashan's frame as he settled beside her on the loveseat. "I don't think she likes me because I am American."

Crandall grimaced, "Yuh tek Shani's attention. Im de ongle son an now im inna love wid yuh. Shani become a mon quickly and preparing fi build a life wid yuh. Mary ave no mo babi. Im sistas dating and now Shani fi marry. One look at yuh an wi aal kno wah mek Shani love yuh. Mary ave no mo babi. Yuh de ooman inna Shani life now."

Teran remained skeptical, "I can understand that but when she thought I had people in the islands she was friendlier toward me than when she realized I don't know that side of my family and had never been there for a visit. The few times I have been at her home she has been cordial for a few minutes but then she starts telling Shan to take me home or don't keep me out late or saying that young women should be home at a certain hour. Ivee doesn't seem to care for me either. She brought up Martina, Shan's ex-girlfriend, in front of me. I don't like to go over there, and I don't like to be mistreated.

Only you and Mentha seem to accept me for who and what I am. I am grateful for that, thank you."

Crandall nodded, clearly impressed with Teran. "Whetha dem waan fi be accepting or nuh dem must gat ova whateva dis ah. Ih nuh rite and dey mus gat to kno yuh as a person an as Shani's wife. I will nuh ave yuh mistreated. Dat nuh ou I waan mi fambily fi behave."

Bashan squeezed Teran closer to him. "Tank yuh fah yuh support Dadi. Mumi should tink dat shi gat a dawta instead of losing mi. Teran sweet and makes mi happy. Shi will be a wonderful addition fi de fambily."

"Yes, thank you Pe'r Crandall. It's not easy coming into a family and the cultural difference can make it even harder, but I do love your son. I want to be a positive addition and help in any way that I can."

"Nuh fret bout a ting, I will fix aal dis." He reached for his remote and turned on the television.

Bashan leaned forward, "Wi need fi chat suh wi will be inna de basement." Crandall nodded and Bashan led them out of the den.

----------◊◊◊----------

The basement was cool, so Bashan found a comforter to wrap around them. He also turned on a space heater. "Okay, Miss, I believe yuh ave sum tings fi explain."

Teran leaned back against Bashan's chest. "Let's see … my mother left City College after a year and went to Xavier University in New Orleans in 1963 to study music. She could play the trumpet like nobody's business. At Xavier, she met my father and she told me that all the ladies were crazy about him on campus. She auditioned at a few jazz clubs in the city and was able to work while she went to school. She even worked at the Half Note on Spring and Hudson Streets in Manhattan when I was little. She met Butch when she was working there and then Yana and later Talib came so her music career went defunct."

"Yuh romp wid de instruments?"

"Non mo shou, I didn't get that gene. My dad also went to Xavier, and he was a business major. He was smart, got good grades, and graduated with honors despite the mess he made of things. The whole story is twisted and a little seedy, but three girls came out of it. My Granmè Mazie helped raise us and made sure we knew our Creole family and culture. We spent plenty summers down there in Cloutierville, Louisiana. From what I know, my mom and my dad weren't serious about one another. I came along unexpectedly so my mother couldn't be rid of him like she thought. My mother wasn't trying to be serious then. I will show you some pictures of her; she was very pretty and so I know she had her pick of men. I heard Butch wore her out chasing her down to finally get her to marry him."

"Yuh mada sounds laik a dandimite shorty. Dat ou yuh behaved inna Prep, guh afta wah yuh waan an disregard wah yuh neva waan. Yuh acted suh boldly inna history class and I knew yuh were used to running de show."

"Shan, I returned your stare, nicely I might add. Now you are saying I was too bold."

"Yah, yuh rumpled my note when I treid to taak to yuh and ignored me until I showed yuh wah a mon does inna de relationship. Now yuh sweet and sekkle dung."

Teran laughed, "Yeah, I settled down. I wasn't trying to fight any battles with you. As for my mother, I am not sure how bold she was, but they say she was a trip. My dad must have been attracted because here I am. Now, he was no angel and could be a real stinker at times, but he always showed me love and didn't take any stuff from us. When we were with Granmè and he came through we straightened up quick. We could get away with a lot more with Granmè and he knew she was a pushover with us so he would keep us in line when he was there with us. Sometimes he had to be away on business."

Bashan started playing with her hair. "Was he there often?"

"Pe'r was always around whether we were with Granmè or he was visitng us. He even took Saadri and I to North Carolina to see Veronique and vice versa. He was not having his daughters isolated from him, his family, or one another. I know he took our mothers to court; Pe'r called the shots; he did not play at all."

"He sounds laik he nuh romp. Who do yuh look more laik, him or yuh mada?"

"I definitely look like my father, so does Saadri. Veronique looks like him but more like her mother who is also Creole. Nique's mother is the one the family thought he'd marry because they grew up together. Veronique's mother was in love with my father. Now talk about a triangle, my dad was in love with Saadri's mother and from what I know they were nearly married. My mother and father never loved one another so marriage never entered the equation, especially when she found out about my sisters."

"That must 'ave been haad pon everyone and den for yuh and yuh sistas to come into dat situation. It sounds laik yuh grandmada did help kip tings good for yuh and dem and dat was for di best. Yuh 'ave a good relationship wid yuh fada?"

"Pe'r was a businessman and a really good one, but he was a little hard as a father. He was matter of fact and didn't often change his mind, if he said something that was it. Even Granmè would get on him about us 'Damas, *tô piti çe femèl.*' She would tell him his children were female. He didn't back off though because he said the world was hard and he wanted us to be ready to handle it and not let it get the best of us. He is still that way today. The situation wasn't the best, but he has been our father. Granmè still spoils us, and we go down from time to time although we haven't been down there together since junior high school. I was last there in tenth grade. Maybe we could take a trip down. She would love that, and I know she would love you."

"Dat wud make mi happy, Teran. I waan to kno everyting bout yuh." He nodded with a smile. "Let mi hear yuh speak mo Creole. It did suh pretty di likkle mi hear inna di van."

Teran grinned. "Let me see, oh, listen to this…

Nouzòt Popá, ki dan syèl-la. Tokin nom, li sinkifyè, n'ap spéré pou to rwayomm arivé, é n'a fé ça t'olé dan syèl; paréy si la tèr Donné-nou jordi dipin tou yé jou, é pardon nouzòt péshé paréy nou pardon lê moun ki fé nouzòt sikombé tentasyon-la, Mé délivré nou depi mal.

That was the Lord's Prayer and I learned it by the time I was three or four."

Bashan lowered his voice and pulled Teran into his embrace. "Wah else yuh know inna Creole? Dem did teach yuh ou fi seh ih time fi mek up." Her scent ignited a flame within him.

Teran spoke softly in Bashan's ear. "*Mo oulé fé lainm twa.*"

He grinned through lowered lids, "Wah does dat mean?"

Teran approached his mouth, "Some things are better left demonstrated."

----------◊◊◊----------

Monuments

For a change of pace Teran decided to spend some time with Bashan in Brooklyn. She guided them from Brownsville to downtown Brooklyn and Fort Greene Park. As they entered the park Teran led Bashan to a grand marble staircase.

"I never knew this was here."

Teran shook her head playfully. "You wouldn't while making a bee line for the train station like you did. I told you Brooklyn is a beautiful and important place." They continued up to the top of the steps and walked across a broad platform leading into a plaza flanked with four miniature columns each holding eagles. She led them to a bench.

Bashan examined the plaza; Teran sat as he spun around, hands behind his back, appraising the area. "Welcome to the Prison Ship Martyrs Monument."

"Suh, ih has a name. How do you come to know bout disya place?" Bashan sat down, placing an arm behind Teran so she would lean against him, "Wah yuh know bout disya place? And, yes, I tink dis a beautiful place. Aldough, ih could duh for some fixing up."

"Yeah, it's condition is sad and that makes me sad because this place is personal. During the Revolutionary War, the British and Americans fought the Battle of Long Island not too far from here at Wallabout Bay. The Navy Yard surrounds the bay now, but then this park was a fort and Wallabout Bay was accessible through the Wallabout neighborhood. This city has strong Dutch roots pre-dating the war."

"Listen to my scholar!" Bashan kissed Teran's cheek, and she sat up, turning her body partially toward him.

"This is where the story gets interesting."

"I was interested fram de start. I nuh know any of dis."

"Okay, here goes, so in 1783 an enslaved man; yes, New York had enslaved people. They passed a law in 1817 that slaves born before 1799 would be free by 1827 and so would their children. By 1840 there was no more slavery in New York."

Bashan added, "Slavery fully ended in Jamaica in 1838. De times dey dictated change, ih seems."

"It would seem so; back to 1783. An enslaved man named Joris Jackson was digging graves on the beach for bodies that kept washing up at Wallabout Bay. During the Battle of Long Island, which the British won, the Royal Navy captured men, women, children, black, and white and imprisoned them on ships in the bay. They were starved to death, died of disease, and mistreated. When the prisoners died their bodies were tossed into the bay. But the bay gave them up, sent them back home, and people had to dig graves for them. There were shallow graves dug along the Bay and my grandfather was part of burying those bodies. Another grandfather moved them to a different site in 1808, and yet another grandfather moved them to this monument. Inside, there is a vault with the bones of people who died on those ships."

Bashan snorted, "Nuh too many people know dere family history laik that here inna de States."

"I know, and that's because of the ravages of slavery here to the families. I am fortunate that my grandfather's family kept this alive."

"Suh, his name, Joris?"

Teran shook her head. "His name was Joris Jansen, his Dutch slave owner named him after a popular man in Brooklyn back when the Dutch had control. But the British pronounced it to sound like George Jackson and that's how the Jackson family name originated. Jansen was also pronounced like Johnson then somehow shortened to John. One of my grandfathers was John George Jackson; another was George John Jackson. The names flipped around but Jackson stayed as the last name and this side of the family has stayed in New York."

Leaning into the bench Bashan deduced, "Jackson nuh Buard, so dis statue ah history from yuh mada's fambily." Teran nodded and he continued, "Is yuh fada's fambily suh colorful."

Teran laughed, "Yeah, full of color, but that is a story we will save for later. I know we have a day planned and you are itching to get out of Brooklyn."

As they left the plaza Bashan wrapped an arm around her shoulder. "Disya place ah personal for mi too, now."

CHAPTER NINE
Who Am I?

Fall 1984

With summer over, everyone settled down to business and Teran entered Hunter College, at night, to major in Education while holding onto her position with the Department of Finance. Bashan applied to the Grumman Aerospace Minority Mentoring Program that Reggie spoke with him about while he worked at the airport and attended night classes at Nassau Community College. The couple's schedules decreased the time they spent with one another, but they maintained regular contact via telephone.

----------◊◊◊----------

Reggie and Fawn moved their wedding date to October, but the wedding still came upon them quickly. Fawn's dress was altered to accommodate her bulging five-months pregnant stomach. Pearl chiffon and beaded lace draped bright tan skin surrounded by golden brown hair. Fawn looked angelic as she stood for Teran's inspection. The fall afternoon air was crisp while the sun danced off the white lace curtains hanging in the Crown Heights window. As Fawn took her father's arm, she wore a look of fulfillment. Her mother tearfully expressed happiness over her daughter's day of transition. Upon hearing the music, all fell into formation. An usher led Fawn's mother to her seat and Teran positioned herself behind two bridesmaids just in front of Fawn. Prior to following the bridesmaids' entrance Teran turned to Fawn, "This is your day in the sun girl – shine!"

Bashan watched Reggie stand coolly in front of the group awaiting the bride's arrival. His grey tuxedo looked picturesque against the fall afternoon's glistening rays. Bashan allowed his mind to envision him and Teran's day until attendees standing drew his attention to the procession. He admired the shades of grey that moved into the converted space. When the darkest shade appeared, he swallowed. A nickel-colored dress accentuated all Teran's shapely beauty – modest bosom, curved waist, flat stomach, and round hips. Bashan shuddered as he watched with pride. His reverie jolted at the sound of, "I'm going to have a headache tonight! I can't believe how she is wearing that dress! Looks like the thing wants to melt off her she's so hot."

He looked two rows behind and into the eyes of a light complected young man with a definite bad boy edge. Their eyes communicated equal readiness to accept any challenge. "*Sitoplé* Najid! You are too loud, Be." Bashan turned in the direction of the voice and staggered; he looked at the face of Teran's twin. A snicker then drew Bashan's attention to the beige face of a blond and light brown-haired bombshell who brought back the term *brickhouse*. A light of recognition dawned. He snorted and turned to watch Teran.

Fawn arrived, the picture of beauty, simply radiant under the sun-filled converted living room. Reggie proudly took his fiancé from her father. Teran positioned herself at an angle with the rest of the bridesmaids and Bashan caught a view of her alluring profile and flawless feet in a pair of matching nickel pumps. Again, he heard a comment, "Good grief, all y'all got them curves!"

Bashan turned toward the same young man, and they stared off. Najid nodded his head toward the exit and Bashan was about to move but the young lady the bad boy was with spoke to him. "Najid *arété* please. You are such a trip!"

The blonde bombshell chimed in with, "Be quiet Hood Rat and stop talking so loud." They snickered and settled down.

Bashan snorted and turned his attention to the ceremony. He couldn't keep his eyes off Teran. He envisioned their upcoming special day – how she would look in a wedding dress and what she'd wear on their honeymoon night. As he openly smiled another guest leaned over and said, "She does look beautiful, doesn't she?" Bashan turned toward a grey-eyed woman standing next to him. He hadn't noticed her earlier.

Still smiling he responded with, "Yah, shi ah gorgeous," referring to Teran.

"Her belly looks so cute in that dress." Bashan realized the young lady spoke of Fawn.

Surprised, he responded, "Oh, oh, yah, shi sticking out now."

----------◇◇◇----------

The ceremony was short and simple. Everyone cheered for Reggie as he kissed his new bride, even the young man Bashan stared at gave an encouraging, "Yeah boy!" The guests moved down into the basement where tables were arranged both inside and in the back yard under a tent ready with heaters for the unpredictable October weather. Outside there were

Who Am I?

two food tables filled with delicacies, a portable bar, and a small dance area. As Bashan moved with the group, the young woman moved a little closer and spoke, "I'm Andrea Calverte; friends call me Drea. What ya go by?"

"Bashan Watts, my friends call mi Shan."

Andrea smiled and Bashan found it an attractive feature. "Let me see, Shan, you are Jamaican?"

He lifted a brow, "Yah, I am Jamaican. Gud guess." They settled at a table under the tent at an angle where Bashan would be able to see Teran. As they sat, he saw the threesome from the ceremony enter the yard. He stood from the table. "Excuse mi, Andrea." He walked over to the group.

Najid watched his approach and spoke to Saadri, "Hey, Candy, you and your sister step away a minute. I might have to check this clown once and for all."

Saadri warned, "Najid he is a pretty big guy, and you are not going to ruin this wedding with this stuff. Both of you were staring at one another and both of you shouldn't have been at someone else's affair acting like that. Come on now, please don't start out here." Najid looked at Saadri and she became silent and lowered her eyes.

Bashan saw the silencing exchange and became skeptical as to whether he would be able to get along with the hardened young man.

Veronique voiced Bashan's concern, "Don't shut her down like that! She's right and you'd better not act fool out here tonight."

Bashan could tell the young man was not used to being confronted in such fashion. He decided to break the ice. He stepped up to them. "My name ah Bashan but I go by Shan and Teran ah my ooman. Dat wud mek yuh all my fambily cuz wi marry soon."

"Bashan!" Saadri squealed and grabbed him about the waist. He hugged her in return. Veronique joined their embrace with a bright smile.

Bashan looked at Saadri. "Yuh mus be de twin cuz yuh duh look laik Teran suh much." He then looked at Veronique, "And yuh de oldest sista live inna Nort Carolina. Yuh all suh priti."

"I'm Najid and you are all over my woman. What's up man?" He nodded toward Saadri, extended his hand to Bashan and they dapped.

"Gud to meet yuh all. Teran tole mi bout yuh and I am glad yuh here at de wedding. Najid, here yuh ooman!" They shared a laugh. "I am possessive ova Teran too."

Saadri and Veronique chimed, "Yeah, we heard." Bashan frowned and they laughed.

Bashan led them to the table where Andrea was seated. The wedding party was upstairs taking pictures. Calypso started playing and Andrea stood, her Cabotine de Gres perfume emanating from her pulse points. "Okay, Shan, you must dance with me." She pulled him from the table as Veronique and Saadri looked on.

"Now I'm telling you don't nut out at this wedding." Najid leaned in close to Saadri's ear.

Saadri shook her head, "Real funny. But that's my sister's man and homegirl is acting like he is her's."

"Don't worry, this will be her only dance with him and she is finding somewhere else to sit." Veronique was about to get up from the table when Najid's hand stilled her. She shot him a warning look he paid no attention to.

"Sit down Nique. He's a big boy and he knows how to put her in her place. Let it play out and you find out all you need to know." Najid looked at her until she sat.

"How do you do that?" Veronique sat with a thump.

"Do what?" Najid sat back in his seat and put his arm around Saadri.

"You speak without speaking."

Najid shook his head while Saadri answered, "Sè, I've been trying to figure that out forever."

Who Am I?

Veronique watched as Andrea began to dance closer to Bashan. Then the music ceased, and everyone's attention diverted to the entrance of the wedding party. Two bridesmaids, both sets of parents, Reggie's best man, and Teran entered before Reggie and Fawn. As Teran walked toward the wedding party's table she noticed how close Andrea stood beside Bashan. Instead of dwelling on it she decided to give Bashan the benefit of the doubt. The last thing she wanted was a repeat of her birthday night.

----------◊◊◊----------

Everyone had eaten, and the wedding party was free to mingle. Teran searched for the brown suit, white shirt, and black leather tie graced with a herringbone chain she knew belonged to Bashan. When she spotted him, he was at the table laughing with her sisters and Najid. She stilled and watched them. Just weeks ago, she and Bashan had a terrible argument over her failure to tell him about them and there they were enjoying one another like family – her family.

As she recommenced, she noticed Andrea at the table as well. She smarted at the earlier slight; Andrea prevented Teran from dancing with Bashan. In her blaze toward the table, she failed to avoid Elton, Reggie's inebriated brother. *"Weh yuh guh suh quickly, Teran? Mi waan chat wid yuh. Dance wit mi gyal."* He guided her to the floor with his hands on her size twenty-four waist. The Calypso tune had the floor jammed with people. The DJ kept the party going and Teran had never danced so much in her life.

----------◊◊◊----------

Upstairs in Fawn's room Teran spoke, "Make sure you take everything you want because you won't be here for a week."

Fawn, already in her traveling clothes, sat on the bed watching a preoccupied Teran. "Thank you for inviting your sisters, it was so good to see them! That Najid is a cutie; Dri likes the hard rocks, huh? And Veronique! She is a bad mamma-jamma! So pretty! Y'all should be models. Pe'r Damas has a point about being so protective and hard on y'all." When Teran waved her off with a laugh, Fawn continued. "What's going on? Who was that other girl hovering around Bashan?"

Teran faced Fawn, "Don't worry about that. You just make sure you have everything you need for your trip."

Fawn grew more concerned, "I'm together, now will you tell me what's going on?!"

"Absolutely not, Fawn! This is your wedding night for Pete's sake! You will have your own household to run just as soon as you get back from your honeymoon. Speaking of which, you need to hurry up so I can get you out to Reggie." Fawn licked her tongue at Teran, and they shared a laugh.

They walked out of the second-floor bedroom and into Reggie who was pacing in the hall outside. He smiled at the sight of them, "Bout time, mi did start fi worry dat sup'm did wrong." Fawn went into his arms and Teran walked ahead of them and descended the stairs.

As they came into guests' view, confetti flew into the air. Teran ducked and shielded herself as she moved through the shower. She noticed she'd not seen Bashan. Nevertheless, she continued leading the pair toward the front door. Once outside, on the top landing of the staircase she spotted Bashan getting into his car. Through the windshield she could make out another person, a female, in the car.

"*Éou zòt tô bo va, Sè*?" Veronique spoke behind Teran.

"If I knew where he was going, we would both be inside instead of out here with me mad as hell!" Teran turned to walk inside.

Veronique took her by the arm, "Then why not go to the car and ask him where he is going rather than stand here yelling at me for asking the question. I am with you. We can pull that heifer, I see, out of the car and teach her a lesson Buard style."

Teran joked, "Shaer, you're a St. Amant."

Veronique laughed, "Oh yes, an illustrious St. Amant. *Mèsi,* mercy me!"

"*Non Shaer, Merci* on us all!"

"Hey, stop talking about my mother. *Mon Mon* Nadine is no walk in the park!" Veronique placed a manicured hand on her hip.

"Why are you two out here? Everything okay?" Saadri knit her brows together.

"How did you get out here without your bodyguard?" Veronique jibed. Teran burst into laughter.

"Oh, so you two got jokes right now. Where is your big Jamaican, Terry? He's a cutie, I liked him right off. Granmè know about him? Does Pe'r know about him? He said you two were getting married. Is that true? I know I'd better be in my twin's wedding! Later for Nique and Yana, I know I'm your favorite sister. What will your colors be? How does *Mon Mon* Nadine like him? I know Yana has something to say, I'm going to get her for not calling me and telling me. What?"

Teran and Veronique stood silently, watching Saadri. Veronique spoke, "How in the world can you ask so many questions and not let a person get in one answer? Good grief, where's the fire?"

Teran nudged Veronique, "You know she has to get it all in while she's not with Bruiser. He shuts it all down when he comes on the scene." The sisters laughed again. When they saw they may have wounded Saadri they stopped the teasing. Teran offered, "Dri, we both love Najid with his fine self. He's a hardrock for sure, but he loves you and we know he treats you well. That's all we can ask for. Have you two thought about getting married?" Saadri looked pained. "Dri? What's the matter, *Sè?*"

"Umm, I have to tell you something. We ... uh... Najid and I ... well..." The sisters looked at one another before looking at Saadri as if to say, 'out with it!' "Okay, here it is – we got married at the justice of the peace over the summer."

"What?!" The two chorused before Veronique spoke up. "So, when were you planning to tell us? He is your husband – ooh, does Pe'r know?" Saadri shook her head. "Granmè?" Saadri shook again. "Crap, Dri, you've done it now."

"What did she do?" Najid walked up to the threesome.

Teran went to embrace him, "Well my cutie hard-rock, it seems congratulations are in order because you're now my *bofrè*, my brother-in-law." She kissed his cheek.

"Thank you, Gorgeous, I am happy to be part of the family. Now I have three beauties to protect. When Nique came up the last time, it was a headache, but I managed it."

Veronique pushed Najid who grabbed her and kissed her on the cheek. "Let me go you ruffian! Wait, you guys got married over the summer! Before or after I came?"

Najid looked at Saadri and held out his hand. She came to him. "We tied the knot after you left."

Veronique shook her head, "Ya'll are a piece of work! Wait until Pe'r finds out Dri. He's going to have a fit. Can I tell my mother?"

Saadri and Teran responded, "*Non*!"

"Ya'll better stop coming at my mother!" Saadri and Teran laughed.

Najid asked, "What's wrong with Nique's mother?"

Teran quipped, "Just wait until you meet Merci." She smirked and sent a covert look toward Veronique who rolled her eyes. They all went inside to help with clean up.

----------◊◊◊----------

An hour later the doorbell rang and Teran heard Bashan's voice as he spoke with Fawn's mother. He walked into the living room and up to Teran. "Hey, Miss, I kno yuh ah vex but please yuh nuffi cah mi ena dween a gud deed."

Najid asked Saadri, "What did he just say? She can understand him?" Saadri nudged him. He spoke to Bashan. "You know she's pissed, and she should be. You cut out on her, and she didn't know where you were, what's up with that? I'm glad we were here to wait with her."

Teran offered, "Shan, Saadri and Najid are married so you're now talking to my brother-in-law. You two will have to get along so don't start acting crazy in here."

"Laik yuh and my mada, rite, Teran?" Bashan snorted in Teran's direction.

Saadri took the opportunity to break the ice. "Oh Lord, Terry! You have a Merci?"

Veronique volleyed, "Non, she has a Nadine and that's bad enough. We can't all be Sain't Ellen."

"Ooh! So, are we ranking now?" Teran became animated.

The sisters looked at one another and exclaimed, "It's on!"

Bashan turned to Najid, "Ah dey laik dis aal de time. Dey chime inna lacka chorus - dree blind mice!"

"Oh sweat, three blind mice! Ha! I have to get used to your accent but that was good, man." Najid tapped Bashan on the shoulder.

"Don't start you two because we can have a session!" Veronique challenged.

Najid answered with, "Why are you always the ringleader? Do you have a man? You have so much mouth, and I thought Candy had mouth!"

Bashan added, "Teran ah nuh slouch, shi ave much mout!"

Teran added, "Yeah I do, and this mouth is getting ready to go off on you. Who was in your car and why was she in your car?"

"Teran, I took Andrea home. Shi drank a likkle too much an I nuh waan har pon de train laik dat."

"Put the heifer in a cab! You ain't her man! You got my sister here waiting for you and all nasty with us while you trying to play the gentleman with some skeezer!" Saadri pounced. Najid wrapped his arms around her waist and whispered in her ear.

Veronique was about to speak but Najid intercepted. "Nique. Let's get our stuff and let these two handle their business. Come let me talk to you about finding you a good man to keep you preoccupied and calm you down." He laughed when he said the last part because she was baited.

"I don't need you to find a man for me and I am not interested in one of your hoodrat friends." She walked with Saadri and Najid into another room.

Bashan playfully pinched Teran and she rolled her eyes. "Yuh ah almost reddi to go?"

"What about my family? They will need a ride to Saadri and Najid's wherever that is." She went up to Fawn's room to gather her things without waiting for his answer.

Bashan followed the path the others took and found them lounging in the den. "Yuh ah reddi to leave fambily? Najid point mi inna de rite direction and I will tek yuh home."

Najid stood and helped Saadri out of her seat. "You got it Bro-in-law. Come on, Baby. We are going home. Big Mouth you get up and come on too." Veronique sucked her teeth and stood.

"I cyaan get ova how yuh look just laik my babi. I luk pon yuh face and I see Teran." Bashan shook his head in disbelief.

"Well make no mistake, this one here is my Candy. Besides, she's older so Terry looks like her! But we both have good taste because all of them are fine!"

"Dey ah fine indeed." Bashah dapped Najid as Teran walked into the den.

"Is everyone ready?" She looked at the men, "Glad to see the testosterone contest is over." She turned and walked toward the front door.

Who Am I?

Veronique walked up to Bashan, "Ohh, are you in trouble, Big Boy! Terry is pissed. Let's see you take another hussy home."

"Mouth Almighty! Please mind your own business. That man doesn't need you stirring up trouble between him and his woman." Najid steered Saadri out of the den. He looked back and saw Veronique standing beside Bashan and grabbed her hand, then yanked, "Let's go woman before I drag you out of here by your hair. Then you can add cave man to the list of names you call me."

Bashan laughed aloud, "Dat wud be a sight to see!"

"Cool it Reggae Boy! You ain't in the family yet!" Veronique volleyed over her shoulder as Najid pulled her away.

Bashan snorted, "Oh, I am inna de fambily arite. I see de mout runs drough de sistas."

Najid pointed at Veronique, "Yes it does! As pretty as they are and as much mouth as they bring, this is one trait I can do without! And she's the queen!"

"Najid, stop talking about my sisters. Obviously, we need the mouth we have to deal with you two apes!" Saadri took Veronique's arm and continued walking.

Najid lowered his voice, "Don't worry, I know how to shut that mouth."

Bashan howled, "I ave de siem crosses wid Teran. Shi rises up den I affi show har ooo de mon."

Saadri and Veronique yelled, "Terry!"

Teran was on the stoop when she heard them call. "What's going on? Come out of these people's house making all that noise!"

The group said their goodbyes to the Welches and filed out the front door. The drama commenced on the block and a half walk to Bashan's car.

Saadri was by Teran's side. "So, Shan shows you who the man is? 'Cause that's what he said."

Veronique agreed, "He and Hardrock said we have too much mouth and he said he knows how to shut Dri's mouth."

Saadri sucked her teeth. "*Ki fé pensé-yé nouzòt to?*"

Najid jumped in front of the women. "Time! First of all, I had no idea you could speak another language and second say everything in English so we can understand. I have a tough enough time following my man here."

Bashan placed a hand over his heart. "I dought wi were pon de siem side, Najid." He mimicked the way Saadri sucked her teeth. The group laughed.

"Are you trying to go to war, Shan? I said for those who didn't know." She leveled both of them with a glare. "Who did the two of you think we were?"

Bashan put both hands in the air. "Sup'm tells mi wi ago find out." They all laughed as they arrived at the car.

Teran sat in the front seat at Najid's insistence. They settled and she laid into him, "Shan, who was the chick and why did she stick up under you tonight? She didn't even want me to dance with you!"

"T, shi Reggie's coworka and wi met tenight."

"Tonight?! And you drove her home?! Let me just meet someone and go off with him; it would be World War Six, but you go off and don't know her from Eve."

"I was trying to be a gentleman, I knew yuh wud be busy wid de reception and de newlyweds suh I took har home and came rite bak here to yuh. Besides, I knew yuh were here wid fi yuh sistas and Najid. Nutten happened or wud happen. Yuh ah de ongle ooman I luv, T. Be gud fi mi babi and don't quarrel wid mi. I waan taak bout dat dress pon yuh badi."

Najid cut in, "He wants to talk about getting you out of that dress and I don't blame him because you wore the stitches out of it!"

"Najid!" Saadri covered her mouth while Veronique shrieked.

"What?! Candy, if you had worn a dress like that, I would have stopped the wedding, 'Pardon me everyone but I got to take this gift home and unwrap the package'!" The car erupted.

Bashan reached over and caressed Teran's thigh. "See, he undastans mi. Nuhbadi looked laik yuh did inna dat dress. Wah mek mi wud waan sum oda ooman wen I ave yuh? I luv yuh gyal."

Saadri sniffled, "I am so glad my sister has your devotion. Welcome to the family."

Najid chimed in, "Welcome to the family, man. It's good to have a brother who can relate. We have to do some things together."

Three sets of eyes focused on Veronique. Bashan watched her from the rearview mirror. She huddled in a corner and stared out the window. Najid reached behind Saadri and placed a hand on her shoulder, "You okay, Nique?"

"I'm proud of my sisters, welcome to you both." She sighed and continued to watch the passing sights.

----------◊◊◊----------

In the middle of October, Teran was home getting over the flu. Bashan entered the kitchen, beaming, with groceries of soup, crackers, fruit, and juice. Ayana greeted him, "Well, if it isn't the medicine man! What do you have in those bags?

"Yana-love, I ave groceries fi mek my babi feel betta. Weh ah shi? Wah gwan, Mrs. Gregory, how ah yuh today?"

Nadine took the bags from Bashan. "Hi, Shan. You had better stop spoiling her like this. It will be hard to keep up once you're married."

"Shanidoo!" Ten-year-old Talib came into the room and looked at the bags. He was already taller than his mother and shared Ayana's chestnut brown complexion. Like Teran, his smile sported twin dimples.

"Talib ih been a lang time since I've seen yuh. Gimmi a pound."

The stocky boy ran into Bashan, as was their custom, before giving him the dap. "Whatcha buy me?"

Before Nadine could protest, Bashan pulled out a bag full of candy. "Yuh kno I cyaan figet my likkle mon." Talib grabbed the bag with delight as Nadine supervised what he took out and stored the rest, silencing his protest of being treated like a baby.

Long tee shirt, tights, and ponytail stood in the kitchen entrance watching the scene. Bashan became visibly excited upon seeing Teran and the transparency of her shirt. Nadine responded, "Put on a robe, girl, y'all ain't married yet!" Teran left the kitchen.

When she came back Bashan was sitting in the living room on the couch. She walked over and kissed him before seating herself next to him. He made sure she was comfortable. "Ou yuh ah feeling? Yuh ah up to a likkle surprise?"

Teran grinned, "What kind of surprise? I need to go and change first."

Bashan looked her up and down, "Eff yuh mus. Get an ova night bag too."

Teran stood up, giggled "Fresh," and walked out of the room.

Nadine saw Teran head for her bedroom and questioned Bashan. "Are you leaving? Make sure she is dressed warmly. Don't keep her outside too long."

"I will tek gud care of har Mumi Nay." Nadine smiled, nodded, and went into her bedroom.

Teran came out of her bedroom and stated, "Don't wait up for me, Mon Mon."

Nadine looked out of her door and saw Teran's bag. She responded loudly enough for Bashan to hear, "Alright, I already told you two that I don't want any grandchildren right now."

To Teran's surprise Bashan answered with, "Don't fret wi won't be dween dat fah ah while; wi ave too much pon de plate rite now Mumi Nay." With that he took her bag and began to steer her toward the front door.

Who Am I?

---◊◊◊---

They headed toward Queens as they usually did. Bashan drove into Queens Village and Teran thought they were going to his house. When they didn't turn down 91st Avenue Teran began to question, "Where are we going, Shan?"

Bashan gave her strange look, "Mi nuh know."

"Stop playing, Shan! Where are we going?"

In a matter of fact voice he answered, "Wi ago home."

Teran pondered the response then became excited, "Home? You got your own place?!"

Bashan turned toward Teran, "Wi ave our own place now, yes." Teran leaned over and kissed his cheek. Bashan drove into a section called Laurelton off Springfield Blvd. The house was located on the corner of 121st Avenue, which intersected Springfield Blvd. It was a brown brick front, detached, with a front yard, and three entrances adorned with aluminum overhangs; the house was one of the nicest on the block.

Eldrige Edmond was taking out his garbage as Bashan pulled up. Seeing them he waited inside the fence. When Bashan emerged, he called, "Wah gwan, Shani, mi see yuh ave fi yuh wife-to-be wid yuh!"

Proudly grinning, Bashan opened Teran's door and helped her out of the car. He reached in the back seat, took out her bag, grabbed her hand, and walked into the gate to make introductions. "Mista Edmond, dis ah Teran. Babi, dis ah de owna, Mista Edmond."

Eldrige smiled as he looked at the young couple. "Mi ena taking out de trash, nuh mind mi. Pleased fi meet yuh." He gave Teran a hug and talked about the entrances. "De front leads to fi mi part of de ouse while around de side leads to yuh apartment. Yuh can use de yaad, so long as yuh clean ih afta. Just let mi know wen yuh gwan use ih. Mi nah nosey fi mi wife edah, wi rent to Shani cah wi kno he's a gud bwoy an wi hope yuh bote will be appy here." He gave Teran another hug and kissed her on the cheek before leaving the couple alone. His overt familiarity made Teran feel strange.

Bashan led them down the path to the side door. They stepped inside onto a short landing atop a flight of stairs. The stairs led into a living room followed by a kitchen area. Off to the left of the living room was a bathroom and finally a bedroom. The apartment was small but enough for them to make a start. Teran stood in the middle of the living room taking in the details of the space. Baseboard heaters made the apartment very cozy. Bashan walked up behind her and wrapped his arms around her waist, "Yuh laik ih babi? I kno ih likkle but wi ah just starting out. I will get yuh de 'ouse before long, but ih de best I cyan duh fah now."

Teran turned in his embrace and smiled, "I love it baby! It's perfect, the best thing I've ever had besides you."

He looked at her a while before stating, "I luv yuh suh much, Miss."

Teran purred, "I love you too, baby." After a brief kiss, they went through the apartment making plans for decorating.

Teran entered the bedroom, "Don't have a stitch of furniture but you got the bed."

Bashan sat on it and watched her a moment. "Yuh kip saying mi Teran. Dis ah our apartment, dis ah fah us."

"I mean to say we, but right now it feels more like you. I'll get used to us once we are married."

"Ih sounds laik yuh nuh serious bout marrying mi; yuh trying to tell mi sup'm?"

Teran threw her hands in the air. "Shan, there you go reading into things. I ain't said nothing about not wanting to marry you."

Bashan wouldn't give up. "It is nah wat yuh seh, it is wat yuh do. Yuh act like yuh ah backed into a corner. Yuh ave a choice an nuh ave to look fah a way out."

Teran shifted her weight to her right hip. "I just finished telling you how much I love you. I was excited about the apartment, and because I say you, instead of we, about the bed, I'm looking for a way out?! You get all worked up over nothing – I just gotta get used to the idea of us having an apartment. That's all there is to it Bashan, plain and simple." Teran stood with hands on her hips waiting for Bashan's reply.

Bashan stared at her and nodded, "Cum sit by mi, I waan to tell yuh sup'm. It's sort of a surprise."

She stood in place. "Do we understand one another?"

Bashan took her by the hands. "I get it now, sit and let mi taak wid yuh. It's funny how I got dis apartment. Rememba wen I got my cyar fram fi mi fada?" Teran affirmed while he continued. "Well, ih turns out a few of months ago I found out Crandall ah nah my real fada. He and my mada gat back togeda when I was one. He de ongle fada I know until recently. Anyway, my real fada found out ooo I was when I was ten. Cyan yuh believe my madda wud kip mi fram knowing him fah dat lang? I cyan imagine nuh knowing bout my pickney. I wud ave a big problem wid de child's mada and wud probably try to raise my pickney myself."

Teran patted his cheek, "Don't worry, you'll know about all of our babies. You're going to be such a good parent."

He grinned, "Wi gwine mek a bunch of babies togeda. But now for de story. My real fada said he saw mi and my mada one day and looked at mi and knew I was his son cah I luk just laik his bredda. But my mada nuh want him round mi wid Crandall inna de picture. Shi neva explain to Crandall bout him cah shi nuh know ou Crandall would tek de news. Den wen dey split up shi nuh know ou to contact my fada. Dat was bak wen I started high school, but Crandall took care of mi still."

Teran fanned herself, "Whew! This is a lot, Shan."

Bashan nodded, "Dere is more to tell. Arite, suh one day, I was out raking my mada's yaad while shi was working in har garden. Dis mon cum to de fence and seh, *'Wah gwan, Mary?'* Shi tung to see de guy and look laik shi will pass out.

Cyan yuh imagine my mada going to pass out?" Teran shook her head in disbelief. "I tap raking and watch de events. De mon aks eff I am de bwoy, says I was getting big, and aks eff dey could taak. Aal dis time, my mada nuh seh a wud! Dey guh into de ouse an I follow alang. Lang story short dis mon ah my fada, Eldrige Edmond. I could ave passed out myself, but I was too mad. Den my mada tells mi nuh be vex wid him cah ih was har fault. Shi introduced us and lef de room. Wi taak sum dat day den spend sum time togeda oda days. I met his fambily and wi seem to get alang as eff wi knew one anoda aal de while. Tings at home gat worse suh he offered mi dis apartment an I took ih."

The older man's friendliness made sense to Teran. "So, the landlord is your father? Wow, baby! How are you doing with all of this? What about Papa Crandall?"

"I am fine and wi will taak bout my fada anoda time. I ave anoda surprise fah yuh." Teran faced him with an expression as if she couldn't take all the news. Chuckling at her actions Bashan reported, "Yuh know dat mentoring program I applied to at Grumman? I got accepted! Training begins inna two weeks an ih paid! Once I pass training dey will pay for mi to go to school and give mi a full-time job."

Teran screamed cheerfully and jumped into Bashan's lap. "Oh, baby, congratulations! My man's gonna be an engineer! I'm so happy for you and for us. I'll be a teacher and you'll be an engineer, we gonna clock some dollars together!"

"Dat mo like it! Wi, wi, wi gwine be arite, I waan celebrate." Bashan held Teran as he spoke.

Attentive, Teran asked, "What do you want to do?"

He pulled her hair out of the ponytail she wore and let it fall around her shoulders and down her back. "Tenight ah going to be special."

CHAPTER TEN
Our World

The fall slipped into winter as everyone settled into their routines. Fawn's parents stayed in Brooklyn awaiting the baby's arrival. Reggie was also accepted into the mentoring program, making him and Bashan co-workers. Fawn continued working at the job her mother secured for her at Merrill Lynch – her mother worked there as well. Teran maintained her college aide position while attending Hunter at night. Bashan and Teran weren't seeing much of one another because of their schedules, and it was causing tension.

On a Thursday night Teran walked out of Thomas Hunter Hall with Jerry Ames – a classmate. They were discussing the night's lecture. Jerry was tall, dark, very attractive and constantly barraged with attention from their female classmates. That she had not thrown herself at him may have been a factor in he and Teran becoming good friends. "So, Teran, thinking about the lecture tonight, what's our responsibility for carrying the Afrocentrism torch in this society?"

"I think the contributions of Africa should be recognized and accepted, and we must mobilize as other cultures have done to see that happen. So, we are talking social, political, and economic mobilization to create a multicultural society accepting of all contributors."

Jerry smiled as he listened, "You one tough sister. Listen, I'm a check you out later. Take it easy, baby." He touched her arm and walked in the direction of Park Avenue while Teran turned opposite to go into the train station.

"Now wah was aal dat bout?!" Bashan stood beside his car with arms folded. Teran startled then smiled and walked toward him. When she tiptoed to kiss him, he gently held her at bey. "Wah was up wid dat? Did I hear him call yuh babi?"

Teran sighed, "His name is Jerry, and we have a class together. He called me baby but not how you would use it. We are friends, classmates, that's all."

"He doesn't affi be inna yuh face and calling yuh babi. A mon doesn't grin at yuh laik dat and call yuh babi unless he likes yuh, suh yuh nuh need to be inna his face. Nuh let mi see him inna yuh face again or it's a problem Teran."

They got in the car as Teran mumbled, "Now you're jealous."

Bashan hit the steering wheel. "Yah, an yuh know dis suh nuh duh nutten to mek mi jealous!"

"I didn't do anything in the first place. We were talking about tonight's lecture. What do you want me to do, go to class with a paper bag on my head?"

"Nuh act simple wid mi cah yuh know what I mean! Yuh ave a way of grinning dat mek a mon waan to try his luck. Yuh smile is sunshine and inviting, suh don't mek mi bruk a mon nek ova yuh, dat include your neck too!" He started the car and drove down 63rd Street toward the east side of Manhattan.

A balladeer crooned for reassurance from his love on the radio. Bashan loved the song. "Yuh ah happy wid mi Teran?"

She sighed, "Not when you act so mean Shan. Jerry is only a classmate. I'm not interested in him, you all the headache I need."

Bashan laughed, "Gud one! Speak of headaches, yuh should see Drea. Yuh should see ou shi carries on at work."

Although he was laughing Teran became visibly upset, "At the job?!"

He turned toward her with a frown, "Yah, shi work at Grumman too. I told yuh at de wedding shi was Reggie's co-worka now shi mine too. And before yuh gat bringly dere ah nutten gwan wid shi and mi. Look, wah mek yuh nuh cum home wid mi suh wi cyan start our weekend early? Yuh ave clodes dere aredi and I miss yuh. Sleeping alone inna dat bed ah driving mi crazy. Wi affi gat marry soon. I will drive yuh to de train inna de mawnin." When she agreed he headed toward the 59th Street Bridge and had them home inside forty minutes.

After parking Bashan announced, "My fada and his wife laik yuh whole heap. Duh yuh want to tap inna an say wah gwan? Ih nah too late cah dem ah still up, dey guh to bed late."

"Okay, that will be fine." Teran held the food they stopped for and waited for Bashan to lock the car. They walked proudly toward the front door.

Nellie Edmond answered the door. "Shani, wah gwan?! El, yuh bwoy dey yah! Gat iz priti likkle gyal wid him."

Eldrige came from the kitchen to greet the couple. "Wah gwan?! Mi bwoy!"

Bashan gave his father a hug. "Mi dought yuh wud laik fi see Teran, suh wi tap by."

Eldrige gave Teran a big hug, "Ih gud fi see yuh Teran, ih been a while. Shani luk suh sad round here widout yuh. Nel, luk pon mi bwoy an iz empress. Isn't shi priti?"

Nellie smiled as she inspected Teran. "She likkle - yuh need mo food. Yuh nyam?"

Teran moved closer to Bashan and held up the bag she carried. "We got something to eat already. Thank you."

Nellie wouldn't be put off. She looked at the bag then at Teran and shook her head. "Wah? Food fram out dere? Ih nah betta dan my food. Yuh need gud food fi kip yuh healdy."

Bashan stepped to Teran's defense. "Shi nuh laik har food too spicy Mumi Nel."

The older woman wore a puzzled expression, "Nuh spice, wah kine of food ah dat? Yuh laik spice an shi mus learn fi cook it. Lawd a massi shi ah marrying a Jamaican mon an nuh laik spice. Cum, pickney, save dat food fah lata an nyam som gud food now." Teran followed Nellie into the kitchen.

Bashan watched Teran walk away, and his father noticed observed. "Eff yuh happy den suh mi Shani. Shi seems fi suit yuh well. Kip har happy."

"Dat gyal ah fi mi world. Shim ah intelligent too yuh know." Bashan sat in an armchair and Eldrige settled nearby.

"Den de two of yuh can duh whole heap togeda. Yuh two can guh far just use fi yuh brains. Tek dis time an build fi yuh savings. Get reddi fi de babies yuh ah sure to mek. Mi ago help yuh as much as mi can as long as yuh duh de rite ting."

"Tenk yuh Dadi."

Eldrige continued, "Wen yuh plan fah de wedding? Yuh know Nel an Mary will waan gat de cakes made..." Bashan's quizzical expression caused Eldrige to lean in. "De ooman dem will make de bridal cakes an kyarri dem fi de reception place just laik in JA."

Bashan sat upright, "My mada nuh seh nutten bout shi waan kip dat custom."

"Truss mi, dey will kip ih suh mek sure Teran know. Dere will most likely be round twelve of dem." Eldrige broke out in laughter as Bashan buried his head in his hands. "Nel an mi waan gat yuh som furniture fi mek de apartment a home fah yuh two."

"Wah wi gwon duh wid twelve cakes? I must let Teran know bout dis soon." Bashan wore a pained expression.

Eldrige clapped him on the shoulder. "Yuh guests will nyam de cake suh nuh worries. Dat gyal ah a beauty an deserve mo cakes too. Weh ah shi fram? Shi looks like shim ah mixed wid sup'm."

Proudly Bashan answered, "Teran ah Creole fram Louisiana an can speak Creole too."

A light of understanding caused Eldrige to sigh, "Now mi get dat priti color an hair an har eyes too dem tun cola nuh dem? Mi saw a hazel an green color fi dem. Shi carries harself well, nuh wonda yuh were attracted to har."

Bashan groaned, "Wi arite eff mi nuh affi kill smadi bout being inna har face."

Just then Nellie called for the men, "Hey, wah gwan, a meeting or sup'm?" The men joined the women in the kitchen.

Eldrige laughed aloud. "Men taak ah aal. Trying fi mek sense of de ooman."

Teran raised her eyebrows but didn't speak. When Bashan saw her, he replied, "Yah, like wah mek yuh cyaan kip de mon outta fi yuh faces."

"Wah yuh ah talking bout, Shani? Teran cyaan ave a Boops?" Nellie teased.

Bashan leaned toward Teran, "Nuh eff shi an de Boops waan fi gat licks."

Eldrige grabbed his son's arm. "Cum now, son, nah gud fi lick fi yuh ooman. Shi waan be luv up nuh lick."

Teran concurred, "Listen to them Shan. The only man I want is you."

Nellied added, "Sidung an nyam, Teran made fi yuh plate fah yuh. Yuh aal shi taak bout shi nuh waan anoda mon." Bashan smiled as he sat down to eat while the older couple talked to them about married life.

----------◊◊◊----------

Two weeks later, Bashan called Teran to make plans for the weekend. She informed him that she was not going to be able to meet him until Saturday. A group of classmates decided to do dinner and a movie and Teran was eager to participate. Bashan agreed to meet her at the train station Saturday afternoon and wished her a good night.

Seven of them went to see a new movie and followed up with a visit to Tad's Steakhouse. On Broadway and 40th Street, the group decided to walk to the east side to catch their respective trains at Grand Central Station. Jerry Ames and another male classmate, Remy Coran, were part of the group. Remy walked with three of the female classmates in front of the threesome comprised of Teran, Jerry, and another female classmate. All were talking and laughing about the movie at a leisurely pace allowed by the unseasonable winter night. They passed the Bentley nightclub and commented about the line to get in. Teran heard a familiar voice. "*Weh yuh guh, Miss?!*"

Teran turned as Bashan stepped off the line and inhaled. Jerry watched her reaction, "Everything okay, Teran?"

Bashan challenged, "Eff ih nuh okay ih my job to mek ih okay cah shi my ooman. Duh yuh ave ah problem wid dat?"

Jerry responded, "I am just making sure my friend is okay."

Bashan snorted, "Yuh friend is my wife-to-be. Yuh let mi fret bout har."

Three other guys left the line and Remy stepped beside Jerry. Wayman spoke to them. "What's up y'all? We got it from here. Teran is fine with us. Good night." They looked at Teran who nodded and said her goodbyes to the group. Wayman moved Bashan aside to calm him down.

Al stepped beside Teran, "What are you doing out here with this dude? Shan gonna kick your behind girl. His head is nice too! We gonna have a headache out here trying to keep him from nuttin straight up!"

Teran left Al with a roll of her eyes and walked toward Bashan who was still in Wayman's sphere of attention. "Baby, we were in a group and went out together as a bunch of school mates. There is no one dating each other in this group. Everybody was laughing and joking, why do you have to act like this embarrassing me and creating a show out here for everyone to see?"

He spun toward Teran, "Yuh kip yuh mout shut and I will deal wid yuh wen wi gat home!" She was shocked and angered to the point of tears as she stepped away from a man she hardly knew.

Wayman watched Teran's retreat and shook his head with dismay. He pulled Bashan further down the street.

Kennith, another in the Queens group spoke to Teran. "Don't pay too much attention to B. He's talking out of his head; you know he has you on a pedestal. Of course, he's jealous because you were walking with dude, yeah it was a group of y'all but dude was the one who spoke up for you, so we know he's the one trying to talk to you. He's probably madder because you don't seem to realize dude is checking you out. Just chill a minute and let us talk to Shan." Teran nodded as Kennith walked over to Bashan and Wayman.

Al chose the opportunity to approach Teran, "You still marrying that dude?" Teran just looked at him. "You don't have no freedom now, what do you think it's gonna be like when you get the ring on the finger? A woman like you needs some breathing space. I noticed that about you as soon as I met you. He got to go nut just cause you out with a group of friends. He must not be doing things right cause he worried somebody gonna take you from him. You need to leave that fool alone. I don't want no answer now. Just think about it. You want somebody that can allow you freedom cause they know they have everything with you on lock. I ain't gotta worry cause you ain't going far once you're mine. Pretty little thing like you, I'd have you spoiled and sprung. He doesn't have you either way, apparently, to act like this. When you ready for some good lovin' let me know." He left and entered the club with Kennith.

Teran stared out into the street disbelieving the level to which Al sank and wondering if she should let Bashan know what he'd said to her. She jumped as someone took her hand and was relieved to see a calmer Bashan standing beside her. "Yuh arite? Let's guh home." Teran nodded as she allowed Bashan to lead her four blocks to where Wayman parked his car. She got in the back and laid across the seat. Closing her eyes so she'd not be disturbed Teran listened to the music of the radio and snippets of the conversation in the front.

"Shan, you better go home and talk to her before you start accusing her of something. She was in a group, and everyone seemed to be maxin' out. It would have been different if it was him and her alone."

"Way, I know, but I ave seen har wid dis dude before. He likes har but shi cyaan see dat. Yuh see how he was reddi to step to mi bout har? I would ave bruk his jaw."

"You know Teran would have had a fit. You wouldn't have wanted her to see you like that. She should never see that side of you man, and we talked about that before. Our woman should never have to see that in us. It's bad enough she had to see you dust off J at the beach; that girl almost lost her mind when she watched you wearing that boy out."

"I know mon, but I will fight fah wah mine. I told har nuh let mi ketch him inna har face again. Group or nuh he was dere and I know he waan har. Teran always taak bout women's intuition but men know oda men as well."

"Well man, I know she ain't no skeezer. You got yourself a good girl there so talk to her. That girl is crazy about your maniac behind so do this right. Check your attitude."

Wayman had them home in thirty-five minutes after leaving the club. Teran awoke to, "*Cum wi guh Miss, wi ah home.*"

Wayman got out of the car with them to give Teran a kiss. As they hugged, Wayman slipped his number in Teran's pocket. "Was you rappin to that dude, T?"

She quickly responded with, "No! We were all hanging out as a group. That's it."

Wayman continued to hug her, "I knew you was a good girl. If Shan does anything stupid, call me. I put my number in your left coat pocket." Teran smiled and nodded as Bashan approached to give Wayman five before he left.

Teran and Bashan entered the yard, walked down the path, descended the stairs, and were well within the apartment before he spoke. "I told yuh I nuh waan dat guy inna yuh face, I neva tell yuh?"

Teran hung up her coat while answering, "Shan, the whole group of us went to the movies and Tad's together. I wasn't out on a date with Jerry; all of us are chill-out partners."

"He acts laik he waan yuh. He was reddi to challenge mi ova yuh!" Bashan threw his coat on the floor.

Teran picked up the coat and walked back to the closet, "He did it as a friend concerned about another friend, like Wayman, Al, and Kenny stepped off the line when they saw you explode. He knows I'm engaged to you. I always talk about you to everyone – now here you come tonight acting like a lunatic! After all I told them about how good you are to me."

"Dat dude waan yuh. He wouldn't mind being mo dan a bredren. And yuh smiling inna his face won't duh nutten but mek his desire stronga. Yuh nuh know men laik I do."

Teran challenged, "Oh you do, do you? Let me tell you what I know! I know you are jealous, and I am tired of having my life turned upside down because of it. I refuse to be locked away in the house because you are worried someone may notice me or like me. I don't have to get married and live like that. We can't control other people, but we can control ourselves. Trust me enough to know I will put them in check when they come with a line or try to come on to me. That's what I do for you, and I expect it in return." Bashan was about to reply but Teran cut him off.

"And what exactly were you going to do in Bentley's? Stand against the wall? You know I know better than that. There are plenty of women in that placed all dressed up and looking for a man and here I am going to a movie and it's a problem. I ain't stupid Shan, I know some skeezer would have been in your face. "

Bashan snorted, "Deres nutten wrang wid mi dancing, de ongle ooman I sleep wid ah yuh."

"And the same goes for me so spare me the double standard! I am not living on pins and needles afraid to go out because Mount Bashan will explode. Stop the madness Shan and trust me. I am marrying you so trust me! Good night!" Teran left the living room for the bathroom and a well-deserved shower.

----------◊◊◊----------

Happy with herself for checking his behavior, Teran felt more settled and confident. She walked into her mother's home and was met with Nadine's. "You need to call your sister; she doesn't sound too good."

"Dri or Nique?" A frown disrupted her peaceful countenance.

Nadine called over her shoulder as she walked to the back of the house. "Saadri!"

Teran dialed her sister's number and didn't wait long for a response. What she heard caused the color to leave her face. She rang off and had a seat in the kitchen.

Nadine returned and looked in her direction. "What's the matter? Is Ellen, okay?" Ellen was Saadri's mother, and she and Nadine had been close friends at one time.

Teran placed her head in her hands and sighed, "The crap has hit the fan big time."

Nadine sat across from her daughter, "Well, what's going on?"

Teran looked up with tears in her eyes, "Pe'r is coming to New York."

Nadine shook her head, "Why is that a bad thing? He is yall's father. What aren't you telling me?"

Teran swallowed, "Mon Mon just hear me out... Saadri is married, she got married back in the summer, but she never told Pe'r. I also have not told him about me and Bashan."

"Lord have mercy! He has every right to run through here like a Mack truck. What were the two of you thinking? Whatever happened between him and Ellen and me, he has still been in your lives. He deserved more than that but then again, you could be his chickens coming home to roost. For you and Saadri to have different mothers you two sure are exactly alike, twins from different wombs." Nadine sat back in her chair and shook her head. Teran looked up at her and she could read the look instantly. "Heck no! I don't feel like fighting with Damas, yet again! Teran, you and Saadri are big girls, and she is a wife, you two handle it."

"Mon Mon, you know you are the only one who was ever a match for Pe'r. You can't just let him come to town and steamroll us! We need your help, and you know it. Come on Mon Mon, you know we can't win with him – ever!" Teran was near hysteria.

Nadine moved from her seat to embrace her daughter, "My lord, girl, stop and calm yourself down. If you're like this, I can only imagine how Saadri is. Ellen doesn't need this stress. Come on and pull yourself together. Let's go to Ellen's, call, and tell Saadri we are on the way. I'll have Yana look after Talib."

----------◊◊◊----------

Ellen Weston opened the door to her apartment and peered into the eyes of Nadine Scott. She inhaled, "Y'all come on in. Saadri told me she and her twin were up to it again, but this is a big one." They entered the apartment and Nadine wanted to embrace the frail woman, but she knew it would never be welcomed. Ellen pointed toward her couch, "Have a seat. Can I get you anything? Dri! Your twin is here."

They sat and Teran asked, "Where's Najid?"

Ellen shook her head, "Who knows? He is a bit of a phantom around here."

Saadri entered the living room and signaled for Teran to end the line of conversation. Teran asked, "Mon Mon Ellie, can I get some iced tea or something?"

Ellen sat at her kitchen table, "You know you are welcomed to get what you need. Go ahead and make sure you get some for your momma."

Nadine got Saadri's attention to thwart any conspiring between the two sisters. "Dri, can you please tell me how you forgot to tell your father you were married? I know he is one crazy Creole by now. How did he find out?"

Ellen chimed in, "How else?"

They looked at one another, shook their heads, and said, "Merci."

Teran handed her mother a glass of tea and spoke, "Nique didn't do it on purpose. She didn't know Dri still hadn't told Pe'r. She only told us at Fawn's wedding."

Ellen laughed, "They stick up for one another don't they, Nay."

Nadine was jolted; it had been a long time since she'd heard Ellen use her nickname. She swallowed more tea and responded, "I know Ellie, we have Miss Mazie to thank for their closeness. Now we have to keep Damas from coming up here and causing havoc."

Saadri and Teran sat next to one another on dining room chairs. Both mothers looked at them and laughed. Ellen remarked, "Remember that picture of them when they were about two? They were all hugged up and smiling like they were little angels when they had just finished getting into mischief. Looked like little Indian babies or something. Now they are sitting there trying to look pitiful and helpless."

Nadine responded, "Yeah I know. They want me to go toe-to-toe with Damas for them. This is their mess!"

"Well..." Ellen shrugged her shoulders.

"Not you too, Ellie! Why me?" Nadine drained her tea and held the cup out for Teran who retrieved more for her, "Just a little more Teran."

Ellen shifted in her seat. "You know full well you are the only who can go toe-to-toe with him. You give as good as you get. He always bullied Merci and, well, you know me."

"Yeah Ellie, I get it. Let the *Queen B* handle it. I know." Nadine also shifted in her seat. "I have to get my head ready for him. You know he is a ball breaker."

Saadri went over to Nadine and hugged her. "Thank you so much, Mon Mon Nay. I just can't do all of that and I sure don't want Pe'r and Najid to lock horns."

Teran and Ellen both echoed, "Oh, no!"

"I say let it be the clash of the Titans and may the best man win," Nadine laughed.

Saadri looked grief stricken and Teran stood by her. "Mon Mon stop, you know that wouldn't be anything but disastrous."

Nadine kept laughing, "Oh, and then I'd let him loose on the Big Jamaican and really see the sparks fly!" Ellen joined in the laughter and the sisters watch helplessly. The longer they stood looking horrified the more the two women laughed.

Catching a breath Ellen reflected, "You always were a trip, Nay. Never a dull moment with you!"

"I miss you too, Ellie-" Nadine lowered her eyes.

The room went silent before Saadri spoke. "Maybe there are some other things that need to be said before Pe'r gets here.

We are going up to see Najid's parents. We'll be back later." She ushered Teran out of the door.

Ellen looked at Nadine and sighed, "It is about that time, isn't it?"

Nadine nodded, "Long overdue."

----------◊◊◊----------

Bashan sat in a chair watching television as Teran descended the stairs. He looked at her in shock, "How yuh gat here?! I dought yuh had school tonight. I was going to call yuh lata wen I felt yuh had gotten home. What's wrong, yuh ah okay? Did smadi duh sup'm fi yuh?"

Teran hung up her coat and sat in his lap. "My father is coming to town Bashan, and this won't be pretty. Saadri never told him she was married and … I never told him about us."

"Wah yuh mean? He nuh know wi ah togeda at aal?"

"No, he knows we are together, he just doesn't know we are getting married."

"Teran! How yuh could kip sup'm laik dis fram yuh fada! Yuh and Saadri really ah twins. De mon mus be angry and disappointed by dis. Yuh and yuh sista ashamed of mi and Najid?"

"Absolutely not Shan, we love you both. We just know our father and we didn't know a good time to tell him. He is a trip, and we didn't know how he would take this type of news."

"De mon has dree dawtas of course him waan fi know ooo dem ah marrying! Yuh two did him dutty and I hope Nique nuh duh dis. Yuh tink bout ou dis mek mi and Najid look? Wi fava wi ave cum inna lacka tief and stole his dawtas. Dis ah bad, really bad, and whole heap of hurt cyan cum fram dis. Wi must speak wid yuh fada mon to mon, mi an Najid. Suh dis ah wah mek mi neva met yuh dadi?"

Teran laid her head in Bashan's neck. "Well, baby, you're about to meet Damas in the flesh. I hope you still want to marry me afterward."

Bashan touched her chin and brought them eye level. "Yuh will be my wife and nuh one will tap dat. Yuh gat drough Mary suh I cyan gat drough Damas. Sup'm tells mi being married to yuh will nuh be boring." He laughed and kissed her lips. "Yuh look suh stressed and I nuh laik dat. Let mi fix a bath fah yuh to soak inna and chill yuh nerves. I cyaan 'ave yuh fall apart pon mi before our wedding."

"Can we call and talk with Saadri first? She is talking to Najid."

Bashan shook his head, "De twins strike again. Gat har pon de phone. Wi may as well be united pon dis front."

The call to Saadri was longer than expected as Najid had much to say. Bashan succeeded in getting him to see the better avenue of not escalating the situation even if Damas was spoiling for it. The women became more nervous as Najid became agitated, so Bashan knew he had to be the one to keep the situation under control. Before they rang off, he and Najid had a newfound respect for one another.

"Yuh and yuh sista marrid de siem mon. Najid ah mi an mi am him, dats wah mek us understand one anoda suh perfectly well. Damas mus undastan wi will nuh let him terrorize our women. Wi will protect our women nuh matta wat or ooo." As Teran lowered her head Bashan picked her up and carried her to the bedroom. "Get reddi fah yuh bath, yuh need to relax. Everiting will wuk out fine, tap worrying. Wi ago drough dis togeda. I luv yuh Teran an nuh one ah going to tap dat."

"Thank you for not yelling at me. I know you wanted to meet my father earlier than this."

"I should put yuh ova my knee and spank yuh, but yuh look suh pitiful I cyaan bring myself to dweet." He laughed at Teran's expression of surprise and kissed her mouth. "How bout wi romp hooky tomorrow an yuh mek it up to mi? Wi have nuh food inna here and wi ave sum cleaning to duh."

She put her hand on her hip, "So you have me playing Suzy Housemaker tomorrow? How is that playing hooky?"

"Dis ah your ouse too and wi need to attend to it. A clean ouse will mek mi feel much betta. Wi cyan guh to a movie afta wi tek care of de home first." Bashan turned toward the bathroom.

Teran called, "Slave driver!" at his back.

He returned with, "Dats rite I waan yuh barefoot, naked, an inna my ouse! Yah, and belly too!", and turned on the water.

----------◊◊◊----------

Bashan awoke Teran at noon Friday morning, "Cum wi must go shopping cah deres nuh food inna here."

Teran stretched, yawned, and turned toward him, "Good morning to you too."

"Mawnin? Ooman ih noon! Yuh sleep laik yuh did dead! I let yuh sleep cah I dought dis whole ting wid yuh fada had yuh stressed out. I nuh laik seeing yuh dis wey Teran; wi cyaan ave yuh feeling laik dis nuh mo."

She looked at the knit brows covering pensive dark brown eyes, placed a hand on Bashan's smooth face and nodded affirmatively "I know you don't like it baby." Then she got out of bed. She stopped at the closet to pick out a pair of jeans Bashan liked for her to wear, grabbed a pull over sweater she favored and entered the bathroom. The growl of her stomach let Teran know it would be a ponytail day.

Bashan ushered Teran out of the apartment and to the supermarket. It didn't take long for them to get the groceries they needed. Within an hour, they were back at the apartment putting the goods away. Bashan fixed them sandwiches while Teran prepared meat for the night's dinner. They settled into a comfortable routine as they ate, cleaned, talked, listened to music, engaged in horseplay, and relaxed in the living room.

At seven, a knock on the door roused the drowsy couple laying together on the bed with the television playing. Bashan ran up the stairs and welcomed Wayman, Delores, Cheri, Al, Kennith and Nina. Everyone said their hellos while Bashan went to his father's house to get folding chairs. Cheri commented on the progress the couple made, "The place is shaping up nice Teran. Did you pick a place for your bridal registry?"

Al shifted on his feet and Teran pretended not to notice as she answered. "We are thinking about A&S, Stern's, and Orbach's. Do you want a tour?" Cheri told her not to bother and took Nina and Delores to view the other rooms. Bashan called for help, so Wayman and Kennith went up the stairs.

Teran braced as Al stepped close, "I don't believe you gonna get married without giving me a chance."

Teran became agitated, "Get real. You hang out with Bashan. What makes you think if I wanted to cheat on him, I'd do it with you? You want a chance? For what? You ain't got a thing to offer me afterward! Get outta my face!"

Al stood watching Teran, his countenance changing. "So, that's how you are playing this?"

Teran shot him a nasty look, "I'm not the one playing. I'm dead serious, I am not now or ever giving you the time of day, so step! Bashan needs to know who his friends are."

Al looked at Teran disapprovingly, "He needs to stop messing around with skeezers!" Teran's buttons were pressed.

Everyone entered the living room to an explosion. "Who are you calling a skeezer?! Who are you talkin about?!"

The room fell silent before Bashan intervened, "Babi, wa'ppun? Did he seh sup'm to yuh?"

Teran continued her tirade, "First, you try to get with me, then when I don't give you no play, I'm a skeezer?! I think you messed with the wrong somebody else's woman!"

Al defensively spat, "Ain't nobody call you a skeezer!"

Delores dissented, "Yes you did! We heard you from the bathroom!"

Cheri added, "And we heard about what you said to her up in Manhattan about Shan."

Al yelled at them, "Y'all need to stop instigatin! I'm just trying to get her to open her eyes and peep the situation."

Teran tasted blood, "Oh really, so you want me to open my eyes and see that, according to you, Shan ain't doing things right. You want me to understand that he can't, but you can! I need to drop him and get with you. Tell him 'Mr. You Can Love Me Right and Give Me Freedom!' Cause he ain't doing that right either according to you."

Kennith looked at Al, "Are you living that foul, man, that you would make a play for homeboy's woman, behind his back and in his house? We all chillin together and you trying to make a play for his woman? You illin man!"

Bashan removed his watch and pulled his shirt out of his pants. Teran saw what he was doing, "Shan, please, he ain't worth it, just put his behind out."

Wayman stepped next to Bashan. "How you gonna smile all up in dude face and you trying to move in on his woman? I should let him bust you up in here but you ain't worth him messin up his crib." Wayman stepped in front of Bashan, "Don't do this man, Teran don't need to see you like this. She's right and she ain't give him no light. You got a good woman, that fool ain't got nuthin, that's why he wanted to make a play for her."

"He has been trying mi fram de start, and fram de dey he met har. Making likkle comments bout Teran like I nuh know he was checking har out, look to any excuse to get next to har or seh sup'm to har. I kno ih nuh Teran, shim ah aal mine and I kno dat but, I let dis clown gat too far an now I am guh fi guh box him."

Al yelled, "Man y'all act like y'all tight like that! You know you got that freak Andrea on the side and Little Miss

Muffet here don't know jack bone about it. Don't act like you innocent, you know we went to the club that night to meet up with that freak and her friends, but plans changed when you saw homegirl out with dude from her school."

Teran had heard enough, "Alright, everybody out! We need privacy, out!"

Wayman and Kennith escorted Al up the stairs and away from Bashan. The ladies gave Teran instructions to lay into Bashan before leaving. Bashan didn't lock the door behind them. He sat in a folding chair with his head in his hands. Teran waited a few minutes before she slapped Bashan so hard her hand stung. "You are a lying two-timing dog! Andrea huh? Works at your job, nothing's going on, yet the name keeps coming up!" Teran continued hitting him about the head and shoulders. Angry and hurt she determined he would feel as she did. "You out screwin around and think I am supposed to stay true-blue-faithful-to-you! You got the wrong one! Al shoulda got it and Jerry too but, I'm about to take care of that! I'm getting mines and it ain't gonna be from you because I ain't gonna be with you and I sure as hell ain't marrying you!"

Bashan jumped up causing Teran to scratch him enough to draw blood. He grabbed her, "Tap it, Teran, nuh vex mi now!"

"Go to hell!" She continued to fight and yell.

Bashan slapped her on the behind, "Ooman tap it! I neva sleep wid har, I told yuh shi only a co-worka. Yuh romp rite into Al's hand, he knows I brought de guys to de club to introduce him to Andrea. I figured eff I could get him interested inna Andrea, I wouldn't kill him ova yuh. I know he waan yuh."

Teran shook her head, "That's it! I have had enough, and I am out! It's over!"

Visibly upset, Bashan grabbed Teran by the arms and began shaking her. "Yuh ah listening to mi at aal? I luv yuh gyal and am nah cheating. I neva cheated pon yuh or waan to be wid anyone but yuh. Aal I eva waan ah yuh! Since school I jus waan yuh!"

His voice escalated along with the shaking, Teran's heart began to race. "And I been running afta yuh dree years, begging and groveling and pleading and convincing yuh I luv ongle yuh. And here yuh tan reddi to lef mi pon wah sum clown ooo tried to gat yuh seh! Yuh believe him ova mi?! And yuh drow sum oda mon inna my face? Yuh nuh eva duh dat again, tell mi yuh will guh sleep wid someone else or allow someone to touch yuh! Aal I eva duh ah fah yuh and mi and us and yuh drow sum oda mon inna my face?! Ah fool yuh tek mi fah? Ooman I nuh 'ave it and yuh won't dweet eva again, yuh undastan?!"

His continued shaking replaced Teran's anger with fear. "Shan!" Tears blinded her as she thought of how out of control things became. "Stop it, you're hurting me!" She looked up at him and his anger terrified her, "Shan, please!"

Eldrige grabbed his son's arm, "Bwoy, yuh waan bruk har nek. Let har guh mon! Lef har alone. Shani, listen mon, let har guh!"

Seeing his father, Bashan let go of Teran who cried uncontrollably and sank to the floor. Nellie reached her before Bashan could kneel and shot him a look. "Bak bak, bwoy!" He watched them leave the room until Eldrige stepped into his view.

"Shani dis ah nuh gud! Mi told yuh before bout dis very ting. Chill yaself." He then took his son outside to cool down. "Wa'ppun inna dere? Suh much yelling an crying, smadi running out. Wi cum inna an see yuh shaking dat gyal suh haad har head ena bobbling bout. De neighbors cyan hear yuh two yelling. Poa Nel did scare a fi death. Shi tink yuh did beat dat gyal an shi crying fi wi help. Dis ah nuh gud Shani, nuh gud ataal! Eff yuh ah bringly, guh an cool off, but nuh hit yuh ooman. Dat gyal ah dung deh crying har yeye out. Tell mi yuh nuh lick or box har, Son?"

Bashan answered quickly, "Nuh, Dadi, nuh! Mi nuh hit Teran an mi neva beat har. Mi grabbed har arms an shook har. Shi was de one ooo lick mi, luk pon fi mi nek." Bashan allowed Eldrige to see the scratches.

Upon inspection Eldrige commented, "Wi get Nel fi dress dem cah de dey luk a likkle deep an yuh nuh waan an infection. Listen mon, mi know I nuh been dere while yuh were a young bwoy but mi dey yah now. Ih still hurts mi, but wi affi move past dat. Yuh always lass de ooman eff yuh lick dem edah physically or mentally, Ih a bad business."

Bashan leaned against a fence shaking his head. "De lass ting mi waan duh ah hurt Teran. Shi means evriting to mi."

Arm around the younger man's shoulder he gave instructions. "Den tell har dat, Son; guh dung deh an yuh tell har dat an den yuh show har dat." Eldrige winked.

They turned toward the door and Nellie approached them with her arms folded. "Shani, yuh ah chill now?"

Bashan nodded affirmatively, "Much betta now Mumi Nel. Tanks fi helping us."

Nellie searched his face, "Dat likkle ting ah dung deh bawling. Yuh did lick har, Shani?"

Again, he defended himself, "Nuh, shi lick mi, luk pon fi mi nek."

Nellie winced when she saw the scratches. "Cum let mi dress dat den yuh guh an mek it up wid har, okay?" Bashan went along quietly.

----------◊◊◊----------

Teran sat on the bed thinking about what Nellie said to her as she tried to go back to Brooklyn. *"Yuh will be marrid soon an dere ah nuh running bak fi mumi den. Tan an wuk it out."*

In the middle of her thoughts, Bashan walked into the room. She looked at him and saw the bandage on his neck, her heart sank. They stared at one another a few seconds before Bashan spoke, "I know yuh must be tinking yuh ave a wild mon pon yuh hands."

Teran chuckled, "Seems like we have traded places. You were the calmer one in school. Now you can be so hard to manage. Your jealousy makes me nervous; you get so crazy."

Bashan knelt beside the bed. "Babi, I will neva inna my life touch yuh again. I will leave an chill dung before I act outta anga. My lass intention ah fah hurting yuh." He gently took her hands in his and kissed them while staring into her eyes. Teran began to cry. Bashan sat on the bed and wrapped his arms around her. "Eff yuh eva stopped loving mi, I wud crumble, gyal, I luv yuh dat much. I knew I wud luv yuh laik dat fram de first day I saw yuh inna dat history class."

Teran squeezed his waist tightly as she listened to his words. Through crying induced hoarseness, she answered him. "I baited you and I am sorry but hearing that girl's name again enraged me. I was trying to hurt you. Shan, I never felt like I quite matched your maturity and focus. I am a spoiled youngest daughter and the oldest daughter who is used to getting her way. Then you came along, and I had to start truly considering someone else. Not because it was a chore or responsibility but because I wanted and needed to. To think that I wouldn't be enough for you when you're who I want to make happy above all others is more than I can handle."

Bashan placed his hand under her chin. They were eye to eye. "Show mi an mi ago show yuh." Teran didn't hesitate.

CHAPTER ELEVEN

Help is on the Way

Early November 1984

Damas Buard caused a quiet disturbance at LaGuardia Airport as onlookers debated whether he was someone famous. Used to the attention his appearance garnered, he headed, undisturbed, for the car rental counter. The customer service agent upgraded his vehicle and offered unwritten perks he just winked at. Damas was on a mission. He knew his girls well enough to know they had a strategy for dealing with his arrival, but they didn't know he had a countermove for their maneuver. Once settled in the car, he mentally mapped his itinerary.

----------◊◊◊----------

Bashan answered the phone at eleven o'clock the next morning. His voice quickly changed from languid to alarm. Then he hung up. Teran looked at him through a frown, "What's the matter Shan?"

He placed a hand on her hip, "Yuh fada, he is here. I need to get yuh to Brooklyn, now."

Teran could feel her heartbeat in her throat. "I need to call Saadri."

Bashan stilled her movements, "Too late. Wi need to showa an guh. Yuh mada sound vex."

Teran jumped up, "My mother is upset?! Oh God, he is tearing it up. That Creole is kicking a-!"

Bashan stood and held her, "Wi ago drough dis togeda Teran. I am yuh mon and I protect us, yuh undastan?"

Teran touched his chest, "I know baby, but the thought of you and my father going toe-to-toe makes my stomach churn. And add Naajid to the mix! God, this is a mess. I am so sorry for not handling this better. I knew Pe'r would hit the ceiling. Please forgive me baby. Let's not go, let's just go and get married and then it's done. Then Pe'r won't have much he can do."

Bashan watched her grow toward hysteria. "Teran wi ah getting marrid and nuh one ah stopping dat. I nuh allow yuh fada to tap us from getting marrid. Wi will taak as men but he nuh tap mi fram making yuh my wife. Chill dung, cum wi guh hol a flesh and den guh to yuh mada's ouse." Bashan went into the bathroom.

----------◊◊◊----------

Teran unlocked the door to the Brownsville apartment and was met with, "*Bonjou fiy. Konmen ça va?*"

"Bonjou, Pe'r. Çé bon." She walked into her father's arms and kissed his cheek after telling him she was doing well. "Pe'r, this is Bashan, he has been waiting to meet to you."

Damas raised a brow, "Really? Why have we not met then, mo shou?"

Teran inhaled, "It was my fault, I kept waiting and before I knew it here, we are." The look her father gave her stopped her words.

Damas extended a hand, "I am pleased to finally meet you Bashan. From the look of my daughter, I owe her happiness to you. I would like to talk, man-to-man, you know?"

Bashan smiled and met his handshake. "Good to meet you, Mista Buard. I am very glad to finally meet yuh."

"*Mo fé tendé mâ mô tit-fiy?*" A petite, fair woman appeared in the hall asking if she heard her granddaughter's voice.

Teran gasped, "Granmè! Bonjou!" She turned to her father, "Pe'r, you didn't say you were bringing Granmè with you." The look on Damas' face let Teran know he'd meant to leave that bit of information out. She groaned inwardly but reached for Bashan's hand. "Granmè, çe mâ bo, Bashan." She brought Bashan to stand in front of Mazie and coached him to say hello.

Mazie watched the tall young man in front of her for a moment before smiling and embracing him. "Bonjou, pleased to meet you."

"Granmè, you are speaking English now?"

"For him shaer, wi."

They all walked into the living room to meet Ellen, Saadri, Najid, and Nadine. Teran commented, "The gang's all here I see."

Saadri answered, "Bonjou, Sè. Come sit by me. Hi, Bashan." Saadri held out her arms and Bashan walked into her embrace.

As they greeted, Najid spoke into Bashan's ear, "Old Man's a trip and he has these girls on lockdown. We gonna have to step up to the plate with him or he will try to punk us out for real."

Bashan nodded, "Gat yuh back; wi a nuh guh out like dat."

Najid grinned, "My man," and clapped him on the back. They resettled on the couch with the sisters between them.

Mazie looked at the foursome and smiled, "Tou ma ti piti."

Saadri interpreted softly, "She likes you two, she called you her little children." She looked up into her father's green storm clouds.

Damas folded his arms and bore down. "I am not a man to beat around the bush. I am more than ticked with this whole situation. My daughters are up here running wild, and I hear about things after they have happened. Are one or both of you pregnant?!"

Nadine sucked her teeth, "You know, you are about as subtle as a hurricane!"

He glared at Nadine, "And you are letting Teran run around here like the original Wild Woman of Borneo! At least Saadri is married!"

Teran lowered her head and Bashan tensed but Nadine volleyed. "Our daughter has done nothing to be ashamed of, she is not being wild."

"She just spent the night out and came in with him and I am supposed to be happy that my daughter is playing house?!"

"Sir, we are getting married this spring. We are working and saving for the wedding now." Bashan's movements were hindered by the weight of Teran's deflated body.

Damas pointed at Bashan, "You are telling me? You didn't ask me like a gentleman for my daughter's hand! Just like that one just took my daughter like I didn't matter."

"Mr. Buard, I love your daughter and I wanted to make a commitment to her to show her how much I love her." Najid wanted to stand but Saadri wrapped her arms around his waist. Her rapid heartbeat angered him.

Damas looked from Najid to Bashan. "I am not an absent parent! Those are my babies, and I should have been informed along the way! This is not what I expected, and I am not about to come up here and act like everything is peachy because it's not!"

"Mo shagrin, Pe'r" Teran rasped out before she broke into a sob. Bashan held his breath to keep from exploding as he comforted her.

"Mo .... shagrin," Saadri broke as she spoke and Najid consoled her, thankful for the diversion.

"Damas, you've made them cry." Ellen was near tears.

Nadine fired, "You come in kicking butt and taking no prisoners, but you don't stop to see what's obvious and that is your daughters have men that love them just as much as you love them. Stop acting like a crazy Creole long enough to get to know these young men because they are solid and thank God for some sons."

He faced her and she stood. "You act like I don't have a right to be mad about how this has gone down! I saved some for you too because you didn't tell me a word!"

"I didn't have to because Merci was only too happy to let you know!"

"Well Nay, at least she gave a doggone enough about me to tell me!" He and Nadine stood face to face. The foursome on the couch watched the match of wills with awe. Ellen shook her head and wiped tears.

Najid whispered, "Daag, they ain't no joke."

Bashan conspired, "Teran gat ih honest."

"Damas, ça asé." Mazie's voice and statement of enough stopped her son's diatribe. The room fell silent. Mazie pointed toward a seat, "Nadine, asi en lashèj-la." Nadine complied by taking a seat and the act left the foursome open-mouthed. Mazie looked at her son and made the sign for quiet. "Damas, fèrmé tô ladjèl."

Nadine mumbled, "Yeah, shut up." The foursome and Ellen snickered until Mazie looked around the room.

"We are family. Make up." The matriarch waved her arms as if pushing them together.

The women calmed, and Najid stood to address Damas. "Mr. Buard, we," he pointed between he and Bashan, "would like to talk to you. Is that possible?" Bashan stood next to Najid as Saadri and Teran huddled together.

Damas looked at the young men and his daughters before he spoke, "I think it's long overdue." He turned toward Nadine, "Where can we go to make this happen?"

"You can stay here and talk. We are going back to Ellen's house to warm up dinner. You have exactly one hour. Damas, don't tear up my house. You are not as young as you used to be, and these dudes are solid."

Damas laughed, "Woman your mouth should be outlawed in these fifty states. Men talk ain't none of your business."

Nadine ushered the women out of the room. As Ellen passed Damas gave her a hug. "We also need to talk, right?" She nodded.

"Nothing changes, huh? I get you up in my face and Ellie gets the sweet, we need to talk. Just don't tear up my stuff. One hour and no more."

"Woman, leave! The only time you quiet is when - Just go so I can talk to these young men, Nadine. Have the dinner warm."

Nadine rolled her eyes, "Male chauvinist pig."

Damas laughed, "Barefoot and in the kitchen, Nay, when I get there, you hear me?" She slammed the door and he laughed as he locked it. He came into the living room as the young men gave one another dap.

They all sat and faced each other a minute. "So, who are these men that came in and took mô fiy?" He leaned back in the armchair commanding the respect in the room.

----------◊◊◊----------

Bashan spoke up, "Lawd a mercy Teran ah har fada's pickney! Straight to de point laik an arrow and cut laik a razor."

Najid concurred, "Yeah Terry and Nique are definitely their father's daughters. Saadri is more like Miss Ellen, and

I am happy about that. I can't take all of the mouth." He turned to Damas, "You and Miss Nadine, I don't get it, but I do understand Miss Ellen, I don't know Nique's mother."

"They are all a story for another time. You are both men and the Lord will bless you with children one day. If you had daughters that did to you what has happened to me, how would you feel?"

"That's fair Mr. Buard," Najid leaned forward. "I first saw Saadri when she was about sixteen. I had known her before then, she was always good friends with my brother Rasheen. But I saw her when she was sixteen. I didn't approach her until she was eighteen and coming out of school. I got to know her, I dated her, I pursued her, and I married her over the summer. I honestly thought you were not in the picture. I only saw Miss Ellen and I knew her grandparents were dead. She spoke briefly about your mother, Miss Mazie, but that was it."

"Siem here, I tried to gat Teran to tell mi bout har fambily but shi wouldn't. I used to gat frustrated trying to gat har to taak bout you aal. Wi almost nuh gat marrid because of de way I found out bout har being Creole and yuh being har fada and nuh de fada of Talib and Ayana. Wi met at school, shi was inna de siem history class. I saw har round de school - beautiful and haad to handle. De fellas couldn't duh nutten wid har quick and biting tongue! I watched har and dought bout har until I couldn't tap tinking bout har. Den a day came wen wi caught one anoda's yeye and afta dat ih was ova cah I knew shi was fah mi. Now wi ah set to marry inna May."

Damas remained silent. Najid addressed his concern. "I work at the stock exchange, sir. Some nights I go to college up in Manhattan. I make a pretty good salary; it's enough for me and Saadri. I plan to save up enough to move us out of Miss Ellen's apartment and into a house. Maybe we'll go to Long Island, who knows. The fact is, as long as Saadri is with me, we can go wherever. I am sorry things worked out the way they did, but I do my best to take care of your daughter. I would like it if we could get to know one another, sir?"

Damas looked at Bashan as if to say, your turn. The young men looked at one another before Bashan spoke. "Rite now I am in a training program at Grumman. Dey ah sending mi to school. Wi ave an apartment in Laurelton, and Teran will live dere afta de wedding. Meanwhile, wi ah saving an preparing for our lives togeda. I wud like a blessing for your dawta's hand in marriage."

"I know it's late, but I too would like your blessing, sir. Saadri and I love one another, and we want to know that you accept our love."

Damas sighed, "Mô fiy have made good choices, of that I can be proud. This generation is different, and you take more chances, more independent. My generation helped you to be able to do that. I'm glad you two have it together, I don't have to worry over mô fiy. You have my blessings. Now we have to get down to business."

The young men thanked Damas and looked at one another. They thought they were taking care of business.

----------◊◊◊----------

Ayana walked into the house and peered into the living room, "Ma?" Behind her were Talib and a man who could only have been Butch. Ayana looked at Damas and squinted, "Pe'r Damas?"

"Bonjou, Poupé!" He stood and opened his arms for Ayana who flew into them without hesitation.

Talib stood beside his father but said hello as he looked around the room. He spotted Bashan and yelled, "Shanidoo!" and walked over to him.

"Likkle Mon, wah gwan?" He nodded toward Butch. "Wah gwan?"

Help is on the Way

Najid nodded toward Butch, "Hey, how are you doing?" He then gave dap to Talib.

Butch spoke, "Where's Nadine?"

Damas held onto Ayana, "They over Ellen's fixing dinner, and it's time we made our way over. Meet my sons-in-law, Najid and Bashan. Najid married Saadri over the summer and Bashan is marrying Teran in the spring. This is Butch y'all, Nadine's husband."

Ayana left Damas' embrace and hugged Najid, "Welcome to the family." She left the living room to answer the telephone and took Talib with her.

"Why are y'all here?" Butch stepped into the room.

Damas sat down but Najid and Bashan remained standing. Najid stared at Butch and their eyes met. Bashan watched a recognition dawn between them and wondered what it was all about. Damas also caught the exchange; he announced, "Butch come on with us over to Ellie's, she and Nadine cooked, and they both can burn, you can meet my mother."

"I'm trying to figure out why she left you here if she is there." Butch remained in place.

Damas finished his drink. "Family business to take care of; Nay provided us with a space to talk, but that's neither here nor there. It's time to eat." He stood from the table. "Fellas, finish those drinks and let's head over to Ellie's."

Ayana entered the kitchen, "Pe'r Damas, are you going to Mon Mon Ellie's because my mother said for me and Talib to come with you, Bashan, and Najid. Daddy, are you coming? Mommy said there is plenty food."

Talib stood in the hall with his coat on, "Come on, Daddy, don't go yet."

----------◊◊◊----------

Teran answered Ellen's door, "I'm glad you are all here because Mon Mon was about to go off on you Pe'r."

Damas entered the apartment first, "Mo lainm twa fiy, but your mother makes me want to choke her." He kissed his daughter and took off his coat then threw it over his shoulder, "She's Butch's concern now."

Teran laughed as Ayana entered next and bent to her ear, "You know they had a Mexican stand-off in the kitchen." Teran motioned to ask who, and Ayana tipped her head toward Butch who walked in behind Talib.

"Hey, Dove!" Butch kissed Teran's forehead.

"Hey yourself, you look well. Mon Mon said you might come, and I am glad you're here. Did you meet my fiancé?" Teran queried as she looked around the tall man and spotted Bashan.

Butch turned in the direction of Teran's attention and smiled again. "Bashan and I talked a little on the way over. He seems to have a good head on his shoulders. Good choice."

"Tenk yuh, Mista Gregory. I cyaan wait fah dis beautiful ooman to be my wife." Bashan walked up to Teran and kissed her mouth. She grinned.

Najid walked in and slapped Bashan on the back, "Control yourself my man! I know you want to throw her over your shoulder and carry her out of here." Laughing, he and Bashan high fived one another then he inquired, "Where's Candy?"

"She's in the kitchen or in the back. Everyone was busy with something, so I got the door." He nodded and walked into the apartment after kissing Teran's cheek.

Teran yelled, "Sè! Tâ ma mari çe li-minn pou twa!" She held Bashan by the hand and led him to an enclave of seats with tray tables set up.

"Yuh must tell mi wat yuh ah saying," Bashan spoke as he sat. "And wat your fada said to yuh, I heard dat before. Yuh said dat to mi."

Teran smiled and kissed him again. "I just called my sister and told her that her husband was looking for her. My father said he loves me, but he could choke my mother." They both laughed at the last part.

Bashan added, "Outta everyone inna dis room, I believe your fada respects your mada de most. I know he loves har but dey could neva ave been married." They looked at one another and shook their heads.

"They would have killed one another, and I would have been an orphan going between downtown and Cloutierville." The couple laughed before Teran left him to help in the kitchen.

Saadri escorted Najid over to a seat next to Bashan's. He looked up and laughed, "Saadri, yuh have to hide de evidence, your lipstick ah smeared." He then looked at Najid and teased, "Wa'ppun to control, bredda?"

They clasped hands and laughed as Najid sat, "You know these sisters are irresistible, they make a brother lose it."

Bashan snorted, "Yah mon! Dat's wah mek us ave taken dem off de markit suh quick."

Najid nodded, "Got that right! I been scopin mine a while and caught her at the right time. Naw, I can't even entertain the thought of no other dude even trying to rap to her. I will nut out if somebody try to step to my wife. That girl is my world, and I would do anything for her."

"Yuh kno wen wi first met I nuh tink wi wud gat alang, but wi ah two sides of de siem coin. Teran ah my world and I would kill fah har." Najid held out his hand and Bashan slapped it.

"You good people, man. We need to hang out and talk about some things." Najid leaned in. "Let's make that happen."

"Yah mon, wi will mek ih happen soon." Bashan sensed a turning point in their relationship.

----------◊◊◊----------

Nadine put the last of the food on a table set up for the occasion. Over her shoulder she spoke, "Did you behave yourself?"

Butch put a hand to his chest. "Me? What makes you think I wouldn't behave myself?"

"Terrence Gregory don't play with me; I know you too well." Nadine sucked her teeth.

He touched her shoulder. "You do know me, Mrs. Gregory. Of that I have no doubt."

"Butch, were you cool?"

He became exasperated, "Nay, ain't nobody thinkin about that red nigga! I was cool. Me and him got an understanding. He is cock of his walk, and I am cock of mine."

Nadine removed his hand, "Boy, don't get on my nerves tonight. It's time for us to eat. Sit down and act civilized for once." She brushed by him and called everyone to the meal. He laughed as she walked by. He knew his wife.

----------◊◊◊----------

Ellen sat Damas in a chair in her room while she sat on the bed. "You're looking good, Damas."

Damas lowered his head briefly before speaking, "Ellie, woman I still love you and I will never stop but you have crushed me with this Saadri being married and not telling me. If I could turn back the hands of time things would be different."

"You wouldn't have your girls and you know you wouldn't change them being here. Look, I know you're upset but I wasn't trying to hurt you. So much happened with my health that I just prayed Saadri and Najid would make it. I am not long for this world, and I needed to know she would be alright given these decisions she was making." Ellen breathed in deeply. "Don't waste time being angry. Enjoy the addition of two young men to the family and support your daughters. They love you and it would crush them if you didn't accept those boys."

Damas nodded, "You are absolutely right Ellie. They have made their decisions. Marry me so I can take care of you. We have been on hold and cast aside so long. Marry me and let's ride this out together Ellie."

"Damas, I don't have long, and I couldn't do that to you. You know I love you and I am sorry I wasted so much time being hurt and trying to hurt you that I didn't do what would have been best for all of us. Now my prayer is for Saadri and Najid and that God sends you the one you can love and who will love you."

"Ellie, I don't care about the time because I have loved and waited for you my entire adulthood. Look, I can come here, and we can stay. I can close up the house in Texas. Who knows, if you feel up to it, we can go there. I want to take you to the doctor's appointments and take care of you. I can finally relieve some of the strain on Saadri. I know it's been hard on her. Baby, just tell me you'll think about it." Damas was seated beside her on the bed before she realized it.

"Okay, I'll think about it."

----------◊◊◊----------

Everyone gathered around the dining table for the blessing of the food. Damas readied himself when Saadri interrupted, "Sitoplé Pe'r, pèrmèt Granmè priyé."

Mazie stood up and recited the Lord's Prayer as Teran had done for Bashan. Afterward she waved her arms over the food and announced, "Astè lésé nou-diné!"

Damas repeated, "She said let us eat, so let us eat!" and started cutting into the roast that Nadine prepared.

"I enjoy hearing yuh and your fambily speak de Creole. Will yuh teach ih to our pickney?" Bashan spoke into Teran's ear.

Teran smiled at him, "I recited the Lord's Prayer for you before, remember? I don't sound like Granmè though. I can teach our kids, but they may not have much occasion to practice. Granmè is older and so are her siblings, they are starting to die off and not many are speaking the language anymore. Pe'r speaks but he speaks English more. So, our kids may not be as fluent as my sisters and I." She finished making Bashan's plate and seated him.

CHAPTER TWELVE

Holidays

With the Christmas holidays upon them, Bashan and Teran spent several days together buying gifts. Much transpired after the early winter showdown. Butch and Nadine entered stages of reconciliation, Ellen consented to marrying Damas, Saadri grew concerned about Najid and Veronique spoke with her sisters about having a boyfriend. Damas planned to come back for Christmas and the extended family planned a big celebration to be hosted at the home of Teran's grandparents.

Times were also exciting for Bashan's family. Mary and Crandall were also working their way through their marital problems. Armentha introduced her boyfriend to the family. Crandall was going to be at the Queens house for the holiday. Eldrige's sons and their families were expected to come to Laurelton to spend Christmas with their parents and were eager to meet Teran.

Bashan and Teran sat in their living room on folding chairs wrapping gifts and talking. "Teran, I hope yuh kno Christmas will be hectic. Wi will be running to de ends trying to visit everyone. Maybe wi should let Reggie kno wi nuh able to see dem pon dat day. Wi should plan fah a gat togeda afta."

"I think you're right; it will be enough getting to the ones who expect us to be there. We can't tell your parents or mine that we are not coming. Pe'r is being really nice, and I want to keep him happy." Teran laid a completed gift with a red bow in one corner of the living room.

Bashan snorted, "Mek him happy and neglect mi! Wen is he going back to Louisiana suh I cyan gat my babi back? Nuh luvin, nuh snuggling, nuh attention, I am sleeping in a cold bed. Dis ah starting aredi and wi ah nuh even married."

Teran laughed, "Shan! Don't act like that. I want to respect my father and you know he doesn't approve of me staying overnight."

"Here ah your home, weh I am ah your home. I am taking his present back to de store!" Bashan jumped up and grabbed a wrapped box marked for Damas.

Teran doubled with laughter. "Oh my God, I don't believe you are acting like this! You are throwing a temper tantrum."

"Wah mek mi cyaan act laik dis, yuh drough tantrums aal de while!" Bashan hit his chest.

"Stop." Teran gasped through tears. "This is too funny."

"Suh I am funny now? I will show yuh funny." He grabbed Teran out of the chair, threw her over his shoulders, and headed to the back of the apartment.

----------◊◊◊----------

Christmas morning Bashan and Teran spoke on the phone to reaffirm their plans. He went upstairs and shared a meal with his father's family. Nellie prepared ackee, callaloo, beef liver and boiled green bananas, bacon, ham, fried plantains, soft-boiled eggs, fried dumplings, roasted & fried breadfruit, fried bammy, homemade hot chocolate, and coffee. The group sat down and feasted with jovial banter.

Between bites Eldrige inquired, "Weh Teran? Yuh two ah spending tideh togeda? Shi nuh been round lately. Ah evriting okay? Mi dought shi would jine wi fi breakfast. Ah evriting okay wid yuh two?"

"Teran's fada is here and he ah a strict Cadolic mon. He nuh waan har staying de night." Bashan stuffed his mouth with food.

Everett, Eldrige's second oldest son, joked. "Shani yuh duh sound as eff yuh a Yankee dis morning. Teran ah rubbing off!" Then sobered, "Eff yuh had a dawta yuh wud nuh waan dat edah. Har poppa ah doing wat im ah suppose fi duh and protect iz dawta."

"Teran ah guh fi guh be fi mi wife and mi protect har." Bashan asserted.

"Eeee, im bak!" Everett leaned in his direction. "Nuh rite now. Shi belongs fi har fada until im releases har fi yuh at de wedding, suh chill yourself."

Bashan sucked his teeth and Neil laughed. "Daddy mussi cum inna de way of fi yuh romp time."

The men burst into laughter. Bashan, good naturedly added, "Ih mus show."

----------◊◊◊----------

At eleven thirty, Bashan was knocking on Nadine's door. Butch answered, "Merry Christmas, Bashan. I hope you're hungry because I made breakfast. Do you like pancakes? Let me help you with those gifts man."

"Merry Christmas, Mista Gregory. My fada's wife made a whole heap, suh I am stuffed." They walked into the living room and put the packages down.

"Bon Krismis, Be!" Teran announced and jumped into Bashan's arms. Forgetting Butch was in the room with them they greeted one another with a passionate kiss.

"Well, I'll be – ahem! It's a Merry Christmas indeed." Butch walked out of the living room and announced, "How many pancakes?" Answers came from all parts of the apartment.

Teran laughed as the color returned to her face. "I missed you."

Bashan grimaced, "Wen duh yuh fada leave?"

"Stop it Shan and you better be on your best behavior when we go over to Mon Mon Ellie's. I don't want you and my father getting into it."

"Nuh fret bout mi; it's Butch yuh fada ave de bad blood wid." He pulled her closer conspiratorially, "Mi an Najid hung out a while ago and he told mi sum tings I need to let yuh know, but nuh now."

Teran leaned in, "Yeah, he knows Butch from the streets. I'm not even touching that with my mother. She's a big girl; she can deal with it because he's back in the house now. I can't wait for us to be married; it's crowded in here."

"What are you two over there whispering about? Merry Christmas, Bashan." Nadine walked into the living room and hugged her prospective son-in-law. "Have you seen your mother yet? Please tell everyone I said Merry Christmas."

"I will Mumi Nay. My mada ah home. Wi see my fambily dis evening. Today ah fah Teran's fambily." Bashan kissed her cheek as Butch entered the living room.

"Man, you love kissing the women." He joked.

Bashan smiled, "Nuh, I just laik to kiss Teran."

Teran wrapped her arm around Bashan's waist, "Let's go into the kitchen. I know Butch threw down."

Bashan looked at Teran and answered. "I will nyam off your plate. Mumi Nel made ah feast at de ouse and ah still cooking food fi tenight."

Holidays

----------◊◊◊----------

At one o'clock they were walking through Ellen's door. Saadri led them into the living room where Ellen stood holding out her hand and Damas stood by grinning.

Nadine announced, "Did you two finally do it? Is that a wedding ring?"

Ellen nodded with tears down her face, "Yes, Nay, we got married."

"Well about time! Congratulations Mr. and Mrs. Buard!" Nadine grabbed them both in a hug that lasted several seconds before the group realized she was talking to them.

Saadri led the rest into the kitchen where Teran began questions. "Sè, how does it feel to have your parents married? When did they do this? Where's Najid? Don't they look happy? Where's Pe'r going to live? Here? Are they moving to Texas?"

Bashan snorted, "Your fada lives inna Texas?"

Butch broke in, "So many questions, Teran? Which do you want her to answer first?"

Saadri laughed, "I know, right?!"

Teran laughed and was about to speak when they heard Damas looking for them, "*Aou zòt mô fiy?*"

The sisters answered, "En lakizinn–la, Pe'r"

Damas walked into the kitchen and hugged Teran, "You still love me, Shaer?"

Teran kissed her father's cheek, "Of course Pe'r. You and Mon Mon never would have worked. Mon Mon Ellie is more to your liking."

Butch laughed, "Me and Nadine barely work!"

Nadine yelled, "And we won't if you keep putting your foot in your mouth!"

Bashan laughed aloud and Butch turned to him. "Don't be too entertained, you are marrying her daughter. The fruit doesn't fall far from the tree."

Bashan countered, "Teran and mi ave an undastandin, rite babi, cah shi know I nuh romp dat!"

Teran swatted Bashan's arm and Damas spoke, "That's it Son, you have to know how to handle them. That one in there," he nodded in Nadine's direction, "is pure fire and will scorch you! Butch, you have my sympathy."

Butch laughed and the women appeared in the kitchen. Nadine's head cocked to the side toward Butch who held up his arms in surrender. "That was Damas!"

She looked at Damas who still embraced Teran and said, "Merry Christmas to you too! Let me get a picture of this moment, you two, stay right there." After she snapped a picture, she had everyone strike different poses. The kitchen exploded with laughter when Ayana got Nadine and Damas to pose nicely for a picture. The last photo they captured was Damas holding Ellen around the waist. Their smiles spoke of their sublime happiness.

Teran stood next to Saadri and whispered, "Aou çé tâ mari?

Saadri pulled Teran into her room, "I don't know where he is Sè. Lately he has been more elusive, and I can't ask him about what's going on without him getting upset and talking about he's a man and don't question him like he's a child. So, I just stay quiet and focus on other things and my mother. I don't want Pe'r asking any questions, but he'll be around more. I just don't know, Teran."

"What's the matter, Candy?" The ladies jumped; they never heard his approach. Najid smiled, hugged Teran, and took Saadri in his arms; he stared at her until Saadri nodded affirmatively. He then descended on Saadri's lips in a kiss that winded Teran, the man was raw virility.

Awed by proof of what Veronique told her about Najid being able to communicate without speaking, Teran blinked. "Bon Krismis, Najid."

He grinned and wrapped an arm around each sister. Damas stepped into the doorway. "We head downtown in ten minutes, *piti*." He looked from Saadri to Najid to make sure all was well before he returned to the living room. Teran followed her father and joined the rest of the family.

Three carloads traveled thirty minutes to the Jackson's downtown home in Clinton Hill, Brooklyn. In the Monte Carlo, the couples, Bashan, Teran, Najid, and Saadri, listened to WBLS play Christmas songs by R&B artists. The foursome sang along as they coasted down Atlantic Avenue. Najid held Saadri close, kissed her several times and spoke, "Yo B, man, we have to chill more often. We were maxin and I enjoyed that man."

"Anytime mon, wi cyan chill anytime." Bashan looked at Najid through the rearview mirror.

Teran looked back at her sister, "Did you know they went out together, Sè?" Saadri shook her head.

"Teran, wat de problem? Yuh tink wi affi tell yuh wen wi ah going out? "

Najid blew out a breath, "You buggin! Our names ain't Butch!"

"Najid, that wasn't nice!" Saadri hit his arm and he returned a look that said she'd better not do it again. She emphasized meekly, "That was uncalled for."

Teran was irritated by Najid's treatment of her sister and his attitude. "I am not buggin and I didn't say anyone had to tell me. I was surprised when Shan told me that you two had gone out so don't get all cave man on us. And what do you have against Butch? The temperature goes down twenty degrees when you two get around one another."

Najid cocked his head, "I seen dude around and he ain't squeaky clean but I'm a parlay in the cut cause he's your mom's husband." He leaned against Saadri.

Teran turned her body toward him, "Don't play me to the left either. What do you know?"

Saadri sat up from their embrace and looked at him. Najid looked between them. "You see this, B? They double teaming me with this twin thing back here. It's buggin me out because they look so much alike."

Stopped at a light, Bashan watched the scene and laughed, "Nuh dem perfected dat double team? Yuh cyaan get outta dat trap." He continued to drive.

"Okay, so I know dude uses and I just hope your moms won't have any grief because of it." Najid held his hands forward as if to say that's it.

Teran turned back around, "It makes sense why he had to leave the last time."

Saadri touched her shoulder, "Mo shagrin, Sè."

Teran grabbed her sister's hand. "It's okay, *Sè. For all my mother's kick butt attitude about life it seems it hasn't always worked for her. She ends up with this additional set of headaches. Well, I can't do anything about* that, but I can marry my baby and live my life in better circumstances."

"Yuh gat dat rite! I am moving yuh into a ouse pon de ahland as soon as I can. Yuh will gimmi sum pickney an I am coming home to yuh everi night."

Najid reached up and clapped Bashan's shoulder. "That's what I'm talkin about boy! Get these women hooked up in a nice crib somewhere and make love to them without everybody hearing and make a house full of kids. Bring that check home, have a hot meal cooked – that's the life. Shoot, we can be neighbors, you let me know where you are going on the Island. You want to go on the Island, Candy?"

Saadri laughed, "Oh you top billing today! We are going on the Island now. Sure, you take me there, I will go." She and Teran laughed.

"Wi may nuh waan dem dat close to one anoda. Dem will be able to double team us everi day." Bashan feigned a grimace as he spoke.

Najid leaned up to Bashan's seat, "But yo, check it, we know how to slam dunk on them. They know who wears the pants and puts the lights out."

The sisters squealed. Teran spoke first, "You so fresh Najid! And don't be agreeing with him Shan!"

Bashan spoke "Nuh affi cah yuh kno I romp haad."

"Oh Lord! Y'all romp in the romper room!" Saadri commented as she and Najid burst into laughter.

Teran turned toward her sister, "Yeah and you get your lights put out! I'm telling Pe'r!"

Saadri laughed enough to have tears in her eyes. "Brat!" She couldn't stop laughing. After a moment Teran joined in too. Bashan got them to the Clinton Hill home in a fit of laughter. The other carloads met them at the door.

Damas saw the foursome and asked, "What's going on?"

Najid answered, "Folks just rompin lights out that's all." They sniggered but then broke into unbridled laughter after watching Damas' expression of confusion.

Ellen touched her husband's arm. "Leave them baby. It's young people talk; I don't always understand them either."

----------◊◊◊----------

The smell of good home cooking and Mrs. Jackson's perfume met them as they walked through the door. The silver-haired brown woman kissed and hugged everyone. Mr. Jackson called from a back room where the men of the family assembled. The group walked to the room and greeted everyone. Mr. Jackson saw Damas and stood from his chair, "What ya say, it's our own long-lost Creole! Damas, you ain't dead yet? I ain't see you boy!"

Damas laughed and grabbed Mr. Jackson in a bear-hug. "It's good to see you, Gordon. I brought my wife with me."

Gordon Jackson looked around and said, "Where is she?" Damas pointed to Ellen and Mr. Jackson was shocked. "After all these years you finally wore Ellie down! Come here and give me some sugar my little Chocolate Drop!" He gingerly kissed the obviously frail Ellen.

"How are you Mr. G?" Ellen laid a manicured hand on Mr. Jackson's chest. "You are looking well. It's good to see you."

Gordon replied, "It's always good to see you, Ellie." He looked at Damas and said, "You make sure you take care of my Chocolate Drop because she needs tender love and care. She's a lady you know." He smiled and released Ellen to Damas. "Speaking of which, where is my Amazon child? Nadine! Your daddy doesn't get a Merry Christmas?!" Nadine yelled greetings from the kitchen.

Teran laughed and stepped in front of her grandfather with Bashan, "Merry Christmas, Granddaddy. I brought Bashan with me."

Bashan joked, "Shi brought mi, but I drove de cyar. Merry Christmas, Mr. Jackson!" They slapped one another's shoulders and laughed.

Saadri came next, "Merry Christmas, Granddaddy. This is my husband Najid."

"Husband! When did all of this happen?" Mr. Jackson looked completely shocked.

Damas answered with, "Imagine how I felt when I found out. They went to the justice of the peace last summer."

Gordon Jackson shook his head, "You don't say. Well welcome to the family-"

Saadri answered with, "Najid, Granddaddy."

"Najid, welcome. So, are you an Indian or something? You are named like the musician." Gordon grasped his hand and pumped vigorously.

Najid grinned, "Hello, Sir, it's good to meet you. My family is from Texas and the musician is not Najid like I am."

Gordon joked, "The U.N. don't have a thing on my family: Creole, Jamaican, and now Texas."

Saadri frowned, "Granddaddy, Texas is not another country, it is part of the United States."

"No, ma'am, Texas is its own country!" Gordon broke into a peal of laughter.

Holidays

Najid agreed, "You have a point there."

Gordon sat back in his recliner as Ayana and Talib came in to greet him before they went back out to spend time with similar-aged cousins in attendance at the Jackson home. He became comfortable and declared, "Damas go on over there to the bar and fix us up. Fellas," he nodded to Bashan and Najid, "take a load off. Let me show you what good music sounds like. Terry, you and Dri go and please get that wife of mine to speed it up. Look, try to bring me a sandwich or something to keep me from starving back here." The sisters exited with Ellen, laughing at Mr. Jackson's usual antics, as Butch entered the room and they heard Gordon wish him a Merry Christmas.

----------◊◊◊----------

At five, Teran and Bashan said goodbye with a promise to come over again within the next few days. Najid and Saadri left with them to be dropped off in Brownsville so they could spend time with the Raeniers. Najid's parents hosted extended family from Texas and the local area at their home; the family was also celebrating the newlyweds. Mrs. Jackson sent the couples along with food and desert. Teran and Saadri got into the back seat together.

"You see this, B. They kicked me out of the back seat. I wanted to snuggle with my baby." Najid closed the door after he made sure the young women were in securely.

Bashan turned to the sisters and said, "Dis double team bizniz mus tap."

Teran rejoined, "You have been with the men all afternoon so, stay with your boy up there and leave us to our girl talk."

Bashan looked at Najid and the two of them laughed as Najid commented. "Oh man, they are jealous, so they are giving us the cold shoulder." Najid rubbed a gloved hand over his face and leaned his head back against the seat.

"Dats okay, taak now an wi romp lata." He started the car.

Najid rolled with laughter, "You a wild boy, B! Candy, you know what time it is!"

The ladies sucked their teeth as the fellas laughed in the front seat. Bashan enjoyed his time with them. "Teran, duh yuh want to tap an see Fawn an Reggie fi a short while?"

Saadri answered, "That would be nice; we haven't seen them since the wedding. She must be ready to pop any day now."

Najid shook his head, "And you answer for one another too. Y'all should have been twins and made life easier on everyone. How do you assume we are invited, Mrs. Raenier?"

Saadri leaned toward her husband, "Since you have to know everything, Mr. Raenier, they live in Crown Heights which is on our way home. It makes no sense to pass their house to drop us off to double back and then come back in the same direction to go out to Queens." She and Teran gave each other a high five.

Najid turned around and looked at his wife. He smiled, "When the lights are out, I am going to make you eat those words."

Saadri inhaled, "You aren't playing fair."

Najid winked at her, "I play for keeps."

----------◊◊◊----------

Reggie answered the door in good spirits. "Cha! Mi bredren!" He spied Bashan and held his hand out for a dap. "Wa'ppun mi key?" They greeted one another before Reggie called again, "Fawn, cum yah!"

Fawn wobbled toward the door to greet them. "Teran! Saadri! Shan! Saadri's husband!"

Everyone laughed as Najid bent to kiss Fawn, "Hi, Fawn, it's Najid."

Holidays

Fawn held onto his arm, "I am so sorry, but since I have been pregnant it seems like my brain cells have gone on vacation."

Teran hugged her, "No, that's not the reason. I told you to stop hanging out with 'the young and the foolish'." She nodded toward Reggie and Fawn giggled while he grabbed Teran in a bear-hug.

"Wi will ave none of dat! Merry Christmas, Teran."

Saadri wrapped her arm in Fawn's as they walked into the house, "You look so pretty, girl. It's good to see you."

Fawn gushed, "Thanks, Dri! You look good yourself; marriage agrees with you."

"I do what I can." The two ladies laughed as Najid followed behind them.

Everyone settled into the living room and Reggie became the ultimate host. "Cyan mi get mi breddas sup'm fi drink? De gyal dem waan a drink?"

Bashan stretched his long legs as he positioned himself comfortably in an oversized armchair. "Yuh ave beer Reg? Mi could use a Red Stripe."

Teran sat on his lap, "Shan, you had a few drinks at my grandparents' that's why we left so late. I wanted to make sure you were good to drive."

Bashan looked from Teran to Reggie, "Mi empress nuh waan mi fi drink suh mi ave a cola. Dis a gud day mi nuh waan spile it."

Najid relaxed on the loveseat and gently guided Saadri to sit next to him. "I could use a beer though, I ain't driving." Saadri looked at him but said nothing. Najid watched her and returned an exasperated look at Reggie. "Never mind man, bring me some soda or something. The Mrs. don't want me to drink anymore either."

"I didn't say anything Najid." Saadri grinned. The room laughed.

"Yuh usband kno yuh, Twin, suh don't behave as eff im nuh kno wah blowing out yuh breat mean cah unu undastan dat!" Everyone laughed again as Reggie left the living room to retrieve refreshments.

Teran examined Fawn and exclaimed. "Girl, when are you going in? You look like you are about to bust!"

"Sè! That was rude. She knows she is growing; she has to live with it." Najid looked at his wife with pride.

Fawn replied. "It's good having you around Saadri because you know Teran never knows what to say. You're right, I'll be glad when this is over. We are counting the days down."

"Yuh look beautiful Fawn. Yuh will be a gud mada. Wi ah happy fah yuh and Reg." He cradled Teran's body as he spoke.

Fawn stretched on the couch and placed her feet on an ottoman. "Thanks Bashan, so what is everyone up to?" Reggie came back with drinks and snacks.

Teran excitedly caught her up on the last few months. "We really have lost touch, so much has happened. Pe'r came to town back in November and he was pissed!"

Saadri added, "He had us quaking in our skin, but we were to blame because we didn't tell him about Najid and Bashan."

Fawn sat forward, "What?! Oh, I know Pe'r Damas went ape on your behinds! I missed it, shoot! Oooh, did he and Miss Nadine-"

Najid cut in, "Head-to-head! That was a treat. Miss Nadine is no joke, and she will take Mr. B on in a heartbeat!" Bashan burst into laughter and dapped Najid again. The sisters looked at them as if they were foreign beings.

Teran elbowed his rib cage, but Bashan went on undisturbed, "Likkle Mumi Nay inna Mista Buard face and im vex but shi nuh care. Mi dought dem wud box!"

"Wa'ppen? Dem box inna de ouse? Teran mada box har daddy? Mi cyan imagine dat scene." Reggie shook his head and chuckled.

"Oh, it was a real treat, Reg!" Najid sat forward. "I have big respect for Miss Nadine though. She was defending her girls and Mr. B really couldn't come back at her on the points she was making. Then he turned on me and B, but we handled ours too! We knew our turn was coming."

Reggie asked, "Yuh large up yuself, eh?" He made a motion of standing taller so Najid could better catch his meaning.

"Yeah man, you know we did. Bottom line is they are our women and Pops or no Pops we weren't going to let him get but so far. They were petro and you know a man won't stand by and let his woman get bullied by nobody, so we had to respectfully let Pops know we got this." He made a hand motion between he and Bashan.

Reggie sat back on the couch and placed Fawn's legs in his lap. "Yah mon. De gyal dem nuh undastan ou haad fi be a mon cyan be, whole heap de respons."

Bashan nodded his head as he joined in, "Mi told Teran dat very ting. Reg, Santa did bring yuh wat yuh waan?"

Reggie brightened and removed his wife's legs to her dismay. "Bredren cum yah, wi ago inna de basement. Mi show yuh ting an ting." The men left the room without a word to the women.

Teran broke the silence following their abrupt departure. "So, we have our apartment in Laurelton, I got a raise on the job, I am thinking about taking the civil service test, school is going well, we set the wedding for May, our families are helping a lot with the festivities and have given us many things for the apartment, and we are saving money."

Fawn nodded her head and smiled. "You two have been productive, that's good. I'm glad things are going so well. So, the wedding is in May. I hope I can lose enough weight to look decent in my dress. I am standing with Damas' two oldest supermodels, Nique and Saadri, and I don't want to look like the homely housewife."

Saadri laughed, "Stop it girl. We are not supermodels, and you could never look like a homely anything. When is the baby due?"

"The doctors said the middle of February. I hope it is on time because I have to get my body back together." Fawn looked at them and lowered her voice. "I am glad they are gone because I have something to tell you." The sisters leaned forward as she continued, "We have a situation on our hands. This co-worker of Reggie's named Andrea."

"That was the skeezer at the wedding Sè, remember, the one Bashan drove home?"

Saadri affirmed, "Yes, I remember now. We also had to keep Veronique from clocking her. Maybe we should have let her loose."

A frowned appeared on Fawn's face, "What in the world? At my wedding?" The sisters nodded as she continued, "Well it seems the skeezer strikes again because she bought my husband a g-string for Christmas and from what Reggie told me she bought some for all of the men on the job." With the revelation, Fawn raised her eyebrow.

Two pairs of eyes looked in Teran's direction; she could feel a headache mounting. "How many times must I hear this skeezer's name?"

Saadri stared wide-eyed, "Well, how many times have you heard it and why haven't you told me?"

Teran knew her sister would feel betrayed if she thought she was deliberately left out. "Dri, you have had so much to deal with, and Bashan and I have been weathering storms and riding waves. I didn't say anything because we are trying to keep things within our relationship, you know, not bringing everyone into what we alone should be dealing with. But we had a pretty big fight over this chick. One of his so-called friends dimed him out that they were meeting her and some of her friends up at Bentley's. I went off but Shan maintained that he was going up there to introduce her and this so-called friend, who by the way was trying to make a play for me. Two of Shan's friends had to get the guy out of the apartment before Shan destroyed him. Then we started fighting and his father and stepmother had to break us up."

"Did he put his hands on you, Terry?!" Saadri stood up. "The bigger they come the harder they fall. I will shoot him myself!"

Teran jumped to her sister's side, wide-eyed with alarm. "Dri, no, no. He didn't hit me. I hit him, quite a few times. He grabbed me to shake me and stop me from fighting him, but I went ballistic."

"Just like Miss Nadine and Pe'r Damas, a chip off the old block." Fawn shook her head and reclined on the couch. "Teran, what can you do with that mountain of a man but get shook? You my girl and got much heart but you are a trip. I guess you would have to be just like your parents because neither of them fears much including each other!" Fawn started laughing.

Saadri watched Fawn a moment. "I guess you have a point there." She too found it amusing.

Teran sat in the chair she'd vacated. "Later for both of you, back to this skeezer. Shan didn't say anything to me about any drawers and we've been together all day." She closed her eyes and breathed a few deep breaths.

Saadri walked over and gathered Teran to her chest. Teran wrapped her arms around her older sister. Fawn spoke as their consolation continued. "I guess there is no other way to find out than to ask. I went off this morning when Reggie showed them to me."

The men walked into the living room as the scene unfolded and Najid voiced for them. "I guess we all know about the freaky deaky Christmas gift. From where I stand, this is obviously a case of homegirl not understanding her place. I say the fellas need to make her know where she stands with them once and for all. Personally, I would not wear dental floss up my butt and would not appreciate that type of gift."

A peal of hoots emitted from all as the last statement replayed in their minds. Bashan looked at Teran's tears and walked over to where she sat. He bent in front of her and looked at Saadri who moved to give them a moment. "Babi, yuh believe mi nuh liad wen I seh I nuh know bout nuh present? Wi been togedda aal di while todeh an aal my presents at de ouse fah us to open lata. Teran, I nuh waan nuh present laik dat fram anoda ooman. Andrea nuh easy."

She looked at her fiancé and smiled despite her throbbing heart. "I just keep hearing her name, Shan, and I am tired of it. Set her straight like Najid said, once and for all."

"Yes, you set her straight or I will. No one is upsetting my sister like this, and I stand by and let it happen. I will come up to Grumman and wait for her to come out for lunch or after work and if she doesn't say what I want to hear I will knock the taste buds out of her mouth." Saadri loomed over Bashan's knelt frame.

"Whoa, Candy! Baby, what's the matter with you? You all over B like you are trying to step to him. He didn't know that freak was going to do that. They work with her so let them handle it the right way. Who are you supposed to be – Kung Fu Mama?" Najid moved her to the side so they could talk in private.

Teran snickered, "He is full of jokes tonight, isn't he?" Fawn hid her laughter as well.

"Teran, Andrea did rudeness and mi vex. Truss mi, Babi, I will tek care of dat." Bashan grabbed Teran into his arms and approached her lips. She did not disappoint him.

Najid whispered into Saadri's ear, "See, what did I tell you?" He nudged her forward.

"Ahem." Bashan looked up from the elongated kiss he shared with his fiancé into Saadri's identical face. "I am sorry for going off on you."

Bashan stood and embraced her, "Yuh ah my sista suh I cyaan get bringly wit yuh. Yuh duh luv Teran." He then looked at Teran and declared, "Babi, my luv fah yuh cyaan done."

Najid walked up behind Saadri and wrapped his arms around her waist. "See, Baby, he's not mad and your sister got that boy's heart."

Teran answered, "He has mine too."

----------◊◊◊----------

By eight they were headed for Queens. Teran was quiet in the car; Bashan reached over and grabbed her hand. "Yuh gud?"

She smiled at him. "This has been a long, eventful day and I am a little of tired."

"Nuh get tired pon mi now. Wi visiting my parents still." Bashan squeezed Teran's thigh as he made quick work of the Belt Parkway and sped them toward Queens Village while she napped.

They pulled up on the Watts' block and Teran admired how the Christmas lights illuminated the snow-covered street. Bashan had to park several houses away, so they huddled together as they carried packages to the door. Teran saw the curtain move in the anteroom window when they opened the gate. "I think they have been watching for us baby."

Ivee opened the front door. "Ku pon ooo show up! Merry Christmas, yuh two. Leggo di packages fi mi ago help yuh."

Teran gladly released some of her load to Ivee and took the opportunity to kiss her cheek. "Bon Krismis, Ivee."

Ivee turned to Teran and smiled, "Tanks mi sista! Mumi, Daddy, Mentha dem yah!"

Bashan came in behind Teran, "Merry Christmas, Ivee." He and his sister exchanged smiles and kisses as she led them into the living room. Bashan stopped as he saw a scene, he never thought he would see again.

Crandall sat in his favorite chair in a tee shirt, sweats, and socks. Mary was in the chair next to his, separated only by a small lamp table. "Yuh did gone aal day, Son, mi dought yuh nuh gwan cum by."

Bashan placed the gifts under the tree and walked over to greet his parents. "Merry Christmas. Wi did tan in Brooklyn langer dan expected. Nex year wi ah starting wit mi fambily an den ago Teran fambily." At the mention of her name, Bashan extended his hand to beckon her from the tree to where he was standing by his parents.

She crossed the room and took Bashan's hand. "Bon Krismis, P'er Crandall and Mon Mon Mary."

Mary beamed at Teran's initial use of the moniker. She stood and embraced the petite beauty soon to become her daughter-in-law. Bashan and Crandall beamed with pride over the women. "Teran mi suh glad yuh call me yuh mada cah mi waan be suh fi yuh. Merry Christmas, dawta!"

Crandall kissed Teran on the lips and received a mild tongue-lashing from Bashan and Mary. Teran left the trio and settled next to Armentha on the couch. "Hey, Mentha! Merry Christmas! I have missed you."

Mentha kissed Teran's cheek. "Yuh nuh ave time fah mi, Shani ave aal yuh attention. Yuh cyan call mi fram time to time."

"You got it girl. We should go shopping together." Teran excitedly spoke and would have said more if not for the interjection that followed.

"Yuh nuh spend aal mi funds. Mi ago tap dat trip short, yuh will ave limited spending money." Bashan pulled a pocket inside out to emphasize his lack of money.

They laughed as he sat on the floor next to Teran's seat on the couch while all opened presents. Armentha began a conversation. "Shani, mi know yuh an Teran get nuff of gifts dis year. Enjoy dis now cuz wen mi niece an nephew cum mi drowin yuh both fi de side!"

Holidays

"Yah Mentha, wi did get nuff. Wi nuh kno wah fi aks at de wedding." Bashan looked up from his pile of gifts and laid his head against Teran's nearby legs as she answered.

"I don't know where to put the stuff we have now. I will have to think about what should go where. I know Shan won't help me with the decorating stuff because he feels it's woman's work. Would you come over and help?" Teran rested a hand on Bashan's head as she spoke. Mentha affirmed she would.

Crandall offered, "'Im right it ah wuk fah de ooman dem. De mon brings de funds. A mon comes home fram wuk an waan a welcoming home wid a welcoming wife."

Mary sucked her teeth, "Dat ah nuh wah im really waan seh. Im waan belly, barefoot, inna de kitchen an eff nuh belly, den naked."

Teran gasped, "That's Shan!"

Crandall grinned, "Mi kno, he's mi bwoy." The men gave one another satisfied nods as the women shook their heads. The elder Watts then changed subjects, "Mary an mi getting bak togedda. Shim lang fah mi an mi lang fah har."

The room went silent before Ivee responded, "Jah bless, ih nuh too soon."

Bashan questioned, "Weh yuh deh a guh live, inna which house?"

"Mi wi cum bak home." Crandall looked over at Mary who bowed her head and cried.

Teran swallowed as she looked at the scene. Bashan reached up and covered the hand that still touched his head. Mentha continued questioning. "Wah yuh ago duh wid de ouse inna Baldwin?"

Crandall answered, "Shani and Teran wedding present."

"What? Oh my God I don't believe this! A whole house, oh my God!" Teran grabbed Bashan and screamed.

Bashan looked at his father, "Yuh sure dat yuh waan fi duh dat, Dadi? Wi neva expect dat."

Mary held her husband's hand, "Yuh know evriting nuh outta de basement. Guh dung deh sometime an tek a luk. Wah yuh still need?"

Teran thought as Bashan repositioned himself on the couch beside her. "Furniture now and a nice set of dishes. I don't know if we should register anywhere since we have so much."

Ivee stated, "Yuh ah tinkin laik yuh inna de apartment but yuh ave a house now. Dere many rooms fi decorate."

Bashan, "Yah, but nobody will buy furniture fi wi."

A chorus of "Yuh nuh kno dat. Yuh cyaan seh dat" met his assertion and Bashan held his peace.

Crandall announced, "Mi waan sup'm sweet besides mi wife," stood and walked toward the kitchen. The group followed.

"Dere nuff of food, yuh two hungry?" Mary uncovered pots and announced the bill of fare as Teran, and Bashan prepared to partake. Teran put a little of everything that would fit onto Bashan's plate as he settled at the table. She took small portions on her own plate and stayed away from the very spicy dishes.

Mary teased, "Lawd a merci! Dis likkle gyal nyam like a bud. Wah, Shani nuh waan yuh fi nyam? Im waan yuh winji?"

Teran looked at Bashan who said, "Winji means too skinny, Babi. Mumi, Teran nuh nyam suh much."

"Shi fine de way shi, Mary." Crandall announced as he devoured his egg custard.

"Well, mi ave a likkle dawta now mi affi watch ova, welcome mi Lilly Bud." Mary kissed Teran's forehead. Teran stood and embraced her. Everyone looked on with delight.

----------◊◊◊----------

At eleven Bashan announced they were leaving to his family's chagrin. Although they understood his need to allow Teran to see Eldrige before the night was over, they made the couple promise to return the next afternoon. Before letting them go, the family loaded them down with food to take home. Mary stated, "Mi bwoy cyan nyam his own mada's food." Bashan had Teran take the food before he ushered them out of the door, laden with gifts, to his car which he left double parked and idling when they prepared to leave.

Armentha helped them bring things to the car. Bashan opened the trunk and she let out a feigned shriek, "Rhaatid! Ku pon dis. Weh yuh deh a guh put aal of dem yah tings? Dere too much food. Teran nuh cook. Yuh mus mek har cook!"

Teran laughed, "Girl, put that stuff in that car wherever you find room. I am on vacation, so don't mess it up for me."

As they loaded Mentha quipped, "Yuh see dat, Shani, yuh spile har." They finished putting everything in the car and Bashan hugged his favorite sister before getting into the car. Armentha stepped over to Teran who stood inside the car door and embraced her. "Welcome to de family, Lilly Bud. "

Teran asked, "Is that my nickname now? Little Bird?"

Mentha nodded, "Yah, dat ah yuh name." She leaned into the car so that Bashan could hear her and counseled, "Nuh eva lass de luv between yuh. Merry Christmas." With a tap to the hood of the car she walked back toward the house.

The couple watched her enter, "Now yuh undastan wah mek shi ah mi favorite sista."

Teran answered with, "I totally get it Shan. She is my favorite too." She leaned over and kissed his lips. He smiled and put the car in gear.

CHAPTER THIRTEEN
Bon Krismis

"Teran, babi, wi at our gates. Stir yuhself, babi."
Bashan was already at her door when she started gathering her things. They made several trips to store gifts and put food away before going up to Eldrige and Nellie's part of the house. As they walked in, Neil was dancing with his mother. Teran let out a whoop upon seeing Nellie work her body into a wind.

Eldrige raised his arms, "Wi tink Mary kip yuh hostage! Merry Christmas! Mi call har an shi seh yuh did pon de way home." He sucked his teeth, "Shi nuh waan fi mek time fi wi to be togedda? Ave mi nuh miss enuf time!"

Bashan ushered Teran to the tree to place presents and immediately went to his father. They embraced a few seconds before he assured, "Wi ago spend mo time here suh wi spend a likkle extra time wid Mumi. Nuh worries, wi live dung inna de basement."

The answer seemed to calm Eldrige who announced, "Cum yah Bud an kiss yuh Dadi. Mary seh pon de phone, 'Shani an Lilly Bud pon de way El.' Wi ago call yuh Bud as well." Bashan shook his head at his father's reasoning and smiled as Teran received a hearty embrace.

"Bon Krismis, Pe'r El." Teran smiled into the older man's face and saw Bashan reflected in his expression for the first time.

"Peer? Is fi fada? Wah tongue is dat?" Eldrige held Teran at an angle where he could look at her face.

"That's Kreyol and yes it's father. I'm Kreyol."

Nellie ended her embrace with Bashan and joined, "Mi tol yuh, El, dat gyal did affi be mix wid sup'm. Mi kno shi did nuh one ting. Kreyol yuh sey, fram Haiti?"

Teran shook her head as she embraced Nellie, "Down the line but now from Louisiana. My father and his family are from Lousiana." Nellie nodded as her son Neil grabbed Teran around the waist.

"Nuh wonda wi nuh see Shani aal day. Wid a gorgeous ting laik yuh mi wud be haad fi find too. Mi Neil, Shani olda bredda." Although the man more resembled Nellie, he was clearly a son of Eldrige. He smiled down at Teran and hugged her before kissing her on the cheek.

"An mi Everett de oldest bredda. Ih gud fi meet yuh an welcome to de fambily." He removed Teran from Neil's arms and kissed her forehead. "Wi 'ave no sistas, suh yuh ah ih. Dat a gud position fi be inna, spile and protect by aal de men."

Bashan put a hand to his head, "Wah mek yuh fi tink mi waan har spile mo? Mi nuh need mo headache. Shi spile enuff rite now." They laughed as Teran swatted Bashan's arm.

Neil turned up the music and said, "Miss Kreyol, gyal cum drop legs wid mi." He walked toward her with fingers wiggling.

Teran watched Neil and turned to Bashan who answered, "Lef mi ooman alone mon, weh ah yuh wife?"

"Mi waan fi dance wid mi sista." Neil continued toward Teran who grew visibly nervous.

Bashan wrapped his arms around her, "Shi nuh kno ou yet."

Neil stopped, "Wah yuh mean? Teach har den! Wah yuh waitin pon?" He waved his arms to signal his younger brother into action.

Bashan proudly explained to Teran, "Deh nutten laik wen de gyal dem wine dem bodies. Cum wi ago drop legs." Bashan led her to the area where his family danced. "Nuh worry mi ago teach yuh." He moved his pelvis into her body seductively causing her to bury her head into his chest.

Neil watched, "Nuh be shy, gyal, move yuh body fi de riddim. Fala yuh usband, dat a rite."

Teran moved in sync with Bashan, and he cheered. "Dat ah ih, Babi, wine fi Dadi." The dancing progressed, the group partnered off, and she was feeling very comfortable until Bashan moved against her with such seduction that heat rose in her face and ears. She moved away and left the dance area.

"Weh yuh guh, Teran! Cum ya an dance wid yuh bredda." Neil was on her again.

"Lef har alone, yuh nuh see har face ah red, shi embarrassed." Everett stepped between them. "Wah mek fi yuh face suh red, Teran? Yuh dance fine. Nuh need fi be embarrass."

"I just need time to get used to dancing like this." Teran fanned herself as Everett motioned for his wife to get her something to drink.

Neil teased, "Eeee, but yuh duh dance wid Shani laik dis. Mi kno yuh dance wid mi bredda laik suh cah mi know mi bredda." He laughed even as Everett shot him a warning look.

"Don't mine Neil, im nuh easy. Yuh ah a lady, propa. Shani tole wi yuh ave fambily inna de BVI. Dem propa people an yuh duh behave laik dat. Tan a lady an pay no mind to Neil." He handed her the drink his wife brought out. Teran swallowed and smiled. Everett enjoyed her reaction, "Dat de bes ginja beer, mi wife fi mek it."

Neil teased again, "Dat drink mek yuh ready suh yuh an Shani cyan dance lata." Teran made to choke on the drink and Neil guffawed, "Mi kno yuh a propa BVI lady, but mi know yuh marry mi bredda an 'im nuh propa! Well, propa in de propa place!" Teran reddened again and Neil embraced her. "Mi ah de bredda dat ah de jokesta, yuh kno? Sweet an propa browning." He kissed her cheek and announced, "Wi ago fi de party pon Francis Lewis. Shani yuh cum fi de bashment wid wi?"

"Mi an Teran nuh cum cah tenight. Wi 'ave been pon de cyar fi de ends an wi gwaan rest tenight. Ave fun." Bashan took some of Teran's ginger beer.

"Eeee, bwoy yuh tink mi baan yestaday? Yuh gwaan dung inna fi yuh ouse an dance a likkle mo." Neil slapped his brother on the shoulder.

Bashan grinned and Teran braced herself. "Mi ago teach har mo fi wine fi mi."

Teran shook her head and moved to sit on the couch. Eldrige laughed at the banter as Everett sucked his teeth and went upstairs. Nellie spoke up, "Enuff mon. Teran yuh nyam? Yuh nuh waan sup'm?"

"Mumi Nell, I am stuffed, and I can't eat anymore. We have eaten too much today. I probably won't eat anything for the next week. We brought food home too." Teran rubbed her stomach.

"Yuh nyam likkle mo here?" Nellie laughed as she watched Teran's gesture. "Nuh need fi badda bout yuh weight. Yuh suh likkle now wi nuh waan yuh winji."

Teran made to go into the kitchen with Nellie but announced as she went, "I am not winji I just come from small built people. Both my parents are thin and my grandmothers and many of my cousins. I have a thin family and trust me I am not by any way the thinnest. My older sister is thinner than I am."

"Nuh tru fi dat yuh fi de tinniest inna dis fambily?" Nellie led the way to the kitchen. The men watched them go and laughed. Neil went upstairs to change for the club and Eldrige helped Bashan take gifts downstairs to the apartment.

Teran fell across the bed after her shower. Bashan found her there asleep when he came out of the bathroom and smiled. He lifted her dainty body and placed her under the covers before moving to his side and turning out the light.

----------◊◊◊----------

The next morning, Bashan rolled over and sat up with a disappointed stretch. "Ooman, weh yuh guh?! Wah mek fi yuh lef de bed??"

Teran appeared in the doorway, "You notice that you don't even try to speak American English to me anymore?"

Bashan snorted, "Nuh need fi yuh undastan mi well."

"I know but you also speak it less around my family too and they don't always understand everything you say." Teran cocked her head to the side and smiled. "Get up man, we have several unopened presents, and you know we promised Mon Mon Mary and P'er Crandall that we were coming over today. It's already eleven, how long do you plan on staying in the bed?"

"Until mi open mi present mi nuh open lass night." Bashan held his arm out to Teran who walked over and sat next to him.

She laid a hand on his knee and swallowed, "Baby… I need to talk to you…"

Bashan groaned as he brought her closer. "Nuh tru ih yuh fada and he nuh waan yuh out here wid mi rite now?"

Teran lowered her head, but Bashan placed a hand under her chin for her to speak with him eye-to-eye. "Yes, Baby, I just don't feel comfortable, and I don't want to put my mother in a bad position either. They shouldn't be fighting because of what I do. We will be married in May, and I will be all yours then."

Bashan shook his head, "Yuh sey dat wi ave nuh lovin until May? Wah yuh waan mi to duh until den Teran? Dis enuff, yuh fada cum an change aal ting an ting, mi nuh laik dat!" He blew out a breath. "Everett tole mi dis very ting, yuh know? He tole mi I cyaan get vex wid him fah protect his dawta; mi affi respek dat but mi nuh laik it. Yah, wi duh ih de way yuh fada waan wi duh it. Respek."

Teran looked at Bashan's face, "I love you so much. I know this is hard and it's hard on me too. I would rather be here in your arms than in that crowded apartment. But Pe'r is close at hand, and I don't want to cause anymore trouble than is already brewing."

"Wah gwaan, Teran? Yuh nuh sey nutten bout crosses. Weh de crosses?" Bashan slid from under the covers and put a robe on his bare frame to sit beside her. "Tell mi wah or ooo de problem."

Teran sighed, "Pe'r is having a fit about Najid. He is being mysterious of late. Saadri doesn't see him for days at a time then he shows up and won't talk about what he's been doing. She is running out of excuses and reasons to hold Pe'r off. I am nervous about there being an explosion. Then my mother had a close encounter of the ridiculous kind talking about I should let Butch walk me down the aisle at the wedding. A wedding Pe'r is footing a large part of the bill for I may add. Then there's Nique who didn't come for Christmas as Pe'r asked and we all knew Merci was behind it. Pe'r is mad at Nique though and told her she was an adult now and had to grow a backbone. It's a mess that we all put on hold until the holidays are over but there will be post New Year's fireworks."

"Wah bout us? I am sure Damas ave a ting or two fi sey bout us. Wah im sey?" Bashan raised a brow to signal he wanted complete disclosure.

Teran obliged, "Actually, aside from us sleeping together, which he has emphatically stated he wants no more of, he likes you. He feels like you are worthy of his daughter and wishes

Najid were more like you. He knows you are strong and that he would really have to mix it up with you if it came to it, but he doesn't want that. He knows I don't want that either because he laid into me a few weeks ago and I told him if he started anything with you or made you feel anything but welcomed, I would never speak to him again and then I would come live with you."

Bashan burst into laughter, "Wah yuh mean live wid mi?"

"I threatened Pe'r I would stay with you in sin if he acted the fool." Teran nodded for emphasis.

Bashan laughed so hard he fell back on the bed. "Yuh a jokesta now? Teran mi cyaan believe yuh sey dat fi yuh fada; yuh nuh easy Babi!" He stood to get dressed. "Najid mus ave crosses he nuh taak bout? Yuh know he a haad one fi undastan, a haad rock. I neva undastan ou yuh sista tan wid him cah dey seem suh different, but I know dey luv one anoda. I cyan reach out to him and try fi help him cah wi did bredren since wi marry sistas."

"Thank you, Baby, I think you talking to him would help. Najid likes you and he may be able to say to you what he won't to Pe'r and what he can't to Saadri. I am worried about Dri. At least Mon Mon Ellie has Pe'r, but Saadri feels like she is losing her husband. Mind you this is a husband our father did not have a chance to approve. At least Pe'r has met you before we married. On top of all of that, Mon Mon Ellie's health is not the best."

Dressed in a suede and leather sweat suit, Bashan walked into the bathroom. Teran followed him and stood in the doorway as he brushed his teeth. "I will warm something to eat. Something tells me this will be another long day." He nodded and closed the door. She walked into the kitchen and took out the containers deciding to fix a smorgasbord. The telephone rang.

----------◊◊◊----------

"Hello. Bonjou Pe'r... I answered because Shan is in the bathroom, and I am in the kitchen. Si-fe, Pe'r, I understood you... no, please Pe'r, you don't need to come out here. I spoke with him, and he knows where you stand..."

"Gi mi de phone Teran, mi will taak fi yuh fada." Teran turned toward Bashan and gasped as he removed the phone from her hand. "Mista Damas 'ou ah yuh?... Wi taak dis mawnin bout 'ou yuh feel ... Respek, Mista Damas, respek ... yuh protect yuh dawta and I undastan... wi will wait until May den shi aal mine... Yuh ave my word nutten appen laas night... Wi cum home late afta wi visit wid my fada fambily, ih was a lang day an wi were tired suh wi cum dung here an fall asleep... sure, I ave har home dis evening and no mo spend de night... Tank yuh, Mista Damas... ave a gud day."

He hung up the phone and watched Teran so at ease warming the food. He walked behind her and wrapped his arms around her body, "De day wi marry mi ago be suh happy. Yuh belong inna dis kitchen an inna mi arms. Dis nuh home wen yuh nuh here. Ih feel empty and I feel empty too. May is too lang, wi ago fi de justice fi de peace an marry tomorra?"

Teran turned in his arms, "Shan, I would love to do that. I am so sick of this hovering and posturing that my stomach hurts. Everybody is so focused on what they feel their rights are they are forgetting this is my life and my wedding."

Bashan snorted, "Babi, de wedding day fi de bride, but de wedding fi de fambily an aal ooo cum fi watch de ceremony."

"Shan let's just go to the justice of the peace. We can do it at the municipal building. Then we can save money and be done with all this craziness. I think my sister had it right when she married Najid and let everyone know afterwards."

He kissed her long, long enough to feel the tension ebb from her petite frame. "Mi nuh tief Teran, suh mi nuh guh sneak round fi marry yuh. Wi will dweet inna May before our fambily cah dats de rite way fi dweet. Dats wah I waan fi mi own dawta and mi ago dweet fi Damas dawta. Mi luv yuh too much fi tief yuh fram yuh parents."

"Ooh, the food!" Teran turned toward the stove and settled her nerves in a long breath when she realized Bashan had already reached around her and turned off the burner. She smiled and they made their plates.

After the meal, they sat on the living room floor to open presents they'd left wrapped from the previous night. Teran grabbed a small box.

Her arched eyebrow let Bashan know why she'd chosen the present. "Dat de infamous gift?"

Teran nodded, "Open it, Shan."

He sighed and took the box, when he opened it out came a pair of black and white tuxedo G-string underwear. Bashan held them up in total surprise. As he dropped the box a small card slipped out. Teran picked it up and read it – *"I can just about imagine you in these! (Ooh) Drea."* Teran slipped the card into her pants pocket. Then she asked, "What are you going to do with them?"

He peeked from behind the underwear, "Wah yuh waan mi fi duh wid dem?"

Teran gracefully rose, without a word, snatched them out of his hand and went into the kitchen. She took a pair of scissors from a drawer and started cutting them up. Bashan watched in complete shock. He burst into laughter. "Yuh sey mi red yeye, suh wah yuh call yusself?"

Teran stated, "It's not about me being jealous. You need drawers I'll buy them. No man of mine is walking around with drawers some other woman bought him!"

Bashan continued laughing as he walked toward the kitchen. Teran had reduced the underwear to shreds. "Arite, yuh prove yuh point, deh nutten fi cut." Looking down at the small pile of shredded material they both began to howl. Bashan took the scissors, put them down, and led Teran back into the living room. They exchanged gifts and were delighted. Bashan had gotten Teran a total of two pair of pants, two sweaters, a dress, black and brown riding boots, a black leather jacket, and a red negligee set. She gifted him with a pair of slacks, three sweaters, a pair of jeans, a mohair Kangol, nylon underwear, and a gold chain with his name attached in beaten gold.

As they thanked one another the phone rang. Bashan answered, "Mumi, wah gwaan?... Wi open presents fram one anoda... wi a soon cum Mumi... Yah, wi a cum now... bye Mumi." He hung up the phone with a grunt. "De parents getting pon fi wi nerve todeh. Dat did mi mada telling wi fi cum now."

Teran laughed, "Well, you can't talk about my father anymore because your mother is a force to be reckoned with too."

As she made to rise, he pulled her onto his lap. "Wah yuh did at de house laas night did wonderful. Mi an mi fada suh proud of our oomen." He kissed her and stood them up. "Let wi guh before shi calls again."

----------◊◊◊----------

Teran and Bashan were fortunate enough to find a parking spot in front of the house. Armentha answered the door. "Suh nice of yuh fi cum wen wi wait fi yuh aal mawnin."

"Wi neva sey wi wud be here inna de mawnin. Wi neva wake up until eleven an wi still had fi wi presents to open." Bashan kissed her and walked into the anteroom toward the living room.

Teran who walked in ahead of him was engulfed in Crandall's arms. "Well, mi glad mi dawta here, gud afternoon yuh two."

Mary walked into the room, "Gud afternoon, yuh ah hungry?"

Teran and Bashan reached her simultaneously and kissed her on both cheeks. Bashan spoke, "Mumi, wi nyam aready. Wi fi cum to spend time wid yuh and Daddy."

Armentha joked, "De ongle fambily yuh ave ah yuh parents?"

"Nuh wi ave cum fi spend time wid yuh an Ivee too." He grabbed her in a gentle headlock, and she swatted his backside. "Cha, Teran nuh laik nuh oda ooman fi lick mi batty!" They laughed as Teran looked on shaking her head.

Crandall raised his arms, "Wi ago shopping? De pickney need tings fi dem new house. First wi guh fi guh to Baldwin an let dem look at dem gates. Aright?"

"Thank you so much P'er Crandall and Mon Mon Mary! I can't believe this! A husband and a new home. This is too much." Teran gave the older couple another hug and kiss before they called for Ivee and filed out of the Queens Village home.

Bashan steered Teran toward the Monte Carlo and looked at his sister, "Yuh riding wid us Mentha?"

Armentha shook her head, "Mi ago wid Mumi, Dadi and Ivee. Lef de luv buds alone."

Teran laughed, "Yuh mo dan welcome Mentha." Bashan and Armentha looked at Teran in surprise. She corrected, "I mean you can ride with us."

"Teran wi mek a Jamaican ooman out of yuh aredy?" Armentha smiled and patted her shoulder. When Teran lowered her head, she grabbed the young woman in an embrace. "Wi ah yuh fambily now an wi should rub off, yuh know. Wi luv yuh, Teran, an wi happy yuh marry wi Shani." She kissed her cheek and the threesome walked to Bashan's car.

----------◊◊◊----------

At the house in Baldwin, Crandall gave the couple a tour. "Yuh ave dree bedrums an attic plus de basement suh yuh cyan get five inna aal. Nuh feel laik yuh mus kip de furniture cah mi feeling nuh be hurt. Mi getting sum tings fi tek dem wid mi fi Queens."

Mary offered decorating tips as they walked through the second floor before she and Crandall descended the stairs to let the foursome browse. Armentha chose one of the rooms as the one she would stay in when she visited. Teran recognized Ivee was quiet and had been quiet throughout the time at the house, so she spoke to her, "Which room do you want Ivee?"

"Dis nuh mi home suh mi nuh waan nutten."

Armentha chastised her as Teran stared open-mouthed, "Ivee, yeye too red."

Bashan added, "Wah mek yuh sey dat, Ivee? Teran invite yuh fi tan wid wi an yuh taak laik dat?"

Ivee sucked her teeth, "Hush. Mi offended Teran de empress." She walked off.

Teran walked behind Ivee before she could get far, "Don't worry honey, you won't get another invitation from me. You are so nasty that I wouldn't want you under my roof. *To mové kè avèk jalou ti fiy.*" She brushed past Ivee and walked to the first floor.

Crandall turned in the direction of the steps with a smile that dropped when he saw Teran. "Sup'm did wrong, Teran?"

"Yes, Ivee was very rude to me, and I am tired of trying to be nice to her when she doesn't like me for some reason. I didn't come to cause problems, maybe Shan and I need to stay where we are." Teran was near tears when she finished the statement.

Bashan, Mary, Armentha, and Ivee entered the landing as Crandall questioned, "Weh de crosses? Wah mek Teran yeye wata? Lee, fi deh sup'm yuh mus sey? Wah mek Teran fi tink yuh nuh laik har?"

Iverine lowered her eyes, "Dadi, mi nuh ave de answer fi dat."

"Shi nuh feel dis way fi nutten. Wha'ppun upstairs?" Crandall directed everyone into the living room with a wave of his hand.

Bashan sat next to Teran and answered his father, "Mentha choose a room fah wen shi cum an tan wid wi here, an Teran aks Ivee wah room shi choose an Ivee did taak rude to har. Shi sey fi dis nuh har gates suh shi nuh waan nutten." He sighed, "An dis fi nuh de first time Ivee ah rude fi Teran. Shi nuh approve fi Teran fram de start."

Mentha added, "Shi an Mumi, cah Ivee did fala Mumi inna dat way. Mi told har dat har yeye red."

Ivee called out, "Teran nuh innocent, shi did rudeness as well. Shi call mi a name in har language."

Teran answered, "I said you were mean spirited and rude, and I wouldn't want you to come visit."

Iverine challenged, "Yuh sey yuh home cah yuh move in aredy an pretend yuh de empress fi de castle handing out orders fi de peasants. Yuh home did wah yuh sey. Dadi nuh hand de keys ova yet!"

Mary sighed and Crandall placed a hand on her knee to quiet her. "Now mi know yuh fi nuh treat Teran well. Eff mi sey de home did belong fi Shani an Teran den it did belong wid dem, suh wah mek yuh behave suh rude? Yuh tink mi nuh know yuh waan mi fi give yuh a home too. Rite now dem marry, suh mi give dem de home first. Yuh marry an mi give yuh a home at dat time. Nuh need fi yeye red, Iverine. Wah mi give mi son; mi give mi son an mi aks no permission dweet."

Ivee blurted, "Im nuh yuh son, really."

Crandall's expression killed the unspoken words in Ivee's throat. Ivee lowered her head and cried softly. Bashan adjusted on the couch to speak but Teran leaned into him, and he stilled. Mary held her breath and Armentha crossed her legs as she reclined into her chair. The elder Watts' voice lowered, "Mi cyaan tolerate dis bodderation cah ih foolish, dis nuh ou fambily behave. Shani ah mi bwoy, mi son mi raise fram a babi, an dat mek im de son mi taught fi be a mon. Yuh ave nuh bizniz fi taak bout sup'm fi nuh did concern yuh. Yuh ugly outburst tole mi yuh did rudeness fi Shani an Teran an mi nuh tan fi dat."

"Yes, Dadi. Shani an Teran, hush. Mi waan de best life fi yuh, truss mi." Ivee slumped in her seat and wiped her eyes with tissue passed to her by Armentha.

Mary cleared her throat, "Hush, Teran. Shani taak bout dis Teran, Teran, Teran. Dis gyal im taak bout suh much ah special an mi know dat dis nuh de siem fram de oda gyal. Ih scary yuh see yuh bwoy grow up an fall inna luv. Mi kno Shani luv yuh de first time im bring yuh home. Dis likkle ting mek mi bwoy behave suh different. Mi kno mi nuh handle ih wen mi know yuh did luv Shani too. But mi do luv yuh too, Teran, an mi enjoy yuh as mi dawta."

Teran was in tears and leaned against Bashan for support. He spoke, "Ivee, wi nuh fi compete wid de attention Dadi give. Wi waan yuh part fi wi life but nuh laik dis. Wi fambily but sometime yuh mek ih haad fi wi be fambily, see it? Mi luv yuh, Ivee, an mi kno Teran wud luv yuh mo eff yuh allow ih. Nuh tru mi yuh bredda, Ivee, nuh yuh enemy? Mi luv yah, suh tap quarrelin wid wi."

Ivee stood from her seat still crying and moved toward the couple. Bashan stood to receive her, and they embraced a while before Teran stood and spoke to her, "*Mo lainm twa, Sè.*"

Between sniffles Ivee asked, "Wah yuh sey, Teran?"

Bashan answered, "Shi sey shi luv yuh too, an shi call yuh har sister." He beamed proudly at Teran and his family who looked at him with surprise.

Ivee grabbed Teran in an embrace, "Hush."

Teran hugged her back and afterward questioned, "Why does she and Mon Mon keep telling me to be quiet?"

The Wattses laughed as Mentha explained. "Nuh Lilly Bud – hush– ih de way fi sey yuh apologize, sorry." They continued laughing as Teran understood.

"Oh, okay. That makes more sense now because I was saying to myself, how is that I am the one that keeps being told to shut up?" This brought more laughter from the family.

When they settled down Mary asked, "Well, yuh feel laik shopping? Leggo an see wah de ave in de furniture store."

Teran whispered to Bashan, "I hope they have recliners."

Bashan snorted, "Yah mon, mi hope de ave whole heap."

They left Baldwin and went shopping in the Five Towns area where the family blessed the soon-to-be newlyweds with a living room and dining room set. They made sure a recliner was among the purchases.

CHAPTER FOURTEEN

Sisters

The group on the record calling out the name of the female rapper blasted from the speakers and the crowd went wild as the emcee announced, "Alright, alright! Let's give it up for the lovely ladies of Lambda Chi Eta Sorority – Incorporated!!!!!!"

Saadri turned to Teran, "This is Sè's group, right?"

Teran wrinkled her nose, "I think so." They stood along with the rest of the college students packed into the gym of Forsica University where Veronique attended. The cheers were deafening but the young women were having a wonderful time in North Carolina at the Greek Weekend event.

"Çé lá Dell, li zami mé, aou çé nô Sè?" Saadri spotted Veronique's best friend Dell but could not locate her sister. Teran shrugged until they spotted Veronique in another line. The group of ladies danced into the gym as if they owned it. They cheered. "*Kabalé Sè, kabalé,*" for their older sister who invited them down as a peace offering from the Christmas fiasco.

Just behind them a young man gave a wolf call and was joined by others. Teran turned and looked at the handsome face of Bobby Lattimore, Veronique's boyfriend. Beside him was Dell's boyfriend Maurice "Eddie" Eddrington who was a basketball star at the school. The men looked at her and smiled. Teran turned back to the performance as the ladies stepped with precision creating their own version of the song they entered on. "Lambda, Lambda! We know we own these streets. Lambda, Lambda! No others can compete!"

Saadri clapped and cheered for the chant as Eddie commented loud enough for Bobby and the ladies to hear. "I could kiss they Daddy for making these fine thangs! They all fine! What y'all say a few minutes ago?"

Saadri answered, "*Kabalé*, party or dance, celebrate. We told our sister to party hearty." She deliberately addressed the answer to Bobby.

Eddie touched Teran's hair, and she shot him a warning look. "Y'all all have that pretty color and pretty hair too. You didn't get this red out of nobody's bottle."

Teran shook her head as she watched the group's performance. "No, this is all me."

He would have said more but the crowd responded when the ladies sent a barb to a rival sorority. Bobby let out another wolf call and the others followed. Teran looked at Saadri and they giggled before she whispered, "Didn't you tell me to watch out for wolves in sheep's clothing."

Saadri leaned into her and said, "I know, right." They giggled again. "Veronique, *Sè, bon louvraj*!" She shouted as the sorors finished their last step.

Teran shouted, "*Laissez les bon temps rouler!*" Many in the nearby audience turned to look at Teran who in turn waved and sat down. Laughter ensued in her section. The group left and as they ended the show, the audience socialized while awaiting the judges' decision.

Eddie leaned forward, "What that mean, sexy lady?"

Teran turned to him, "Let the good times roll and my name is Teran."

Eddie laughed, "Good times indeed, Teran. And I beg to differ on that sexy note. Lawd y'all some fine sisters. Who's the oldest?"

Saadri answered, "Veronique."

Eddie rejoined, "No, I mean between you and your twin. Who came first?"

They both said, "We're not twins."

Bobby laughed at Eddie's look of disbelief, "Eddie, they aren't, Roni told me they look and act like twins, but they are not. When I saw them, I bugged out too because they are just about identical."

Eddie looked at them, "You don't know which one to pick, they both so fine."

Teran answered, "The answer is, choose door number three because we aren't an option. Besides you have Dell; my sister," she nodded her head toward Saadri, "is married and I have a fiancé."

Bobby laughed as Eddie coughed out, "Married and engaged! I commend those brothers for getting you off the yard, but I am also mad that I didn't get a chance."

Teran responded with, "You never had one."

Bobby and Saadri burst into laughter and Eddie looked at her, "Wow, Miss New York! Are y'all all this blunt?"

"Yes." Teran turned to Saadri who was still laughing.

Saadri looked at Teran and shook her head, "Nadine Jr."

----------◊◊◊----------

Bobby and Eddie were part of the brother fraternity to Veronique and Dell's sorority. The Upsilon Chi Xi fraternity brothers hosted a party in the university's activity center and were doing so in style as the sisters walked into the area. Veronique thanked those attending by giving congratulatory hugs while proudly introducing her younger sisters. Eddie walked around like the king of the hill with his arm possessively around Dell's waist as she too received congratulations.

Bobby walked over and kissed Veronique to the point of drawing attention and comments of praise. The sisters looked on amused. After the kiss, he led them to a table filled with food and drink. Saadri whispered to Teran, "Sè, remember, don't drink after these people. They slip something in your drink and do all sorts of things. If you put that drink down don't pick it up again. And you are not to drink anything stronger than a soda, you hear me?"

Teran hissed, "I don't drink anymore, Dri, gosh, stop being the mother hen, you're as bad as Fawn. You know I am not trusting these people, especially if they are friends with Eddie the Creep. He, I know, would try to take advantage of us. I don't know what Dell sees in him; he is not faithful to her. He probably chases every skirt on this campus."

Saadri nodded, "I know he probably does but think about it, he wants Dell because she is the female basketball star around here and in the most popular sorority. It's all about status. Dude is a bum and I hope she figures that out before he hurts her. They won't end well, and she seems like real good people, I want better for her than that. You think Nique has talked to her yet?"

"Knowing Nique, she did. But we can let her know she needs to talk with her again." Teran looked at Saadri, "By the way, you sound just like that husband of yours." Saadri laughed and they enjoyed the party.

----------◊◊◊----------

Outside the hall where the party was held, Aan inebriated Veronique argued with an equally inebriated Bobby, who wanted her to accompany him home. "*Imbésil*, how many times do I have to say my sisters are here and I am not leaving them? We can get together after they leave tomorrow."

Bobby shouted, "They are not babies, and they know I am your man. And don't call me names, you are a piece of work! Do you know how many females want to spend time with me? I don't have to be out here fighting with you and I am not begging for your attention when I can have so many others."

Teran shook her head and looked at Saadri, "We'd better get her before she burns down the campus." They moved toward their sister and spoke, "Nique."

"*Inkròyab*! I am supposed to jump to be with you and abandon my sisters because you have other *koshons* running after you? So, if I don't do what you want - you will cheat on me? You probably cheated already! *Mô kalin*, huh?!" The sisters reached her and began trying to soothe her agitation.

Bobby could not stand down with his frat brothers providing commentary about how he should handle Veronique. "Speak English, girl! What did you call me?"

Saadri hissed, "She called you her boyfriend, silly. Stop letting your boys egg you on. Both of you are drunk. We are going to take her back to her apartment to sober up. You two need space before you say or do something crazy that you'll regret."

They made to leave with Veronique, but Bobby stepped in front of them. "She better stop acting like she can talk to me any way she wants."

Teran tensed. "She's drunk and so are you or you would see that we are trying to avoid a bunch of confusion. You should talk this out when you are both clear headed. Let us take her home and get her some coffee. Why don't you come too? You both need it."

Bobby hesitated long enough for Saadri to add in her persuasion. "Come on Bobby, we'll even cook something for you. After, the two of you can kiss and make up." She winked and led Bobby away from the building.

The next morning Saadri shook her sister awake because of a heated exchange. "Terry, something is wrong." They hopped from the bed and strode into Veronique's living room to find Bashan and Najid in a faceoff with Bobby.

Teran swallowed, "Shan, what's wrong?"

Bashan looked at the tee shirt she wore that barely covered her curves. "Whole heap wrong yuh did tan dere wid yuh skimpy gown pon yuh badi! Ooo de raas dis?"

Teran shook her head, "That's Bobby, Nique's boyfriend."

Najid demanded, "Why is he opening the door and then questioning us like he y'all's pimp or something? And where the hell are your clothes, Candy?!"

Saadri looked at her belly tee shirt and short shorts and blinked. "We were in bed; you woke us up with your bellowing. Nique is still sleep. Although, I don't know how she is sleeping through this." Bobby looked at them as if he'd accomplished a great success and the three of them laughed.

Teran commented, "You know why she is still asleep after all the craziness last night." The sisters laughed.

"So, when are you going to get some clothes on? When I go off up in here?" Najid stared at Saadri.

Bashan stepped toward Teran, "Yuh had yuh taste of campus life, now ih time fi guh home. Ih look as eff yuh had a time too."

Teran yawned, "I am beat. I didn't get much sleep messing with the two lovebirds."

Saadri called as she went into the bedroom that she and Teran shared, "Nique! Wake up and join World War Six!!!"

Veronique appeared at her bedroom door in a tee shirt and Saadri warned, "Do not come out without putting some clothes on them hips. Najid and Bashan are here."

Veronique yawned, stretched, and spoke loud enough for them to hear. "Why are the Thug and Rasta Man here so early?"

Bashan yelled, "Wi cum fi get our oomen! De party ah ova!"

Najid also shouted, "You've had my wife for the weekend now it's time for her to come home and be my wife again, no more of this college crap!"

Veronique retorted, "Cave Men!"

Bobby joined in the laughter that ensued. "Well since this is one happy family let's get something to eat. Y'all want to go to the diner?!" He yelled toward the rooms the women disappeared into.

Veronique called out, "I have plenty of food; I will cook with my sisters."

Bobby looked at Bashan and Najid, "Why don't you sit and get comfortable. The Supremes are making us breakfast."

Najid grunted, "Supremes, huh?", as he sat.

Bobby offered, "Your wives hit this campus and created quite a stir. Roni is already the heartbreaker but now she has two younger sisters and that upped the game! I call them the Supremes because they are supremely beautiful and supremely close, they do everything together."

Bashan laughed, "Wi know de duh de siem ting aal de time."

Bobby questioned, "Hey man, where are you from?"

Bashan snorted, "Jamaica."

He nodded, "Cool. Hey, let me hop in the shower and hurry Roni out here. I'll see you in a few."

Bashan and Najid looked at one another but didn't speak since Teran and Saadri appeared. Najid got up and walked to Saadri, "Hey Candy, I miss you too much when you are away." He brought his wife into his embrace and kissed her with a passion that spoke what he could not always express. Bashan held out his arms for Teran who did not disappoint as she sat on his lap.

It was to this scene Veronique entered the room. "What is this, the Love Boat?! They were only here a few days; my goodness you act like they have been gone a year!"

Najid answered, "Three days too long for my liking, then they were down here with all the college boys trying to scoop them up! Naw, it's time for my wife to come home so I came to get her with my man B." He walked over, greeted with a hug and kiss, and asked, "Nique, what's up with homeboy?" He nodded his head in the direction from which she came.

"Najid, don't start with me. Bobby is actually a good guy; he treats me well." She swatted his arm as she turned to greet Bashan. "Wah gwan, my bredda, wah gwan?"

"Dat was gud, Nique." He rose, kissed her forehead, but held her in an embrace. "Nuh kno bout dat dude, aldoah."

She exhaled, "Not you too, Shan. Bobby is good people; just get to know him before you try to run him away."

Teran walked into the kitchen and Saadri followed, "Dri and I think you two may need to really work some things out and I don't mean in the bedroom."

Veronique bounced into the kitchen, "Do tell Dr. Joyce Brothers, what do you and your sidekick have to say about me and Bobby when you couldn't even let Pe'r know about your cavemen? Please enlighten my poor third world self."

Saadri slammed a pot on the stove, "But we sure didn't have to wait for Mon Mon Merci to let Pe'r know because Veronique can't stand up to her mother and just had to blab our business."

Veronique was about to lay into her sister when she heard Bashan call out. "Enuff! Yuh had a gud weekend, suh nuh vex one anoda now. Wah done, done an ova. Wi waan breakfast fi nyam." He and Najid walked into the kitchen.

Bobby appeared in the kitchen, "What's wrong? Why are you all yelling at each other? You were thick as thieves last night. You okay, baby?" He walked over to Veronique and brought her into his arms. He leaned his forehead against hers and whispered something that made a dimpled grin appear on the young woman's face. They kissed and turned to stares.

Teran broke the silence, "Nique never brought her boyfriends around us before. This is a first for all of us."

"Terry, I haven't had many boyfriends and no one that serious that I would want you to meet. Were you and Saadri supposed to be the only ones finding good men?" The elder Buard girl walked to the refrigerator and began taking out breakfast items.

Saadri answered, "Of course that's not what she meant Nique."

Veronique turned and pointed at her sisters, "Look, Doublemint, none of that today so pipe down. Fellas out of the kitchen so the Buard sister's can make you a Creole breakfast."

Najid laughed and stood from his leaning position against a wall near the kitchen table, "Doublemint, ha!" Bashan snorted.

Teran sucked her teeth, "I always hated that name." Veronique gave her a hip bump and they fell into a groove preparing items.

Saadri laughed, "We had to be about three when Nique ran to tell Granmè we were getting into devilment, but it came out Doublemint. From then on, the family always used Doublemint to refer to our troublemaking or as they talked about us. That's the day's history lesson; please exit the kitchen if you want breakfast in a timely fashion."

Najid smiled, "Pardon us ma'am, we are leaving the area. By the way, I would like to know if you're already spoken for because I would appreciate being able to keep company with you." He pretended to take off a hat and bowed.

Bobby laughed, "Keep company? Man, where you from? You can't be a New York dude using that term, you have to be southern."

"My family is from Texas, but I was born and raised in New York." He turned and left the kitchen with Bobby following. Bashan made himself comfortable on the couch. Najid commented on his posture. "Yo, B, you know there is limited space, man! Don't hog up the couch!" The ladies laughed at the men's antics.

----------◊◊◊----------

The sisters set about making a meal and holding a conversation among themselves. Veronique teased, "Granmè voyé madlènn li nonk Thélismarté ça fé."

Teran became excited, "You have some of Uncle Thélismarté's Andouille sausage?! Granmè sent it, when? I haven't had that in so long."

"I asked and if you ask you know Granmè will send it. That is if you can come up for air to call her. She asked me if she has more than one granddaughter."

In the cabinets Saadri called out, "Aou you hominy, Sè?"

"I put it in the pantry behind you, Dri." Veronique continued cutting the sausage.

Teran prepared a mixture of cinnamon, egg, and milk. "You always have something smart to say and then when we go at it it's never your fault. Come up for air, maybe the real problem is that I have someone to occupy my time and I want to be with that person."

"Come on you two, don't start. We enjoyed a whole three days without this bickering. Bashan was right." Saadri shook the box of hominy into a mixing bowl and grabbed other ingredients to place in another bowl.

"Well, I guess three days is our limit because it's on and popping now. You think I am jealous of you, Teran?" The oldest sister stopped what she was doing and narrowed her eyes at the youngest daughter.

Teran stopped her mixing as well and faced off. "Look, Merci!"

Veronique was on her way toward Teran who was also closing the gap, but Saadri stepped between them. "Arété sèk!" The sisters stopped and went back to their preparations.

Teran complained, "I didn't start, Dri. I never start." The older sisters looked at Teran who turned toward them, they all started laughing.

"Mo shagrin, Teran. I am being a witch. I guess I am a little jealous of you and Dri."

Saadri gasped, "Why on earth would you be jealous of us?"

"Well for one, you are already married – to a fine thug but fine no less. Then Terry has that chocolate island boy all wrapped up and they will be married this spring." Veronique stirred the sausage, peppers, and onions in a pan. "Dri, your water is boiling over here."

"Nique, you have no business being jealous of us. Me and Bashan are as much of a shock to me as for everyone else. I certainly wasn't thinking about anyone, especially after Russell."

"You know I was looking for him last summer when I came up. I was even asking about him because I know you and Fawn did what you had to do but I wanted to put a Buard Bayou butt whooping on that boy. Saadri even took me by where he lived, and no one had seen him. We would have toasted his marshmallow!" The sisters laughed as Veronique continued in a lowered voice, "Saadri didn't think so, but I believed Najid or one of his friends did something to that boy. He kept telling me not to worry about what was already handled or something like that."

Saadri stirred the hominy mixture and murmured, "Hmmph, he probably did that, and God knows what else."

Teran whispered, "What's going on, Dri? You seem so disturbed around him lately. Things are not better?"

Saadri waved her question away, "Nique, you have Bobby so why would you be jealous of us? Aside from ya'll needing to chill on the liquor because ya'll act like fools when you're drunk, you seem to be good."

Teran agreed, "Ooh, yuh nuh easy when you're drunk."

Veronique's brow arched, "Listen to the island girl! I'm what?"

Teran repeated, "Yuh nuh easy – you are out of control."

Saadri teased, "Hmm, I imagine we'll be learning a lot more island terms in time to come huh?"

Teran licked her tongue. "Nique, what's up? Why are you jealous?"

"Bobby is okay, but I really don't see this going too far. I feel like I'm a mess and I look at the two of you and feel like you could teach me something instead of the other way around. I am the oldest, after all, in college, and the one who should be imparting to you, but I don't."

"As much as I love Granmè and Pe'r I do not like how they always put so much pressure on you. Me and Terry got away with so much, but you had to be almost perfect. I couldn't stand that they did that to you and Mon Mon Merci seemed to go right along with it. You are Nique and you bleed, hurt, and laugh like Doublemint."

Teran groaned, "There's that ridiculous name again," as she placed biscuits in the oven.

Saadri waved at her, "Shut up, Terry! Nique, we are not asking you to be anyone but who you are. You are not perfect, and we don't expect you to be."

"No, you're not, I'm the perfect one."

The older sisters commanded, "Shut up, Terry!" They all laughed.

As they continued putting the meal together Saadri spoke. "Listen, I have been praying."

Teran interrupted, "Dri should have been the St. Amant or the sain't anything because she is up there with God and Jesus all the time. I don't know how she ended up with Najid." Teran looked at her sisters and saw they did not appreciate her comments. "I know, shut up, Terry."

Saadri continued, "If you don't see a future with Bobby, sleeping with him won't change the outcome. Both of you should be sleeping only with your husband. We give up so much of our value when we allow these guys to sleep with us and there's no commitment. They dog us and it's our fault because we let them. Half the time they are sleeping with us and others too."

Veronique asked, "Were you a virgin when you married Najid?"

"My husband is the only man I have ever slept with." Saadri stirred the hominy mixture.

Veronique stared open-mouthed, "Now I really feel terrible that my younger sister is living a purer life than I am."

Teran added, "I feel like a whore, and I have only slept with Shan and Russell."

Saadri shook her head, "I am not saying this to make you feel bad but to get you both to pause. I love my husband but there are things which I cannot talk about that concern me, and we are by no means a perfect couple."

"So, what are you really saying, *Sè?" Veronique made the coffee and began gathering plates and utensils.*

"I don't feel like this is going in a direction that will make us feel any better, Dri." Teran checked on the biscuits and prepared to remove them.

Saadri watched her sister's and smiled. "I beg to differ, what I'm about to offer you will change your life; His name is Jesus."

Veronique sighed, "Girl, we know Jesus! We were all raised Catholic and confirmed, remember?"

Saadri shook her head, "I am talking about a true relationship that transforms your lives. Not religion, but relationship."

Teran defended, "Are you saying our confirmation was not enough?"

"I am saying, Terry and Nique, confirmation doesn't lead to a transformation, a truly changed life. How often do you all attend church or study the Word?"

Veronique turned off the pots and placed a hand on her hip. "Enough! You are sitting here judging us because you're married, and we are not but look at who you are married to.

You know as well as we do that, he is selling drugs and doing whatever else he can manage to do but you sit on your high horse like Saint Ellen and act like you are somehow not part of the problem."

Teran came to Saadri's defense, "Stop it, Merci Junior! You get so put off when someone tells the truth and shines a light on your dirt. She isn't judging us but telling us a hard truth."

Veronique turned on Teran, "And you, Lady Godiva Junior, with your free spirit self don't care one way or the other. You do as you please and everyone else be damned, just like Mon Mon Nadine."

Teran ground out, "And you're mad because you're so tied to your mother's apron strings that you're choking, and you don't have the backbone to get your neck out of the noose. Don't sit there with all that mouth, blustering at me for hitting the nail on the head. Saadri is right whether we like it or not. I am a stubborn free spirit because I am sitting in a house watching my mother throw her life away wasting time on a fool who will cycle in and out because he can't seem to stay clean and sober. You are the victim of a mother who has you in a choke hold because you are the only thing of our father, she has left despite the fact that she has a loving and devoted husband. Saadri was the only one of us who was really wanted, although our father loves us all. Yet, she still had daddy issues that led her into the arms of a thug. You're right Nique, it is enough, enough with the fighting, hiding, and accusing. We are not our mothers and I refuse to keep that crap going with us. You are my sisters and I love you both and if Dri is trying to tell us something, we owe it to her to listen because she is the most levelheaded of us all, it has always been that way. You are the big bad sister who kept us in line and always protected us, I am the brat who enjoyed the attention and guidance but did what I wanted to do. It is what it is, but the bottom line is, we are sisters and that's worth far more than all of the other crap put together. I love you both so shut up, Nique, and let's hear her out."

Saadri stared at Teran then looked at Veronique, "Who is this?"

Veronique laughed, "I know, right? Maybe we have kicked her butt and argued her down long enough for her to finally get some sense. The big bad sister, huh?"

Teran laughed, "And you know it!"

----------◊◊◊----------

Pain Perdu, Andouille sausage, spiced hash browns, creamy grits, fresh baked buttermilk biscuits and chicory coffee garnished the table as three hungry young men almost knocked one another down for seats. Saadri said the grace and for the next half hour not a word was spoken.

The sisters cleaned the kitchen before returning to the living room and their semi-comatose partners. Teran laid across the floor as she did when she was a little girl. Saadri used Teran's backside as a pillow, also a custom from youth, and they stretched in a t-formation. To complete their childhood routine, Veronique sat cross-legged near Teran's head.

Nodding toward the men, Veronique commented, "Looks like the aftereffects from a *faitdodo*." Teran and Saadri agreed.

Najid questioned, "What's that? Faitdodo?"

"It's an all-night party, baby; they are very popular down home. Pe'r would come home from them wiped out; sometimes he had to be brought home and laid out on the porch or on the couch in the living room at Granmè's house."

Teran laughed, "It's like a *bashment,* Shan."

"Awoah!" Bashan kept his eyes closed.

Veronique leaned in, "Remember when Pe'r and Nonk Thélismarté came in so drunk they could hardly stand and fell out in Granmè's den?"

Saadri laughed, "Oh my gosh! Whose idea was it for us to go in there and run through their pockets? We had a good time getting all their money. It's no wonder someone hadn't done it before us that night!"

Teran laughed, "That was Tant Euprosine who said 'Doublemint *alé atravèr yê lapòsh!*'"

The sisters laughed at the memory then settled into a comfortable quiet. Snoring could be heard from at least one of the men. Teran looked at Saadri. "Sè, continue what you were talking to us about in the kitchen."

Saadri smiled at Teran and looked for a sign of agreement in Veronique, which she received. "I want you to live in relationship with Christ; I want my whole family to be saved."

Veronique questioned, "What does that mean, Sè? How do we know what to do and whether we are doing it right? I mean, we were raised Catholic, and we thought we were doing that okay and now you seem to be talking about something different. I can admit that you are different from Terry and I, you always were – aside from being the love child."

"You see, that's what I mean. Here we are, young adults, still carrying around baggage we didn't even create for ourselves. Bottom line, our parents were irresponsible young college students who made decisions that resulted in three little girls coming into this world in less than desirable circumstances. But God gave us Granmè who embraced us and loved us and made sure we grew up as sisters despite distance and our parents' ill-prepared craziness. That is what we need to focus on; God showed us His love through His agent Mazie Buard."

Teran looked at her 'twin.' "God is speaking through you, right now, isn't He? You don't even seem like yourself. You are bolder and more confident, like you know what you're talking about and won't brook anything contrary. Has Jesus being in your life done this for you? You always look so peaceful even after all you deal with. I need this Saadri, tell me what I have to do to get this."

Tearfully Veronique admitted, "I know I need this too. What do we need to do?"

"Don't leave me out, Roni." Bobby sat up from his recline and leaned toward the sibling trio.

Saadri sat up, kept her eyes closed, and prayed as the responses came.

"I dought I had an undastandin wit God now I must question dat. Yuh ah different Saadri, inna de peace aal de time. I waan dat fah mi and Teran." Bashan moved from his chair and sat beside Teran. "Wi duh dis togeda, Empress, arite?" Teran sat up and snuggled next to him.

Najid watched the scene, "This tugs on the heartstrings, but there has to be more than the emotional pull. I've seen too much to the contrary in people claiming to have God's ear."

Saadri nodded and looked directly at him, "It's called faith Najid. You have to believe Him and trust Him to do the transforming work in you. The other people don't matter when it comes to your faith."

She looked around the room at the group assembled, "It's a step of faith to acknowledge that you can no longer go through life thinking you are in control when you know you really aren't. What God demands is that we hand over the reins. He will not fight us for control because He gave us free will and out of that free will, He wants us to make the decision to enter a relationship with Him. He wants us to love Him more than we love the things that get our attention but don't really amount to much. He is more than a fraternity, sorority, crew, job, friends, parties, faitdodos, bashments, more than all of it. But you must take the first step. He said this in His Word, in James 4:8, to draw near to God, and he will draw near to you. Cleanse your hands, you sinners; and purify your hearts, you double minded."

"So, does that mean we have to stop a lot of things to get close to Him?" Bobby wore a look of concern.

Saadri smiled at him, "I sense you are frightened that for the first time in your life you feel like you have something solid and now that's being taken away because you know you need this. You know this moment is life or death for you."

No one said a word and Saadri ventured forward. "It is not me who knows this but the Holy Spirit who knows because God made Him to know and then He uses His agents like me to speak a word of truth into the lives of others. Listen y'all, the good times last only a moment. After those good times are over, we are faced with our same problems and hang-ups. To experience a different outcome, what we need to do is take the first step and then let God do the changing. He will work with us and in us to stop anything He needs to stop if we genuinely want Him. We show Him we want Him by accepting Jesus as our Lord and Savior, by reading His Word, and by getting into a church where we can be taught and be around people who believe like we do."

"Dat ah de point dere den, church. Wah wi need inna de church fah dem tek wi funds." Bashan sucked his teeth and Teran soothed him.

Saadri was not put off, "We have no problem getting together and putting our money in anything else except church. Last night, we paid to get into the step show and after party. We get together with friends and co-workers and family members to throw parties, take trips, and so on, but we won't get together with people who all believe in and serve God and make sure there are funds to do the work of the Lord. The church is supposed to help meet the needs of the community, but no one wants to put a dime into the church so they will have the funds and services and resources to dole out. Churches are housed in buildings with maintenance and upkeep costs, yet no one wants to put a nickel in the offering plate. How can that be the right attitude? Listen, I know some pulpit-fillers have used the church to get over on people but that is not the norm. There are many pastors who genuinely love God's people and do all they can to serve them. It's wrong that many pastors, who are working hard to better people's lives, are the poorest paid and have less than any other people out here."

Bashan nodded his head, "Eeee, Saadri, yuh mek a gud point."

Najid sat behind Saadri and wrapped his arms around her, "This is my baby. Of course, she is making a good point."

Saadri laid her head on Najid's chest for a moment before lifting it. "Would anyone like to enter a relationship with Christ today? Take the step of faith? Realize this is a do or die moment?" She led everyone in the room in the sinner's prayer.

Epilogue

Najid changed the lane as Bashan awoke from a nap. "Weh ah wi?"

"We'll be at the Delaware Memorial Bridge in a few minutes."

"Wi agreed to change seats inna Maryland. Yuh drove de whole while."

"It's cool, B, I had time to connect with my thoughts, or shall I say get in my head. I'm good, man."

Bashan looked at the console. "Wi need gas in New Jersey, suh I can drive fram dere. Tanks for taking most of de trip."

Saadri leaned forward from the back seat where she and Teran reclined, talked, and watched the road. "It's good we are stopping soon. I need to stretch my legs and go to the bathroom."

Teran added, "I am hungry. I don't know how you are not hungry Sè. Shan, we need to stop soon."

"Wil duh de bridge, Babi, and find a stop afta." He turned and winked at Teran. Teran grinned and blew a kiss. His countenance changed.

Saadri chuckled and swatted her hand, "Stop being fresh. You just gave your life to Christ."

Najid looked at his wife through the rear-view mirror. "You were out of sight today, Candy, I am really proud of you. You did not seem like yourself. I watched you and was like, 'Can this really be my woman?'"

She laid a hand on his shoulder. "Thank you, Baby, it wasn't me. It was the Lord using me through His Spirit."

He nodded, "Yeah, I get that. God has a way of getting His way and that is what He did at Nique's place."

Bashan nodded, "Yah, Jah bless us real gud todeh. Tenk yuh Saadri I feel suh much peace, laik evriting will be arite."

Everyone smiled as Teran spoke. "Listen to you sounding all spiritual Najid, but I didn't really think you were agreeing with what Sè was saying because you didn't join us."

Najid looked quickly at Teran before watching the road. "That's what you thought you saw and that's why my beliefs are no one's business. I get tired of the church business with folks thinking they know everything about God when they know next to nothing."

Teran faltered, "Well, excuse me, I will mind my business. I wasn't trying to be rude."

"T, stop!" Najid shot her a look from the mirror. "I am not talking about you. What I am saying is that I already believe, but I don't have to prove that to anyone like those clowns at Saadri's church."

"Be, that was not nice at all. Don't talk about the church like that."

"Candy, you know I am not lying. T, what do you think of that Ma Mary?"

Teran threw up her hands. "I am sorry, Sè, but Mother Mary is one person I can do without because she is nasty and always has something negative to say about everything. Yet, she is always singing about being happy in Jesus. Now, I like Pastor Sailor, but Cedric is a bum! His younger son is cool. I didn't think about church when we gave our lives to God today. I know I am not going there to deal with those people. I can see Shan demolishing Cedric now, because we both know it would be Cedric to try him." She shook her head in disgust.

"Oh, Lord, that would be a mess. But the church is more than them, so I hope you and Shan find some place to worship."

Teran nodded, "Well, next step is getting through all the details for this wedding." She put her head in her hand.

Saadri brought her close. "Sè, whatever you need help with just let me know. This is a happy occasion and I do not want you stressed out."

As Teran sniffled, Bashan answered Saadri. "Ih been hard for us. Yuh Dadi disapprove that wi stay inna de apartment together. He nuh waan Teran dere overnight. Mumi Nadine waan Butch fi have a bigger part in de wedding and Teran nuh waan dat because Damas waan pay fi de wedding. He waan call de shots, but wi pay for de wedding and have our seh."

"Damas is a trip, B, you know you have to stand your ground with him. How did my man Reggie say it, "Large up yourself!"" Najid nodded in Bashan's direction as he made short work of the bridge.

Saadri kissed Teran's forehead. "I will have a talk with Pe'r. He is putting too much pressure on you because I eloped, and Veronique is ignoring him right now. I want you to look forward to your wedding day because it is a big event and one of the most special days you'll ever have."

Bashan agreed, "I kip telling har Saadri. I look for de day mi Empress come down de aisle fi be my wife. De parents dem will have nuh mo seh afta de wedding ova. We get drought dat day and we done cah we marrid and ih about us."

Najid offered, "We are here to support both of you. I feel kind of bad, now, that Candy did not get this special day she talks about with you, T."

"Be, our day was special for me because I was with you. I don't compare us to anyone, so don't you start. Besides, we can teach them a thing or two about marriage."

Najid grinned, "That's MY CANDY! I got the best woman in the world."

"Nuh Bredda dat wud be my ooman! Teran ah my world." They high fived one another and began discussing which exit they would take to pull into a rest area.

Patwah Glossary

Aal – all
Aal dis – all of this
Affi – have to
Affi bodda wid – have to bother with
Afta – after
Alang – along
Anoda – another
Aredi – Already
Arite – alright
Ave – have
Baan – born
Bashment – party
Bikkle – food
Bly – chance
Boderation – irritation, bothering, annoyance
Boops –

Bot – both
Bruk ya – broke your
Bwoy – boy
Cyaan – can't
Cyaan get bringly – can't get upset
Cyar – car
Dan – than
Dat(s) – That(s)
Dat ah wi – dance with me
De – the
Dem – them
Dere – There
Dey – they
Dis – This
Drough – through
Dung – down
Dutty – dirty

Dween – doing
Dweet – do it
Edah – either
Eff – if
Fada – father
Fah – for
Fambily – family
Fi – for
Fi jink – to drink
Flex – relax, chill out
Fram – from
Gaan – gone
Guh – go
Gud – good
Gwine – going
Gwon noweh – going nowhere
Gyal – gal, girl
im – him
Inna she gates – in her home
Jes – just
Jooks – sex
Haad – hard
Har – her
Healdy – healthy
Ih – it
JA – Jamaica
Kyarri dem – carry them
Kip – keep
Lackan – like a
Laik – like
Lass it – lose it
Lata – later
Lef – leave
Leggo – let's go
Likkle – little
Mata – matter
Mek – make
Mi batty – my buttocks
Mi pickney – my kids
Mon – man
Neva – never
Nuh – not
Nuh fret – don't worry
Nuh vex – don't make me mad
Nuh waan – don't want
Nyam – eat
Oda – other
Ongle – only
ooo – who
Ooman – woman
ou – how
Ova – over
Pon de – on the
Pon tim ahland
Rada – rather
Rass – express shock, surprise, or frustration
Rhaatid – damn, hell
Romp around – play around, not serious
Sekkled – settled
Seh – say
Shim eaz haad –
Si dung – sit down
Siem – same
Skettle – whore, prostitute
Smadi – somebody

Patwah Glossary

Spile – spoil
Taak – talk
Tap – stop
Tap aksin – stop asking
Tek – take
Tenk yah – thank you
Tideh – today
Tink – thin
Togedah – together
Tree – three
Tung – turn
Vex – upset, anger
Wah – why
Wah ah wi – what are we?
Waan – want
Wa'ppun – what happened
Weh – where
Wah gwan? – What's going on? (greeting)
Wi – we
Wid – with
Wud – would
Wuk – work
Yaad – yard
Yah – you
Yah nah easy – you are out of control
Yeye too red – jealous
Yuh nuh a skettle – you're not a slut
Yah waan fi tan ova – you want to stay over

Works Cited

FaceBook post by Neale Donald Walsch from Dec 08, 2012

Malcolm X (2015). "The Autobiography of Malcolm X", p.159, Ballantine Books

About the Author

Stephanie Dunlap-Holloman is a native New Yorker and was educated in the gifted programs of NYC Board of Education. There she discovered her love of writing and received numerous creative writing awards. On the postsecondary level Stephanie had two poems published in her college's magazine. Along with writing, Stephanie has a love of learning. She holds a bachelor's degree from Hunter College, a master's degree from Adelphi University and completed doctoral work at Walden University (ABD.) She recently earned a Master of Fine Arts Writing- Fiction from Lindenwood University. A retired educator, Stephanie taught high school English, was a school administrator, program director/coordinator, department chair, college instructor, and taught preschool, elementary, and middle school.

Stephanie hails from a long line of pastors/ministers and educators. She describes herself as an educator by vocation and calling. She is a licensed and ordained minister who pastors a church in Hampton, Virginia with her husband Frank L. Holloman; they have been active in ministry for over twenty years. Stephanie holds a certificate in Professional Life Coaching from Light University and is a Board-Certified Belief Therapist with Therapon Institute. She is dedicated to helping others become better than they thought they could become. As proprietor of MyVoice, LLC. Stephanie desires to see others recognize, tap into, and bring to fruition the potential that is within them. She and her husband have been married over twenty-nine years, have three children, and have three grandchildren.

Purchase on Amazon

BUARD SERIES, BOOK ONE

Available in Paperback and Kindle

Getting to happy is possible.

Facebook: MyVoice@myvoicestephaniedunlapholloman
IG @dunlapholloman
Website: myvoicellc.com

CPSIA information can be obtained
at www.ICGtesting.com
Printed in the USA
LVHW100554220323
742254LV00001B/85